To

Grace Cordero

[signature]

Special thanks to all my family and friends for their help and support. Thanks to my friends at the CC.

Cover by Susan K. Szepanski

www.darkmoonpublishing.com

ISBN 978-0-9797202-1-5

Max and the

Gatekeeper

James Todd

Cochrane

1

To Grandpa's House

"Where are you heading, boy?" the stranger asked in a raspy voice.

"To my grandfather's," Max Rigdon sighed gloomily as he watched the countryside zoom by his bus window. He brushed a lock of wavy brown hair out of his green eyes and adjusted his baseball cap.

"You sound like a condemned man," the traveler said.

"I am."

"Don't like your grandfather?"

"I don't know. I've only met him once."

"Rubbed you the wrong way, did he?"

Max's green eyes flashed. "You might say that." He turned from the window to look at his fellow passenger. Across the aisle, the man had a hood pulled up over his head and was dressed all in black. Max couldn't see his face but it seemed like a shadow hung over him, as if he emitted a kind of darkness. Max shivered.

"Rubbed a lot of people the wrong way, he has," the

man's voice turned cold.

"You know my grandfather?" Max felt a little uneasy and frightened.

"Yes, and I know who you are, Max Rigdon." the stranger hissed.

"Who are you? What do you want?" Max looked around anxiously and noticed they were the only passengers.

"To kill you," the man roared as he lunged for Max. His hood fell away to reveal a hideous, skull-like face. The man's eyes were blood red like the eyes of an albino rat, and his skin was black as night.

Max blinked his eyes as a blinding bolt of lightning lit the bus. A roar of thunder and pounding rain followed. Max's heart raced as he opened his eyes and looked around but the strange passenger had disappeared. "What was that? Where. . ." he muttered.

Even though the man was gone, Max's anxiety increased because he was still traveling to an undesired destination, his grandfather's. Ever since their first meeting at his father's funeral, Max thought of Grandpa Joe as a crazy old man.

Not only that, but he was about to ruin Max's summer. Only two days earlier, his mother had shattered his dream of being the starting pitcher on his little league all-star baseball team when she told him he would be spending the summer with his grandfather.

He was so angry at her for sending him, and furious at his grandfather just for living. He didn't want to be there. He didn't want anything to do with his idiotic grandfather. "How could he do this to me?" he spat. *He. . .I mean she.* No, he was actually mad at *him* and the *him* wasn't his grandfather. Max was upset with his father. *Why did he leave me?*

Max and his mother had some very hard times since his father's death. His mother had been a stay-at-home mom with only a high school education. The accident forced her to be the breadwinner for the family, but her education level kept her in low-paying jobs. Sending Max to live with his grandfather for the summer would help financially.

More lightning flashed outside Max's window followed by raging thunder that shook the vehicle. The downpour echoed through the bus like stampeding cattle. The storm, like the stranger, made him uneasy.

As the bus slowed, Max glanced out the window and saw a large group of people standing on a hill across the road. They appeared to be watching the bus as it pulled into the terminal. Every one of them was dressed in a black cloak with a hood, disturbingly like the stranger.

The squeal of the bus's air brakes broke through the sound of the rain. "We're here," the driver called as the bus came to a stop.

Max retrieved his backpack from the seat next to him, swung it over his shoulder, and walked up the aisle to the front of the bus.

"Any bags below?" the driver asked.

Max shook his head.

The driver opened the door, and a gust of wind slammed into Max. His grandpa was standing there in front of the door, wet gray hair plastered against his head. Max forced his feet to take the last few steps off the bus.

"Hello, Max." His grandfather gave Max a firm handshake with his bony but strong hand.

Max looked up into his grandfather's smiling face and managed a weak smile. "Hello, Grandpa."

The bus pulled away and the brisk wind whipped around them. "Some storm." Grandpa used a handkerchief to wipe the rainwater off his face.

As lightning zipped across the sky, the landscape went from dark to light revealing Grandpa's small town, population thirty-five hundred. The resulting thunder echoed off the surrounding hills and mountains.

The flashes from the electrical storm confirmed what Max had seen from the bus. There was a crowd dressed in black standing in the rain. Max couldn't see their faces, but he could feel their eyes staring at him. Above the sounds of the storm Max thought he could hear moaning or chanting.

"Who are they?" Max nodded in the direction of the strangers.

"This way." His grandfather pointed up the street as if he hadn't heard Max's question. He started marching with his head down and barreled into the storm.

"What about those people?" Max tried again, running to keep up, but got no answer.

Max trudged along behind his grandfather, and the chanting grew in volume. Max glanced over his shoulder to get a better look at the strange people. To his surprise, they were following. Max was amazed that his grandfather didn't seem to notice or was ignoring them altogether. As they continued up the street, they passed through a nice neighborhood. Through the windows of the houses, Max saw more people staring at him.

"COOOOOOMMMMMMMMMEEEEE WIIIIIIIITH USSSSSSSSS," howled the wind and Max whirled around. The crowd moved up the street and gathered in front of the houses. His grandfather continued to march on in an unconcerned manner.

Max was alarmed. An hour ago, he thought this was going to be a boring summer. Now he worried about what might happen before it even began. For reasons he couldn't explain, he felt a strong desire to join the group of strangers.

"Home at last," his grandfather called over the howling wind.

Max was troubled at the sight of his grandfather's house. An old large three-story with a tower on the far side, it reminded him of a house in a horror movie. It stood alone at the end of the street and could easily pass for a condemned building. Several of the windows were cracked and the shutters were missing or damaged and every window on the third floor was boarded up. The wooden structure looked like it hadn't been painted in years. The yard was as bad. Weeds grew everywhere and the trees and shrubs were overgrown. A rusty iron fence surrounded the spacious lot with a gate at the center of the front yard.

"You live here?" Max tried to hide the disappointment in his voice.

"Yes," Grandpa said with a crooked smile as water streamed down his face and off his mustache.

Max could barely hear the skreak of the rusty gate above the rain, wind, and the voices. Yes, there were voices, and they were coming from the strangers.

His grandfather closed the gate behind them and Max followed him up to the house.

At least we're out of the rain. Max waited under the shelter of the porch while his grandpa searched his pockets for his keys.

"Here we go." Max's grandfather unlocked the door and Max followed him into the darkness of the entryway and waited as he fumbled along the wall for the light switch. "Close the door, please."

Max started to close the door and saw the crowd lining up around the fence. "Grandpa, who are those people?" he asked as he held the door slightly ajar.

"People? What people?" Grandpa winked.

"The ones outside! The ones who followed us from the bus station," Max said, raising his voice as he closed the door. His grandfather had to have noticed. He wasn't imagining them.

His grandfather took off his coat and gave it a good shake, spraying rainwater everywhere. He then hung it on the coat rack next to the door. "This way," he motioned.

Max, still hoping that this was some sort of mistake and that he wouldn't have to stay, held onto his jacket and his backpack. He followed his grandfather down a hallway to the left of the main stairs into a large dated kitchen at the back of the house. In the middle of the room was a rectangular table with two place settings and a steaming pot of what Max assumed was dinner. The house, although spacious, felt warm and homey.

"Are you hungry?" his grandfather asked.

"Yes, I'm starved." Max realized that he hadn't eaten in several hours.

"Have a seat then." Grandpa motioned to a chair at the table.

Max set his backpack on the floor and hung his jacket over the chair in which he sat while his grandfather filled two bowls with stew.

"Dig in." Grandpa placed a bowl in front of Max.

Max took a spoonful and blew across its steamy contents before taking a bite. To his astonishment, it was delicious and he devoured the entire bowlful in seconds.

"That hungry?" his grandfather asked. "Well, there's plenty more. Help yourself."

Max started filling his bowl again but paused halfway feeling his grandfather's eyes on him. "What?"

"You remind me of your father when he was your age."

Max resumed stuffing his face in an effort to avoid a conversation about his father. Even though it was four years since his father's death, it was still a painful subject.

His grandfather seemed to sense that the topic was not a good place to start and changed the subject. "How was your trip?"

"It was okay," Max muttered, trying to keep the food he had shoveled into his mouth from falling out. "I slept most of the way," he added, wanting to end that conversation as well. He resented being here. *Look at him. He's wearing a suit right out of a Tom Sawyer novel. Why, he looks just like Mark Twain. All he needs is a corncob pipe.* Max struggled to stifle a laugh.

"You find something amusing, do you?"

"Has anyone ever told you that you look. . .?" Max felt his cheeks flush with embarrassment.

"Like Mark Twain?" his grandfather finished. "All the time. I've even signed autographs as the famed writer."

"You're kidding?"

"Nope. I don't think those crazy people realized he has been dead for almost a hundred years." Grandpa chuckled.

Who's he calling crazy? But Max liked the fact that his grandfather had a sense of humor about his appearance.

"Are you finished?" Grandpa pointed to Max's empty bowl.

"Yeah."

"Good." His grandfather scooped up the dishes and hauled them to the sink. "You can help me do these later. Now I'll give you the grand tour. Bring your backpack."

Max retrieved his stuff and followed his grandfather from the kitchen. He could hear the rain pounding on the windows as they entered the main hallway. "On the right is the front room. As you can see by the sheet-covered furniture, I haven't used it in a long time.

"On the left is my study. You may read any book you want." He then pointed to a door on the side of the staircase. "That leads into the basement. Again, I haven't been down there in years. My room is at the end of the hall by the kitchen. You, on the other hand, are upstairs."

Max followed his grandfather upstairs and into the first room on the left.

"This is your bedroom." Grandpa turned on the light. "You may toss your backpack in here."

Max took a quick look around the clean room, which contained a double bed in the center of one wall. A slight musty smell reached his nostrils as he placed his backpack on an oak dresser beneath the window overlooking the backyard. A movement outside caught his eye. The people. They were still there, standing around the fence in the rain. He had forgotten about them during dinner. "Grandpa. . ."

"This way. There is more to see." Grandpa went out into the hall.

"But those people." Max protested.

"Not everything in this town is as it seems." Grandpa led Max into the next room, which appeared to have a theme. It reminded Max of a science lab. In fact, all of the remaining rooms he saw had their own themes. One was devoted to mathematics, one to history, and even one to weaponry. There were so many rooms with different themes that Max couldn't remember them all.

My grandfather really is loony! Max thought as they left the room devoted to mythology.

"You can explore any of these rooms whenever you like. Feel free to read any of the books in them. I only ask that you put each book back where you found it when you are done."

"Read? Don't you have a T.V.?" Max had no intention of learning or studying anything new during his summer vacation. Didn't his grandpa know that summer is the time to forget everything learned during the previous school year?

"Television." Grandpa snorted. "No, never had one. I never knew anyone who could survive in this world with the things they learned from television."

"No television," Max complained. "What am I going to do this summer?"

"Oh, I have that all taken care of." Grandpa Joe smiled slyly. "Now, for the last room in the house."

They stood at the bottom of the tower where a spiral staircase led up to what Max assumed was the third floor.

"All the rooms in the house you may enter whenever you like. The third floor; however, you may only enter when I'm present," Grandpa said with a stern look.

"Why do spooky old houses always have forbidden rooms?" Max muttered under his breath.

"They are forbidden for your protection."

Max felt his face turn red. He hadn't intended for his grandfather to hear that. He looked up the staircase and saw a landing and a door at the top of the stairs. "Can we go up now?"

"Not today but soon. Now let's go wash up those dishes."

Downstairs, Max washed the dishes while his grandfather dried and put them away. He could see his reflection in the window over the sink until lightning flashed across the sky. He was amazed and afraid to see the people still out there. His grandfather continued to pretend that he either did not notice or did not care.

"Do you like card games?" his grandfather asked.

"I haven't ever really played any."

"Well, maybe I will teach you one after we finish up here."

"Shouldn't I call my mom to tell her I got here okay?"

"Oh, yes. I forgot. I can finish up here. Go, give her a call. There is a phone in the study."

Max hurried to the study, which was a lot larger than he'd realized on the tour. Thousands of books lined the built-in shelves that stretched from the floor to the ceiling on every wall. In the middle of the room was a huge oak desk with a red leather chair. The phone sat on the desk next to an assortment of pictures.

One picture caught Max's eye. It was the last picture taken as a family with his father before he died. There was a picture of his grandfather when he was a lot younger standing next to an attractive woman. *She must be my grandmother.*

Max picked up the phone and dialed. A wave of homesickness washed over him when he heard his mother's voice.

"How are you? Did you arrive safely?" she asked.

"Yeah, I'm fine, Mom."

Max couldn't remember their conversation as he lay on his bed in the dark. Every once in a while, a flash of lightning illuminated the room and a house-shaking boom would overwhelm the sound of the rain tapping against the window. He had never been homesick before. Not only did he miss his mother but he was terrified of the people outside. He could still hear their eerie chanting mingled with the storm. What really scared him was a strong desire to go outside and join them.

Max spent half an hour staring at them after his grandfather said goodnight. He tried to make out their silhouettes every time the lightning flashed. They appeared to be of all shapes and sizes. They were tall and short, fat and skinny, old and young. Why were they out there? What did they want? The longer Max stared at them the greater his desire to join them grew. Their persistence astounded him. After watching them for a time, he started to feel drowsy. The more he watched and the harder he listened the drowsier he felt. All of his muscles were aching and his head was pounding. His discomfort forced him to move to the bed where he lay down and curled into a ball.

Suddenly, Max found himself in his grandfather's front yard without a clue as to how he got there. He stood barefoot in the rain staring at the people on the other side of the fence.

"Come with us," they called and Max walked towards the gate. He had no control over his feet, they moved as if they had a mind of their own. When he reached the gate, he unlatched it and stepped through.

The mysterious group seized Max from all sides, grasped his right arm, and forced him to hold his right hand out with the palm facing up. One of the figures placed a small metallic object, some kind of symbol Max did not recognize, on his open palm. The chanting of the group grew in tempo and intensity, the words dark and biting.

A piercing pain caused Max to gasp as the metal burrowed into his hand. It twisted and turned as if alive. One second it was on the surface of his hand and the next it was beneath the skin.

The chanting changed. With the sound of each strange new word, the symbol now embedded in Max's hand began to glow. At first, he felt a weird tingle, but then it burned fiercely. He screamed and didn't know how much longer he could withstand the pain. The people held him tight as he struggled to free himself.

Max jerked up when the pain became unbearable. He realized he was sitting on his bed as another bolt of lightning flashed outside his bedroom window. The roar of thunder muffled the cry that escaped his lips.

He sat in the dark covered in sweat, or was it rainwater? His hand tingled; his breathing was heavy and his heart was racing. He lay back on the bed and listened for any sound of movement. Max held his hand up before him, to see if there were any marks. He waited for another flash of lightning to provide enough light to see by. The minutes of waiting turned into an hour. His arm grew tired and his hand fell slowly onto the bed.

Max remembered thinking that the rain had stopped before he fell asleep.

2

Not an All-Star Performance

"Get up, sleepy." Grandpa Joe gently shook Max's shoulder.

Max had a hard time waking up. Lack of sleep made his head spin as the room slowly came into focus. It was a bright sunny morning without any trace of yesterday's storm. He squinted and Grandpa Joe's smiling face became recognizable.

"You going to sleep all day?" Grandpa asked.

"What time is it?" Max yawned.

"A little past eight. Breakfast is waiting downstairs."

Max slid out of bed and got dressed before he made his way downstairs and helped himself to pancakes. He had to admit his grandfather was a good cook and two stacks almost didn't seem like enough.

After breakfast, Max couldn't find his grandfather. He didn't want Grandpa to think he was a slacker, so he washed the dishes. As he put the last plate away, he noticed the palm of his right hand. There was a definite mark of some kind, like a faded scar. At first, he thought it might have been dirt, but after having his hand in soapy water for fifteen minutes, there was no question about that.

"It looks familiar," he muttered, gazing at his palm. His grandfather entered the kitchen, startling him.

"What does. . .?" Grandpa looked at him with raised eyebrows.

"I was just putting the dishes away." Max closed the cupboard and wiped his hands with a towel to hide the mark.

"Is something wrong?"

"No."

For the first time, Max heard a serious tone in his grandfather's voice. It was there for one quick moment, replacing his usual happy-go-lucky, everything-was-right-in-the-world tone.

"Thank you for cleaning up," Grandpa said. "I was going to do that, but thank you."

"I can pull my own weight." Max tried to sound responsible.

"I'm glad to hear it," Grandpa smiled. "I do have some things for you to do."

Max felt like he had stepped into a trap. The twinkle in his grandfather's eyes told him he was about to be put to work. *I am going to be my grandfather's slave. Look at this dump. It would take ten Cinderellas with twenty fairy god-mothers working all summer to get this place in shape.*

Suddenly, Grandpa Joe let out the heartiest laugh he had ever heard. Max could have sworn the house was about to come down under the rumble.

"What's so funny?" Max asked.

"The look on your face," Grandpa chuckled. "You look like you just got caught with your hand in the cookie jar. Does the thought of chores scare you that much?"

Max didn't know what to say but the sight of his grandfather laughing made him feel better. The corners of his mouth curled up in a smile. He didn't know why, but he thought he might just like his grandfather.

"I do have some chores for us to do, but they aren't very big. It's summer after all, and summers are supposed to be fun."

Grandpa Joe led Max out to the backyard to what looked like an old barbecue pit. Max wondered how long it had been since it was used last because weeds grew out of it like a monster's tentacles. Two pairs of gloves lay on its edge.

"Today's task is to clean up all the tumbleweeds in the yard," Grandpa said. "We will bring them here to burn."

Max looked around. "Are these last year's weeds?" It was too early for tumbleweeds this year. He was annoyed at the prospect of cleaning the big yard let alone last year's mess.

"Yes, I'm not much of a caretaker," Grandpa admitted. "Now take some gloves and let's get going."

Max took a pair of gloves but he wasn't happy about it.

"You take the front yard and I'll take the back," Grandpa said. "You have younger legs and it will be easier for you to run back and forth and bring the weeds here."

Max hung his head and dragged himself to the front of the house. He would be carrying the weeds the greater distance, plus the front yard was twice the size of the backyard. He sighed and started picking up the large round weeds. He hauled his first load to the back where his grandfather had already created a pile in the pit. He dumped his load on top and headed back to the front.

It was tedious, but Max discovered cleaning up the tumbleweeds was an easier job than he first anticipated. Because of their bulky roundness, he only had to remove two or three of the tumbleweeds to clear a large area.

On one of his trips from the backyard, Max noticed someone watching him. Luckily, it wasn't a creepy crowd of chanting people. Instead, it appeared to be a girl about his age. Her long blonde hair was pulled back into a ponytail that stuck out of the back of a baseball cap, and she wore torn jeans and a white t-shirt. She leaned against the fence surrounding the house across the dirt lane from his grandfather's. She didn't move during the entire time Max worked. She just stood there like a statue and stared.

After an hour of hauling tumbleweeds from the front yard to the back, Max finally picked up the last two weeds. He carried them around back and threw them on one of several piles his grandfather had made. Grandpa wasn't there, but the backyard was clean as well. He pulled off his gloves and grunted at his mud-covered pants and shirt. *The yard actually doesn't look too shabby. With a little more work the place could be pretty nice.*

An old wooden gazebo in need of a new coat of paint stood in the back corner. The yard had lots of rose bushes, and straggly shrubs and trees.

Grandpa Joe came out of the house carrying two glasses of lemonade. "Thirsty?"

"Oh yes." Max gladly accepted the glass and took a long drink.

"So what do you think of the yard?" Grandpa asked. "It looks a lot better than it did this morning."

"I was thinking it could really be a nice yard with just a bit. . ." He stopped, realizing his error.

"Of work." Grandpa chuckled. "Don't worry we're done working for today." He took a box of matches out of his pocket. "Do you want to light the fire?"

"Can I?" Max's eyes shone with excitement.

"Sure, I never knew a boy who didn't want to start a fire." Grandpa produced a folded-up newspaper from his back pocket and handed it and the matches to Max. "Start this first and then throw it into the pit."

Max's mom had always forbidden him to play with matches. He took the items with a smile, snatched a match from the box, and struck it on the side.

"Hold the newspaper away from you and light the end," Grandpa encouraged.

Max followed his grandfather's instructions. He then threw the lit paper into the pit and watched the fire spread to the weeds. Soon a white pillar of smoke billowed over the house.

"Let it burn down a little and then add more weeds." Grandpa indicated the other piles.

The girl, who had been watching, now stood outside the back fence staring at the fire. Max was a little disappointed that his closest neighbor was a girl. He was past the girl-hating stage but he wanted friends he could play baseball with. He wasn't about to play house or dress up.

"That's Cindy, she lives next door," Grandpa said, inclining his head towards her. "Want to come in and help us burn these weeds?" he called to her.

Max thought he saw her blush as she nodded and made her way to the back gate. When she came into the yard, Max was surprised at her shabby appearance. She was different from other girls. All the girls Max knew were into things like make-up and clothes. He had never met a true tomboy before. She wore baggy boy clothes, but he had to admit she was kind of cute. She had soft features with full reddish lips, baby-blue eyes, and her golden blonde hair reflected an unusual amount of sunlight.

"Cindy, this is my grandson, Max," Grandpa said. "He is staying with me for the summer."

"Hello," Max greeted.

"Hi," said Cindy shyly meeting his gaze for a second.

"Well, this is one of the biggest fires I have. . ." said Grandpa. "I say, where are my manners? Cindy, would you like some lemonade?"

She nodded and Grandpa went to fetch another glass.

While Grandpa was in the house, a gang of boys rode their bicycles up to the back fence. A tall gorilla-like boy rode out in front of the others and appeared to be the leader. "What a shame," he spat as he skidded his bike to a halt. "I was hoping the house was on fire, then, we could be rid of that old wacko that lives here."

The rest of the boys laughed and added their own rude remarks.

"Bummer it isn't the house, with the old geezer in it," another boy called.

"This town would be better without that old, beat up thing. The house could stay though."

This comment brought a roar of laughter, which lasted several minutes. Max was shocked and incensed by their crude comments. Even though he had only known his grandfather for two days, Max liked the old guy. He glanced at Cindy. Her face was bright red, but not with embarrassment. She was angry; her fists clenched at her sides.

"Hey, Mindy, who's the wuss?" asked the leader. "Is he your new, no wait, first boyfriend? Or are you paying him to hang out with you?"

Again, the group howled with laughter.

"Shut your face, Larry," Cindy yelled in a stronger voice than Max expected. He didn't think her capable of such volume. "Why don't you idiots go and jump in the sewage pond."

"Don't tell me to shut your—uh—my face! I might have to knock your wuss of a boyfriend out cold," Larry hollered.

Max had seen this boy only a few minutes and during that time his expression hadn't changed once. Even when he laughed, he still looked mad. Max wondered if his face was stuck in that expression of permanent anger.

"What are you kids doing out here?" asked Grandpa as he emerged from the house with Cindy's lemonade.

"Nothing, you old wacko," called Larry as he climbed back on his bike. "Come on, guys. Mindy and her boyfriend need the old geezer to stick up for them." Larry turned his bike around and pedaled away. "You better watch yourself, wuss. You might get your head knocked off in this town," he yelled over his shoulder. The other boys added their agreement as they rode away.

"What was that all about?" asked Max, still stunned by the brazen crudeness of the boys.

"Just kids being kids." Grandpa handed Cindy the lemonade. "You better throw a couple of more weeds on the fire. It's dying down"

"They're worse than that," Cindy's voice was firm and edged with disdain. "They're bullies. They think they own this town. I have been here a year and they still won't call me by my real name, and they're always rude."

"Do they treat all new people like this?" asked Max.

"Actually, no," she said with a funny look. "It's weird. Four other kids moved here after I did, and Larry and his group didn't pick on any of them. Well maybe at first, but then they all became friends."

"Strange," muttered Max.

"Don't worry about them," Grandpa said and they went back to watching the fire.

The next few days were similar to the first. Max and Grandpa Joe started the day with chores and Cindy eventually joined them. Max liked her, she was fun, and he didn't understand why she didn't have any friends. The town was small enough to walk across it in half an hour, but no one ever visited her. He thought she was pretty, but he would never admit it. Even with those eyes and lips, she was one hundred percent tomboy. She would do anything Max could and, to his great surprise, she loved baseball. Everyday, after chores, they played catch until their arms hurt.

Her parents were nice too, but with both of them working, they left Cindy home alone. She seemed happy that Max was here, which reinforced his suspicions about her lack of friends.

Towards the end of Max's first week with Grandpa, Max and Cindy explored the hills behind Grandpa's house. They hiked all over, catching and releasing lizards that scurried everywhere. Twice they climbed the tallest hill and looked down over the town. From there, Max spied the makeshift baseball field. It wasn't a proper baseball diamond with grass, a fence and chalk lines. It was more of a dust bowl with weeds for fences. The two of them sat in silence and watched a group of kids, including the bullies, play baseball. "Do you think they would let us play?" Max asked.

"Are you crazy?" Cindy snorted.

Cindy gave him the dirt on the six boys. There were Jeff, Burt, Sam, Carl, Brad and Larry. Cindy always added an adjective in front of their names to help Max understand each character.

According to Cindy, there was *Jerky Jeff* who was a skinny eleven-year old with a mop of brown hair. *Cry Baby Burt* was also eleven. He had a high squeaky voice and lots of freckles. *Spastic Sam* was the shortest, chubbiest and youngest of the group. *Crater Face Carl* the oldest at thirteen, was a tall skinny boy with pimples. *Brainless Brad* was the dumbest. Cindy said he hadn't ever had an original thought in his life. She really emphasized the adjectives in front of their names. She said it was so fitting to who they really were. Last of all, there was *Loser Larry*.

The bullies became annoying regulars at Grandpa's house during the morning chores. They showed up every day with shouts and jeers. Cindy was the only one who shouted back. Their comments didn't seem to bother Grandpa. Max, however, found them unnerving. Larry was a big kid. Max thought he could probably stand his ground against one, but he didn't want to fight the whole gang.

Max didn't do much during the afternoons, and Grandpa Joe started making subtle suggestions on how Max should spend his time. "Why don't you look at the books in the rooms upstairs," he would say. "Have you checked out any of the maps upstairs?" He even gave Max a book about survival skills. Max found it an interesting book and he read it in the evenings before he went to sleep.

At the beginning of the second week, Max really wanted to play baseball with the other kids. *If they could only see how good I am, maybe they would be nice to me. Or maybe I could destroy them at baseball and they would be so humiliated they would leave me alone.*

He mentioned the idea to Cindy several times but she didn't want to listen. Max wasn't sure if it was her dislike of those boys or if she was afraid for him because the boys always threatened to knock him out or worse. He needed a plan to help him get what he wanted. Cindy respected his grandfather and what he had to say. Maybe Grandpa could convince Cindy.

At dinner, Max put his plan into action. "Do you like baseball?" he asked his grandfather while he dished up his second helping.

"Baseball? Sure I like baseball," Grandpa replied, as if coming out of another thought. "Why do you ask?"

"Well, you see. . ."

"It isn't enough playing catch with Cindy?" Grandpa smiled. "I take it you've noticed the sandlot games down at the old hayfield?"

His grandfather's keen perception really surprised Max sometimes. "Yes, and I want to play but Cindy won't go," he blurted out, forgetting his subtle plan.

"Why doesn't—"

"I think it's because of those boys who come by everyday. They're always there," Max interrupted.

"Aren't you afraid of them?" Grandpa raised an eyebrow.

"Well, maybe a little, but I still want to play."

"I think it's a good idea, but you might have to go without Cindy." Grandpa watched Max's reaction.

"I would feel bad leaving her behind. She is my only friend here."

"So, you were hoping I could get her to go with you, is that it?" Grandpa smiled.

"Would you? I think she'd go with me if you suggested it."

"I'll see what I can do."

Max couldn't sleep that night. Every reaction Cindy could possibly have kept running through his mind. She could be angry, refuse to go and never talk to him again; she could be angry, not go, and still be his friend; or she could be reluctant, go, and still be his friend. He hoped for the latter.

During the next morning's chores, Max expected his grandfather to spring the idea on Cindy, but he didn't. He seemed preoccupied, like always, with other things. Max was beginning to lose his patience. He wanted to play today but it didn't look like it was going to happen. Maybe his grandfather had forgotten. When Grandpa failed to bring up the topic during lunch, Max decided to let it go for the rest of the day.

Later, he and Cindy grabbed their mitts to play their usual game of catch. They headed for the door when Grandpa made his move. "Don't you get bored only playing catch together?"

"What do you mean?" Max acted surprised. He had to turn his back to Cindy to hide his smile.

"Well," Grandpa Joe started, "I just walked up Kennedy Drive and saw a group of kids playing a game of baseball. Maybe you two should head down there and play with them."

"There's a game? Really?" Max continued his charade. Then he realized his mistake. Cindy knew he had seen the games.

Cindy looked at Max and then at Grandpa. Max could see the suspicion in her squinted eyes as she glared at him. She knew he had put his grandfather up to this, but she didn't look angry. No, it was worse. She actually looked hurt. *Why would she be hurt?*

Before he or Cindy could say anything else, Grandpa pushed them out the door. "Hurry, you don't want to be late. Go on now, have fun."

Cindy lowered her head and walked past Max, "Come on." She proceeded so fast that Max had trouble keeping up. "Had to get your grandpa involved, didn't you." she grumbled, marching ahead of him.

Max figured it was best to remain silent. He followed Cindy down a couple of streets to where they could see the field. The kids were in the process of choosing teams. The closer they got to the field, the more nervous Max felt. "How do you want to go in?" he tried to ask but Cindy didn't respond. She continued to march forward.

Then, with a courage Max didn't think Cindy possessed, she walked right up to them. "Do you have room for two more?"

The looks on their faces told Max they weren't happy to see them. They all had fierce expressions of hatred. Everyone had this appearance, everyone but Larry. Larry actually had a grin. It was an evil grin, but still a grin.

"Suuurrrrrrrrrrrrre," Larry said before anyone else could speak. "We've got plenty of room."

The boys exchanged confused looks with Larry. Their eyes met for a moment and then returned to Max. They all had that same wicked grin. It almost seemed creepier than the chanters from his first night in town. "What position do you play?" asked Larry.

"I can play anywhere," offered Cindy, "Max is an all-star pitcher."

"An all-star pitcher," Larry scoffed. "Good. I need batting practice." He laughed and the others joined in. "You two can be on Fred's team. He needs a pitcher and a second baseman."

Fred opened his mouth, but a glare from Larry silenced him. It was obvious who was in charge.

"You're up first, Fred," said Larry, and his team took the field. Larry was the pitcher and he stood on the mound with his usual disgruntled expression. His twisted smirk had disappeared, however.

"You'll bat eighth and ninth." Fred pointed to Max and then to Cindy.

Max watched Fred step up to bat. He leaned over the plate. Larry's first pitch screamed in high, directly toward Fred's head. Fred barely had time to dive out of the way. Picking himself up off the ground, he brushed the dirt off his shirt and pants. Fred moved back into the batter's box but shied away from the plate. The next three pitches were right down the middle. Fred went down swinging, he wasn't even close. Larry had some speed but nothing Max hadn't faced before. Max knew he was a better pitcher than Larry. The next two batters struck out as well.

The teams switched and Max hurried out onto the pitcher's mound. He threw a couple of pitches to loosen up. He felt good and thought he could make a good showing.

Larry walked up to the plate and dug in. He spit a couple of times like a pompous major leaguer. "Give me your best stuff, wuss," he said with his contorted smile.

Max concentrated on the catcher's mitt, wound up, and put every ounce of strength behind it. Then, something strange happened that Max couldn't explain. The whole world went into slow motion. Instead of the ball crossing the plate instantly, it drifted like pollen in a breeze. When the ball finally did reach the plate, Larry crushed it. Time jumped back to normal as Max watched the ball fly out of the field and into the weeds.

"Nice pitch," his teammates called sarcastically. "All-star pitcher, right."

Larry sneered as he rounded the bases with his teammates cheering him on. He arrived at home plate to a swarm of high fives and chest bumping.

The rest of the inning was worse. Every pitch Max threw hung, suspended in time for Larry's team to destroy. At least none of the other boys were as coordinated or as strong as Larry. They didn't manage to smash the ball out of the playing area, which allowed Max's teammates to get the necessary outs. After eight runs, two homers by Larry, three walks, and one triple the nightmare inning finally ended.

Max couldn't even meet the angry glares of his teammates as he walked to the bench. The players on both teams were still shouting out sarcastic comments. Cindy was the only one who wasn't angry with him. Whatever irritation she had about coming to the game had vanished. Max could tell that Cindy wanted to say something but she looked as shocked as he was. She had been playing catch with him long enough to know what he could do.

Another three batters struck out and Max found himself back on the mound. "Hope you have a better inning than the last one," called Fred from shortstop. Max hoped so too, but that wasn't the case. It was worse. Every pitch he threw had the same surreal feeling of slow motion. Larry hit two more home runs, and by the end of the second inning, Max had given up another ten runs.

"Who elected this loser to be our pitcher? My sister pitches better than this wuss." called one of his teammates.

After the first batter struck out, Max stood at the plate staring at Larry's smug ape face. He wanted so desperately to pound the ball out into the weeds. He needed to do something right. Larry wound up and threw the first pitch. Max watched the ball coming towards him. He timed it. But when he went to swing, the bat suddenly got much heavier; it felt like it weighed a ton. He swung it like a sledgehammer, and the ball hit the catcher's glove before he was even halfway there. Strike one.

Max stepped out of the batter's box and took a couple practice swings. The bat felt normal again and his movements felt good. He stepped back up to the plate and got ready. Larry threw the second pitch. It was a semifastball. Max wanted to jump all over it, but again, swinging the bat felt like he was lifting a tree. Strike two crossed the plate. The third strike was the worst. Max didn't even get the bat off his shoulder. He walked dejectedly to the bench, his mind a whirl of confusion. This average pitcher was pitching a no-hitter and Max, the all-star, was getting thumped.

Max managed to lift his head long enough to watch Cindy bat. She leaned over the plate and her expression matched Larry's. The first pitch flew right at her head. She ducked, letting the pitch sail by. When she rose, she actually moved closer to the plate. Cindy's reaction seemed to unnerve Larry. He wound up and let the second pitch fly. Max watched in disbelief as Cindy knocked the ball deep into right field. By the time it came back, Cindy had hit a double. Max was on his feet cheering her on.

Larry was furious and Fred, next up to bat, took the brunt of Larry's anger. The next three pitches were the fastest Larry had thrown all day. Fred didn't stand a chance.

Max retrieved his glove and headed out to the field. As he stepped on the mound, Fred handed him the ball.

"This is your last chance," Fred growled.

Max threw a couple of warm up pitches and then Larry stepped to the plate again. Max concentrated on the outer area of the strike zone away from Larry. He wound up and the ball flew from his hand. Something different happened. Instead of slowing down like the previous innings, the ball, which was heading down and away, turned and moved up and in. Larry didn't budge as the ball slammed into his side. Max heard an array of angry shouts coming from all over the field. "What are you doing? Loser!" yelled the players from both sides.

Max couldn't believe what had happened. He hadn't hit a batter in two years. Larry looked absolutely insane as he dropped the bat and raced towards the mound. Max took a deep breath; he knew he was only going to get one shot. Larry charged like a bull with arms instead of horns. The instant before Larry was on him, Max smashed his fist into Larry's nose. Larry screamed in pain but his momentum carried him into Max, knocking him to the ground. In seconds, sharp shooting pains ignited all over Max's body. He was on the ground with all of the other boys kicking and yelling. Max heard Cindy scream and just before everything went black, a blinding white light exploded before his eyes.

3

The Third Floor

"Max, Max." Grandpa nudged him awake.

The room came into focus, but it took Max several minutes to realize where he was. He lay on his bed and stared up at his grandfather's face.

"How are you feeling?" Grandpa asked.

When Max moved, a groan escaped his lips as a sharp pain shot across his side. "What happened?"

"You took on the entire fifth and sixth grade." Grandpa Joe beamed as he helped him sit up.

"Oh yeah, the baseball game." Max frowned with disappointment. The painful memory of his worst baseball game ever rushed back. He gingerly felt around for bumps and bruises. "Ouch!" he exclaimed as he touched his face. He had a fat lip and a swollen eye.

"You have a nice shiner, there. I need to take a picture of that baby before it goes away."

Max could see pleasure written on his grandfather's face. "Why are you so happy? And how did I get here?"

"I brought you home. I'm smiling because I'm very proud of you."

"Why?"

"You showed great courage. I mean it. It took a lot to go and play in the first place, but to stand and fight against those odds showed real guts. I'll bet Larry feels worse than you do. You busted his nose with that punch."

"You saw that?"

"Yes, I watched the whole game."

"Then you saw how horrible I played." Max sighed. He had been so proud earlier that day but his performance humbled him.

"No, you played well. You are a very good pitcher. Your dad would be proud."

"What game did you watch? They beat me like a piñata. They crushed everything I threw at them." Max did not like his grandfather patronizing him. In his mind, he had stunk.

"Oh, they weren't that good and you weren't that bad." Grandpa Joe moved towards the door. "They cheated." He smiled as he left the room.

"They cheated?" Max called but his grandfather didn't return. "How could they? I was pitching!"

He lay there thinking about the game. *They cheated* kept repeating in his mind. He remembered how his pitches floated slowly through the air. It was as if they were hovering, waiting to be hit. That was a bit weird, but how could they do it? It's not possible. And that heavy bat. They couldn't make a bat feel suddenly heavy. None of it made sense but he was certain of one thing, that game was not normal.

One thing that bothered him even more than the game itself though, was the blinding flash right before he blacked out. What was that light?

A knock on his door jarred him out of his thoughts. *Why would Grandpa knock?* "Come in."

To his surprise, it was Cindy. She carried a tray with milk and cookies.

"You have a black eye!" Max laughed as she entered the room. Cindy's swollen eye bulged outward and the purple and green colors were starting to show.

"Look who's talking. Yours is worse than mine," she fired back. "I brought you a snack." She placed the tray on the nightstand and took a cookie. "How are you feeling?"

"I'm sore," Max admitted, and he wasn't just talking about his body. His pride was hurt more. He took a glass of milk and a couple of cookies. "I'm still confused about how I got home."

"That makes two of us," said Cindy with a mouthful of cookie. "I mean, I know how we got home, but. . .I'm not so sure how we got out of that mess."

"What do you mean?"

Cindy paused a moment and pressed her lips together. "Okay, I'm just going to say it. Ever since you arrived, I've noticed a lot of weird things going on."

"What kind of weird things?" Max was curious. He had the same suspicions but he wanted to hear someone else say it.

"Well, this town is definitely different. At least compared to where I used to live. But ever since your arrival, things have gotten weirder."

"What things?" Max demanded again.

"Take your first night here."

"What about it?" Max had his own memories of that night and he wondered if anyone else had seen the people chanting in the rain.

"Don't tell me you didn't notice those people who followed you home the night you arrived. They surrounded your house all night, chanting in the rain. And then there are the *friendly* neighborhood idiots. They've always been mean and annoying, but since your arrival, their meanness has turned to hatred. And that baseball game was the weirdest thing I have ever seen."

"What about the baseball game?" Max's attention locked on Cindy. Deep down he had been hoping that Cindy had noticed everything he had, which would definitely help his pride.

"Where should I start?" Cindy helped herself to another cookie. "I've been catching for you everyday now for two weeks. You are one of the best pitchers I've ever seen, but every pitch you threw at the game was in slow motion."

"You noticed that, too." Max breathed a sigh of relief and a smile crossed his face.

"What are you smiling about?"

"Nothing. Go on."

"Anyway, that last pitch you threw moved right into Larry as if he wanted it to. Did you see the grin on his face? It was like he caused the ball to hit him so he could start that fight. Oh, that was a great punch, by the way. I didn't think you had it in you."

"Why not?"

"Well, every time they come around shouting at you, you never say anything back. That punch was awesome." Cindy smiled. "I don't think Larry will be back for awhile. Anyway, all of those things were weird, but the way that fight ended topped them all. I knew you were in trouble because, not only was Larry rushing you, both teams charged you at the same time. They looked like lions going for the kill. I dropped my mitt and started after them. I saw you punch Larry and go down in the rush. I jumped on the first back I came to. Someone hit me from the side and I went flying to the ground. I got up to head back in and then I saw a blinding flash of light, like lightning."

"I saw the light too. I assumed I was seeing stars."

"Anyway, when I came to, your grandfather was helping me up. Then I saw the field. Everyone was out cold lying on the ground."

"That *is* weird."

"Wait, there's more. Everybody was lying as if a bomb had gone off and you were at the center." Cindy stared out the window as if she could still picture the scene. "Then, your grandfather picked you up and carried you home."

"Strange," Max agreed. "I'm glad I'm not the only one who's noticed the unusual things happening around here."

"Have you noticed anything else?"

"Only a couple of things, but none as big as what you already mentioned," he offered as he reached for another cookie.

"What sort of things?" Cindy stared at him.

Max noticed that even with the black eye, she was still pretty. He felt himself blush and turned his gaze to his cookie. "Uh, what?"

"What other things have you noticed?" Cindy seemed annoyed that she had to ask twice.

"Um, this house. Have you seen any of the other rooms?"

"No, this is the first time I have been in it. I've talked to your grandfather lots of times, but he's never invited me in before."

"I'll have to give you a tour. This place has about a dozen rooms, and each room has a theme to it."

"What do you mean?"

"Well, there is a room about science, one about weapons, one about astronomy, and other subjects like that. There is a spiral staircase leading to the third floor that I'm not allowed to enter without my grandfather present. He tries to get me to go into these rooms all the time. He even gave me a book on survival skills." Max paused and watched Cindy's reaction.

She stood there thinking about what Max had told her. "Weird. I think there is something big going on in this house and in this town. And why are there always forbidden rooms in old houses?"

"That's what I said." Max smiled with satisfaction.

Grandpa Joe walked into the room. "From the smiles on your faces, it looks like everyone is feeling better. Do you think you can come downstairs for lunch?"

"Sure," said Max.

The next few days were fairly normal, except that the neighborhood bullies didn't come around. Grandpa said Larry was too embarrassed about his broken nose. The bullies' absence didn't disappoint Max in the least. He tried several times to ask Grandpa what he meant when he had accused Larry and his friends of cheating. Grandpa always danced around the subject.

They spent their mornings doing chores as usual. Max and Cindy couldn't play catch, because Max was still recovering from the fight. Their black eyes were now nice shades of blue, yellow and green, but the swelling had gone down.

During Max's third week, the rain returned. Max normally wouldn't have thought of rain as being strange, but this time, along with the rain came a pain in the palm of his hand, and the strange mark grew darker. Grandpa went to the store and left Cindy and Max to clean the front room. They removed the protective sheets from the furniture and took them to the laundry room. This task put so much dust in the air that they sat in the hall waiting for it to settle.

"Now what should we do?" Cindy asked.

"I know." Max's face lit up with enthusiasm. "I'll show you the rooms I was telling you about." He figured it was going to be a boring day because of the rain and the strange rooms offered entertainment.

"Okay," Cindy agreed. "I forgot about them. With all of the other unusual things going on, they didn't seem important. Where do you want to start?"

"Let's start at the opposite end of the tower and work our way along," Max suggested, getting to his feet with a groan. Even a week after the fight, he was still sore.

"Your Grandpa won't mind, will he?"

"Nah, I told you, he tries to get me to go into those rooms all the time." Max headed up the stairs.

"Why do you think he wants you to go into them?"

"I'm not sure. Maybe he wants me to learn something." Max led Cindy to the room at the end of the hall. He opened the door to a room filled with ancient artifacts.

"Wow!" exclaimed Cindy as they entered. A desk covered with scrolls sat in the center of the room. There were wooden masks and clay pots lining the shelves against the left wall. On the right wall, there were more shelves, but the items on them were things neither of them had seen before. Made of gold and brass, some looked like weapons, while others appeared to be instruments or tools. Piled on the floor next to the window were several boxes of photographs.

Max walked to the gold items and examined an object that resembled a compass. It was a clear round ball with a round flat disk inside. The disk had strange markings around the outer edge and three golden spindles pointing outward like hands on a clock. "This is a strange looking object." Max tried to see how it worked.

Cindy went to the boxes and began looking at the pictures. "Wow, your Grandpa sure has traveled a lot."

"What?"

"Your grandfather sure has traveled. There are pictures from all over the place." Cindy flipped through a photo album. "Here he is in front of the pyramids and another one in front of the sphinx."

"Really?" Max placed the object back on the shelf and joined Cindy. "Wow, that's cool," he said looking over her shoulder. "Wait a second." Max studied the picture of the pyramids. "This has to be some kind of joke."

"Why?"

"There is grass around the pyramids and snow capped mountains in the background." Max pointed. "The pyramids are in the desert."

"Oh, yeah," Cindy said. "Why would he have a fake picture like this?"

Max thought she sounded disappointed. "Maybe he got it at an amusement park," Max offered. "You know someplace where they do those caricature type drawings."

"Probably. But this is a real photograph. Those drawings are usually done in chalk."

"Well, maybe he has a photography room. I don't remember every room. Maybe he made that picture himself."

Max gave up on the photos and walked over to the desk. He spread open a few scrolls. The writing was in a foreign language. In the center of a scroll, a symbol caught Max's eye. It was the same as the mark on his hand. He turned his hand over. The mark was faint, but it was definitely the same symbol.

"Did you find something?" Cindy asked.

"No." Max flipped his hand over to hide the mark. "It's all written in different languages."

Something in him wanted to keep the mark on his hand a secret. He didn't know why, but he didn't want anyone to know. Out of everything that had happened since he arrived, the mark and how he got it was the weirdest.

Max rolled up the scrolls. "Do you want to go look at another room?"

"Sure." Cindy placed the photo album back in the box.

The next room was devoted to astronomy. A painting of the solar system decorated the ceiling with a round crystal chandelier representing the sun. Again, on both sides of the room there were shelves containing books, charts, models of spacecrafts and satellites. By the window were more boxes with pictures.

Cindy walked straight to the pictures. Max could tell by her demeanor that she wanted to see if there were any more odd photographs. *She finds these rooms a lot stranger than I do.*

Max headed for the models. Many looked like they'd come directly from NASA, but most appeared to be from science fiction movies.

"Check out these pictures." Cindy cradled a photo album on her lap as she sat on the floor.

"Did you find more carnival pictures?" Max called over his shoulder as he studied a saucer-shaped spacecraft.

"I don't know if they are carnival pictures, but they don't make sense either."

The tone of her voice caused Max to look at her. She had an expression of serious concentration on her face. She leaned so close to a picture that her nose was almost touching it. Max joined her by the window.

"Is that a—" she mumbled.

"Is that a what?" Max tried to look at the picture over her shoulder.

"It looks like your grandfather has been on the moon or another planet." She handed the picture to Max.

"Well that's impossible, only a few men have been on the moon and no one has been on another planet." Max took the picture. His grandfather was dressed in a curious space suit and stood on a rocky surface devoid of plants. He wore a helmet, but his face was visible through the faceplate. It was definitely his grandfather, but he was younger. He was smiling and waving to the photographer. In the background was a city covered by a clear dome.

"I know it isn't possible," Cindy paused. "But what if. . .? This is getting weirder all the time."

"What was she looking at?" Max whispered to himself as he studied the picture intently, trying to see what Cindy had seen.

"What?"

"You were looking at something. I wondered what it was."

"It's nothing."

"Come on. You saw something. What was it?"

"I thought I could see something nonhuman in the reflection of your grandfather's helmet," she blurted out.

Max looked at her in time to see her blush like she couldn't believe what she had said. The words did sound ridiculous.

"I know that sounds dumb."

Max found himself with his nose almost stuck to the picture. What is that? It appeared to have human form, with grayish skin and smooth features. It was wearing a suit similar to his grandfather's, but with no helmet. "It looks like it has cat's eyes."

"Yes, that's what I thought, too."

"Did you notice that this picture is. . .well, old? Look how the colors have faded, and my grandfather is a lot younger."

"Why would he have so many of these weird pictures?" Cindy asked.

"I don't know, but let's go look for pictures in the other rooms."

"I agree. I could understand someone having one or two gag pictures, but your grandfather seems to have more than the average person." Cindy climbed to her feet.

Max placed the album back in the box and they went to the next room devoted to zoology. There were books about animals and figures of animals on the shelves. On the floor by the window were more photo albums.

Neither one of them went for the pictures this time. The sight of the animal figures was too alluring. "Wow, look at all the animals!" Max took an elephant from a shelf.

Cindy walked to a different section of shelves. "Max." She stood with her mouth open staring at a slew of mystical creatures in front of her.

"They're only figurines. You honestly don't think they are models of real creatures? Do you?"

"No." Cindy blushed. "These things can't be real. There has to be a logical explanation for all of this." She went to look through the photos on the floor.

Max moved to where the strange animals were. A section with dragons, unicorns, monsters, and other mythological creatures stared back at him. He counted a large number of monsters. "This stuff looks like it came right out of a nightmare."

Cindy flipped through a photo album. "These are normal pictures."

"Gee, you actually sound disappointed." Max grinned.

"Actually, I. . ." she stopped mid-sentence; her eyes riveted on the picture in front of her.

"Actually you what?" Max continued examining the monster figures.

"You have to see this. And I'm not disappointed anymore."

Max peered at her. "Found more strange pictures?"

"Yes, and this picture has all the others beat." Cindy didn't wait for Max to come to her. She carried the photo album to him and held it out for him to see.

"Holy cow! That can't be real." In the picture his grandfather stood at the edge of a few trees. He was younger than in the space-suit picture, but it was him. Behind him in a clearing was a Tyrannosaurus Rex eating a fresh kill.

"There is no way this is real." Max turned the page and saw more pictures of several different kinds of dinosaurs. Many of the pictures had people in them. Then, Max noticed the people. They were rather odd-looking. Most of them didn't look like people at all. They looked like aliens from another planet.

Suddenly, the sound of the front door slamming shut startled them. Max closed the album as if he had been caught doing something wrong. He handed the album to Cindy and moved to the door, peeking into the hall.

Grandpa bounded up the stairs, seemingly preoccupied with something, turned left and shot down the opposite end of the hall. Max was surprised he could move so quickly for an old man.

"He went up to the third floor," Max whispered.

"Why are you whispering?" Cindy placed the album back in the box and joined him. "You said he tries to get you to come into these rooms all the time."

"Yes, but with all these strange pictures, I feel like we're snooping." Max spoke in a normal tone.

"No, snooping would be going to see what he is doing up there," Cindy said with a mischievous grin.

"I don't think we should do that," Max said, surprised by Cindy's suggestion. "He said the third floor was forbidden."

"That's not what you said before. You said it was forbidden without him. Well, he's up there now."

Cindy smiled innocently and her blue eyes sparkled. Max stared at her for a moment thinking how pretty she looked, then turned his attention back to the hall to hide his flushed cheeks.

A creaking noise followed by an electrical hum echoed through the house. "What is that?" asked Max.

"Let's find out." Cindy pushed past Max into the hall.

Max didn't think they should, but Cindy seemed determined to get to the bottom of everything. Max was surprised as Cindy zipped ahead of him. It was his impression, when going to spy, you move slowly and cautiously. Cindy was at the spiral staircase in a matter of seconds. Max wanted to tell her to slow down but before he could speak, she sprang up the stairs. She had the same fearlessness as when she had gone up to bat against Larry.

The humming pulsated and rose in intensity. Max wanted to comment on the sound but decided against it. If they were going to spy, he didn't want Grandpa to catch them doing it.

The top of the stairs had a small landing with a door slightly ajar. Cindy approached the door in a crouched position. She moved at an angle so Grandpa couldn't see her unless he stood on the other side right next to the door. Max followed her lead.

They both peered into a room that ran the entire width and length of the house. The pulsing, which at first was a mild sensation, now made the floor vibrate. Max felt a tickle all through his body as they knelt on the floor.

Five tall silver metallic stands stood in a circle around the large room and appeared to be generating a transparent force field. Grandpa Joe stood next to a type of control panel, but it wasn't like any Max had ever seen. It had switches, dials, and lights all over it. Grandpa Joe and the terminal were inside the force field along with a brilliant light. The light hovered in the center of the room about an inch off the floor. The force field spread from the cylinder-like stands to form a prismatic dome, which completely covered everything in the room.

"What is that?" Cindy's whisper was barely audible above the humming.

Grandpa Joe made adjustments to the terminal. He was too preoccupied with what he was doing to notice Max and Cindy watching. The room had no other furnishings. A single light bulb hung from the ceiling, its light flickering in time with the pulsating hum. The string, to turn the bulb on and off, bounced around on the top surface of the force field like a jumping jack.

"What's he doing?" Max tried to see the top of the terminal. Knowing his grandfather was too busy to notice him, he risked standing up for a better view. Grandpa was studying notes written in a pocket-sized notepad. He kept looking from the notepad to the terminal, rapidly turning dials and flipping switches.

After a few more adjustments, Grandpa stuffed the notepad into his pocket and walked toward the bright light. Before Max knew what was happening, Grandpa walked directly into the light. The light grew so intense that Max and Cindy shielded their eyes. When Max could finally see again, Grandpa was gone!

4

Destiny

Max and Cindy looked at each other, mouths agape. They stood in shock, wondering what they had just seen. Grandpa Joe had vanished right in front of their eyes.

"What happened? And what is that light?" Cindy pointed at the glowing ball.

"I have no idea." Max was as confused as she was. "Whatever it is, Grandpa hasn't used it since I've been here. I mean, this humming can probably be heard from three blocks away."

"Now that you mention it, I have heard it before." Cindy pushed the door the rest of the way open and entered the room.

"Oh, great. No wonder everyone thinks my grandfather is crazy."

"No, it's not what you think. It's barely noticeable at my house."

"*Barely noticeable.* What does that mean?" Max's voice rose in agitation.

"Calm down. Why are you so mad?"

Max wasn't upset but he felt panicky. Although he hadn't wanted to stay with his grandfather this summer, he had bonded with him. "I'm not angry, but my grandfather just disappeared! In a ball of light!"

"I'm sure he's okay."

"How do you know?"

"It looked like he knew what he was doing. No one made him go into that light. He did that on his own and he didn't act afraid."

"Yeah, I guess so," Max agreed, feeling slightly better.

They surveyed the dome which looked like a giant soap bubble with swirling transparent colors gliding across its surface. "What do you think it is?" Max tried to stay calm.

"Well, it looks like a big light surrounded by some kind of force field," Cindy stated the obvious as she moved closer and extended her finger.

"What are you doing?" Max asked anxiously.

"I only want to see what it is."

"Don't touch it with your finger. Find something else."

"I don't have anything with me." Cindy held her finger inches away from it.

"Wait, I have an idea." Max took off his shoe. "I'll throw my shoe at it."

"Good idea." Cindy stepped out of his way. "Throw it as hard as you can."

Max held the shoe in his hand as he studied the dome-shaped force field. Max stared at a spot directly in front of him, wound up, and threw his shoe as hard as he could.

What happened next would cause laughter on Cindy's part throughout the rest of Max's stay at Grandpa's.

The shoe flew through the air and hit the force field. It bounced back directly at Max, but with greater velocity. The sole of the shoe landed smack in the middle of Max's forehead, knocking him to the ground.

"Are you okay?" Cindy stepped to Max's side and helped him up.

"Yes, just feeling stupid."

Cindy exploded with laughter. Her face turned red as she wrapped her arms around her stomach and doubled over. She leaned against the wall to keep from falling.

"What's so funny?" Max was annoyed that she found the incident comical.

"The sole of your shoe is imprinted on your forehead." She pointed and continued to laugh. "And the way it knocked you flat. You flew almost six feet!"

"I'm glad you find it so amusing." Max glared, but then cracked a smile realizing how ridiculous he must have looked. He ran his hand across his forehead and, sure enough, he could feel the imprint of his shoe.

Cindy's laughter quieted as the light grew bright enough to blind. Cindy and Max covered their eyes. Then, Grandpa appeared. He looked shocked to see them staring at him from outside the force field.

They all sat in silence at lunch. Max didn't know what to say. Grandpa ate his sandwich while staring off into space. Cindy, for all of her previous bravery, reverted into the shy girl Max met his first day. She hadn't raised her eyes to a level above anyone's shoulders since they sat down. Max had remained silent, but he tried to make eye contact with both of them. He kept looking to Grandpa, wanting an answer, and then to Cindy, hoping for backup.

Max couldn't read his grandfather. He couldn't tell if he was angry or disappointed. His grandfather hadn't said anything about them being in the room on the third floor.

"What happened to your forehead?" Grandpa studied Max's face.

Before Max could answer, Cindy started choking on her sandwich with laughter. Max couldn't help himself and started to laugh as well.

"Did I miss something?" Grandpa asked.

Cindy's hilarity gave Max the opening he was looking for. It broke the silence and unstopped the dam of questions he had.

"Well," Max stammered. "I hit myself in the head with my shoe." He couldn't help himself and continued to laugh. He hadn't thought it was that funny before but it became more so when he heard himself say it.

"You hit yourself, in the head, with your shoe?"

Tears streamed down Cindy's cheeks and Max was laughing hard. Grandpa smiled at them and looked like he wanted to know more.

"Would one of you please tell me what's so funny?" Grandpa demanded.

Cindy was laughing uncontrollably so Max started to explain. "We were wondering if that thing upstairs was a force field. Cindy was going to touch it with her finger, when I suggested throwing my shoe at it."

"You should have seen it, Grandpa," Cindy gasped. She had started calling him 'Grandpa' from day one. "He threw his shoe as hard as he could. It bounced back, smacked him right in the forehead and knocked him flat."

Grandpa started to chuckle.

"Look, you can still see the imprint on his forehead." Cindy pointed. Grandpa laughed out loud as he noticed the markings. Max was laughing, but not as hard as they were. After all, it was at his expense.

"Grandpa, what is that machine?" Max asked.

The kitchen became silent. Grandpa looked at Max while Cindy and Max eyed him.

"Well," Grandpa explained. "It's a gateway."

"A gateway?" Max and Cindy asked simultaneously.

"Yes, a gateway."

"To where?" Max asked, his attention glued on Grandpa.

"To hundreds of worlds." Grandpa leaned closer towards them. "It opens doors into other dimensions that exist right here on this planet."

"So," started Cindy, "all those pictures upstairs are real? You have actually seen all those things and traveled to those places?"

"Yes, anything you can imagine exists in other dimensions."

"Dinosaurs?" Max's voice rose with excitement.

"Yes. Dinosaurs, dragons, interplanetary space travel, and even magic," Grandpa explained with a sparkle in his eye.

"Magic?" asked Max. "What kind of magic?"

"Well, like this," Grandpa winked. "*Pridi.*" The saltshaker flew from the center of the table into his hand.

"Wow," said Max.

"Cool," whispered Cindy.

Later that night as Max prepared for bed, Grandpa Joe came into his room. "I thought I told you not to go up to the third floor without me." He sat on the edge of Max's bed with a disappointed look in his eyes.

"I'm sorry, Grandpa. It's my fault." Max accepted the blame because he didn't want to get Cindy into trouble. "We were cleaning the front room, but the dust got too thick. While it settled, we decided to explore the other rooms. We found a lot of strange photographs and objects that gave us the idea that something strange was going on. Then you came home and ran up to the third floor like something was wrong. That, and the fact that there was this noisy humming, was more than we could stand."

"Well, I can't blame you there. I would want to see what was happening as well." Grandpa paused. "There is more going on than I explained at lunch. Things I've wanted to tell you but didn't know how."

"Like what?"

"Important things. Dangerous, evil things. I think Cindy needs to hear about them too. They will affect her family as well."

"What do you mean?" Max felt uneasy. "What will affect her and her family?"

"The evil. Cindy and her family live in this town. They are in as much danger as you and I and in some ways even more."

"What's going on?"

"More than you could ever imagine. I will explain it all tomorrow. I've decided to tell Cindy as well. I wasn't going to tell her, but I think she can help and I don't want to make the same mistake I made with your father."

"My father?"

"It can wait until tomorrow."

"You can't start talking about danger and evil and. . .and my father, and then just stop and walk out," Max protested. "Do you think I will be able to sleep after all that?"

"Yes." Grandpa Joe smiled.

Max heard his grandfather utter a strange word, "*Zaspi*," and Max slipped off to dreamland.

The next morning, Max found breakfast waiting on the table. He ate two plates of waffles and then began clearing the table. Grandpa had yet to show his face and Max was ready for answers.

After he washed the dishes, he went out the back door expecting to find Grandpa preparing for the morning chores. There was no sign of him in the backyard, so he went to the front just as Cindy entered the gate.

"Morning, Max." Cindy closed the gate behind her.

"Have you seen Grandpa?"

"Nope." She walked up the path.

"Hey, wuss." The call from the street caused both Max and Cindy to turn around. Larry and his gang were approaching, accompanied by two adults. Max and Cindy waited as they drew near. They hadn't seen Larry and the gang for over a week and were surprised to see them now.

"What do they want?" Cindy hissed.

"I don't know," answered Max. He was as annoyed as Cindy. "Who are the adults?"

"What do you want, Larry?" Max asked as the group stopped outside the gate. One of the men was dressed in an expensive suit and the other was a police officer.

"My Da. . ." Larry stuttered. "I mean my lawyer and the sheriff need to talk to your grandfather."

"About what?" Max asked.

"About you," the sheriff sneered.

"About me?" Max's jaw dropped in disbelief.

"Yes, we take assault very seriously around here, son," the officer said.

The officer wore a serious expression with a hint of viciousness in his eyes that frightened Max. The man in the suit was obviously Larry's father. He was a tall, bulky man with black hair and the same facial features as his son.

"We can't have kids moving to our town and starting fights," Larry's father said with the same evil grin that Larry always had.

"Starting fights?" Cindy blurted out with disbelief.

"What's going on, Alan?" Grandpa came out of the house and hustled to join them at the fence.

"Joe," responded Alan. "Your grandson beat up my boy and I'm going to register a formal complaint. We don't want any delinquents in our peaceful town."

"Oh." Grandpa rubbed his chin as if analyzing the situation.

"We know your grandson broke Larry's nose during a friendly baseball game the other day," the sheriff said. "All these boys have testified on Larry's behalf."

"This couldn't be a case of Larry being embarrassed because he lost a fight he started?" Grandpa raised his eyebrows.

"That's not the way these boys explained it," the sheriff pointed out. "They said your grandson was upset because he was pitching a bad game. He began pushing everyone around and when Larry tried to calm him down, Max punched him."

Everyone but Grandpa and Cindy was staring at Max. They looked like wolves waiting for a piece of the kill. Cindy looked disgusted. Grandpa, on the other hand, had a slight smile on his face.

"I always thought Larry was the toughest kid in town," Grandpa mumbled to himself but loud enough for all to hear. The words startled Max but it also eased his fears.

"That isn't the issue here." Alan stepped closer to the gate, his fist knotted at his sides and his teeth clenched. "This is about Max assaulting my son."

"I disagree. This is very much about Larry. I find it interesting that he isn't the toughest kid in town," Grandpa said.

"This isn't about the strength of my son. This is about your grandson attacking my boy." Alan snarled. "I don't really care if my son is tough or weak."

"Oh, my apologies. I thought you were concerned that you were raising a wimp." Grandpa stared at Larry.

"Hey, I'm not a wimp," Larry erupted angrily.

"Larry, shut up," Alan ordered. "My son is not a wimp."

"You don't sound very convinced. I always thought you took pride in the fact that your son was the toughest, strongest kid around. I merely find it interesting that you think he is, in fact, a wimp."

"Dad," roared Larry. "I'm not a wimp. I can take any kid in town."

"Apparently, you couldn't take Max," Grandpa razzed Larry. "You're always calling him a wuss. If he whipped you, that would make you a. . ."

"He didn't whip me," Larry exploded. "That wimp always has to have Mindy stick up for him."

"Larry," Alan shouted.

"It's true, Dad. *She's* tougher than that wimp."

"I know," Grandpa agreed. "I was there the other day. Cindy is the only one on Fred's team who hit Larry the whole game. Isn't that right, Larry?"

"Yes, this wimp couldn't hit me, only Mindy," Larry spat.

"Then it's agreed," Grandpa said with a smirk. "Cindy broke Larry's nose."

"What?"

Grandpa's claim had startled everyone. For the first time, no one was staring at Max. Instead, their eyes were fixed on Grandpa.

"Larry agreed that Cindy was the only one who hit him that day. Didn't you, Larry?" Grandpa said before anyone else could speak.

"Yes, but...," started Larry, however, Grandpa was too quick.

"You see, he said *Yes*," Grandpa finished.

Larry started to protest, but his father shot him a look that silenced him. Alan whirled on Grandpa, his face red with rage. "You can't protect him, just like you couldn't protect his father," Alan hissed through his teeth. He then turned and headed down the street. "Come on."

The sheriff and the rest of the boys followed him, all except Larry. He stared at Max through the gate. "You better not let me catch you alone."

"You don't scare anyone," Max said. "A girl broke your nose."

Larry growled and tried to grab Max through the bars of the gate. As he did, the bars of the gate turned white-hot and the sleeve of Larry's shirt ignited into flames. Larry screamed and wrenched his arm back quickly. Everyone looked around at the noise and saw Larry flailing his arm through the air. Larry stopped waving his arm and stared at his smoking sleeve, the fire no longer visible.

"Let's go, Larry." Alan yelled and Larry followed, nursing his arm.

Max, Cindy, and Grandpa laughed throughout the day about the way Grandpa made it look like Cindy broke Larry's nose. They finished cleaning the front room and were enjoying a glass of lemonade. Max was amazed at the way he pulled it off. "Ego," Grandpa said. "I was only playing with Larry's ego which, by the way, is huge."

"Grandpa, will you tell us what's going on now?" Max asked.

"Yes, I've wanted to tell you since your first day here. I just wasn't sure where to begin."

"We know some things," Cindy offered.

"Yes, I know you do. You're smart kids. Cindy, I am glad you are here. I think Max will need a friend in this, and your family is in danger as well," Grandpa paused.

"My parents are in danger?" Cindy asked and Max could see the blood drain out of her face.

"Yes, but don't worry. There are ways of protecting them."

"How?"

"I will teach you." Grandpa patted her trembling hands. "But first, where to begin?"

"How about with that thing upstairs? What is it? Where did it come from?" Max asked.

"What about the danger?" Cindy asked.

"I will get to that, Cindy. I think I'd better start further back though. When I was a young man, I was hired by the government to work on several scientific projects," he began to explain. "One project dealt with gateways into other worlds."

"Like the machine upstairs?" Max interrupted.

"Yes. The government wanted it for the information and the technology other worlds had to offer."

"What sort of technologies?" Cindy asked with raised eyebrows her face still very pale.

"Like today's space program, computers, advanced medicine and weapons. All of them came from other worlds. Many things we use today came from those worlds."

"How come you have the machine now?" Max asked. "Why doesn't the government have it?"

"The original machine and the designs were destroyed in a fire. Right after the fire a new uninterested administration took office."

"Then how did you get yours?" Max asked.

"I secretly made a copy of the designs and snuck them out. My colleagues and I discovered there was more at stake than knowledge. The life of every man, woman, and child was in danger. We learned about many things going on in our own world by visiting other worlds."

"That doesn't make any sense," said Max, and Cindy nodded.

"Let's see if I can describe it better. We weren't the only people who were entering other worlds and bringing back knowledge. Other people had been entering those worlds for hundreds of years. They, on the other hand, were not bringing back technology, they were bringing back magic." Grandpa took a drink of his lemonade.

"What? How?" Max and Cindy asked together.

"Witches, wizards, and warlocks have been learning magic from different worlds for centuries. The funny thing we discovered is that our world has greater magical powers than any other world. Only most people don't know how to tap into this power. These worlds have beings that teach humans how to use magic. It was beings from other worlds, using their magical power to enter our world, that taught the original witches and wizards of this world about magic," he paused to see if Max and Cindy understood.

"These beings, are they human or something else?" Cindy asked thoughtfully.

"Some are and some aren't. And some of them are good while others are evil. The evil ones, if unchecked, would destroy our world. They want absolute power here. My colleagues and I decided that we needed to protect the unaware and unknowing public. There are beings more powerful than you could possibly imagine. It was our goal, our mission, to keep them from gaining control of this world and others. Now, there are only a few of us left. That's why I need you, Max. I need someone to carry on the fight once I am gone."

"Me? I'm only twelve!" Max protested. "What can *I* do?"

"I am afraid there's no one else, Max. And you'd be surprised at what you can do. I need you because you are young and haven't been influenced by this world. Most adults are already set in their ways and would use the machine to gain power or money. We can teach you. You will understand the need to keep this machine and what it does a secret. We can train you to protect our world. I think Cindy can help you. I don't know who else to turn to."

For the first time Max thought Grandpa looked worried. Usually, he was cheerful and upbeat and never looked old, but in the last few minutes he seemed to have aged right before their eyes. The change frightened Max.

"What is it that you want me to do?" Max asked nervously.

"First, I need to finish the story. There are people who know about the machine and what it does."

"Let me guess," said Cindy. "Almost the whole town?"

"Why, yes," Grandpa said with a puzzled look.

"She saw the people the night I arrived," Max explained.

"Oh. Well, I'm sorry to say that almost everyone in town is against us. They are evil. They practice black magic, and they want to bring more powerful beings into our world."

"I thought you said that people could use magic to travel to other worlds. Why don't these evil beings just use magic to come here?" Max asked.

"Very perceptive," Grandpa smiled with a flicker of his old self shining in his eyes. "Magic can help a being cross into another world for only a short time. It takes powerful magic to do it. In the end, though, that being's body is still tied to its original world and it has to return. After four or five days, they become weak and risk death if they continue to stay. The only way they can recover is if they go back to their own world. Unless. . ."

"You have a gateway," Max offered.

"Good," Grandpa said with a nod. "Yes, with the gateway we can travel to other worlds and stay as long as we want without risk of losing our strength or dying. It also means that we can bring someone or something back. The people in this town and the creatures in other worlds will kill to get their hands on that machine. They want to bring evil beings back and not just for a short visit. They want to control our world."

"Why don't we see any of these beings in our world, even if they are only temporary?" Cindy asked.

"Lots of beings have been seen but they are usually dismissed as hallucinations or nightmares. You've heard of Bigfoot and other such legends. The one they really want to bring back is a being my colleagues and I trapped in a world almost void of magic. Still others come to teach their allies, but this is done in secret. I was only a scientist but, when I realized what we were up against, I learned magic to protect myself. We have allies in other worlds that help us. We have to help them as well. This battle is not limited to our world only, but also affects hundreds of others. Some of them do not have laws or governments to enforce rules. If the gateway fell into their hands, all would be lost."

"So what would happen to us if we went to those worlds?" Max asked apprehensively.

"If you are unprepared and they catch you, they will kill you." Grandpa replied, his face reflecting the seriousness of the situation. "I can teach you, both of you, if you are up to the challenge. You are both in danger already; Max, because you are my heir and Cindy, because you live here."

"What do you mean?" Cindy asked nervously.

"I'm sorry to say, Cindy, without some sort of protection you and your family will surrender to this dark magic. The influence of evil is too strong in this town. Eventually, everyone succumbs to it, and they don't even know it has happened. I can teach you how to protect yourself and your parents. You already saw what happened when Larry tried to cross into my yard. You must trust me. Max, you have seen their hatred from day one. They will try to get rid of you any way they can. Especially now they know you are my grandson."

"Can you protect my yard with the same spell?" Cindy pleaded.

"That would place your parents in greater danger than they are in already. If the enemy discovered such a spell, they would think your parents were on my side and knew more than they know. They would be open for an attack and not know how to protect themselves. Right now, the enemy thinks they know nothing and therefore will assume their usual methods of conversion will work. I can teach you other ways to protect them."

"Did they know about me before I arrived?" Max asked in a shaky voice. He couldn't tell if he was angry or scared or both.

"No," Grandpa said. "That is why you haven't seen me much over the years. I tried to keep you safe by keeping my distance. But now I'm desperate. I only made contact with your mother a couple of months ago and somehow the enemy found out about it. I think that is why they were waiting when you arrived."

"What are you saying?" Max asked.

"You're the only one I can trust. All of my colleagues are too old. I don't have anyone else."

"I am willing to do whatever it takes to save my family," Cindy swallowed.

Max struggled with the enormity of what his grandfather had just said. Grandpa was asking him to save the world. Cindy seemed willing to help, but then she was going to be saving herself and her family; not the entire world.

"I have friends in other places waiting to help us. Waiting to teach you," Grandpa said.

"Please! There must be someone else!" Max wanted to help, he really did, but this was too much for him. He had already accepted what his grandfather told him was true because of all the strange events he witnessed. He didn't want the responsibility.

"Max," Grandpa said softly. "You really don't have a choice anymore."

"What do you mean *I don't have a choice*?"

"They will find you wherever you go. I know they marked you."

"Marked me?"

"On your hand. They marked you the first night you were here. They put it there so they would know where you are at all times. Whether you are in this world or another, they will find you."

Max looked at his hand and the faint symbol. Cindy leaned towards him and stared at his hand. He wondered if she was upset that he had kept the mark hidden from her.

"Max," Grandpa said. "I am sorry I got you into this, but you are my only hope. My friends and I will teach you what you need to know to survive."

Max wasn't feeling very well. He thought this was supposed to be a get-to-know-your-grandfather summer. He wasn't expecting, *I need you to keep the world safe and oh, by the way, evil people with magical powers want to destroy you.* He really wanted to see his mother. Why did she send him here? Did she know what Grandpa wanted? Just then he thought of his father. Had Dad known about this? He had never really understood his father's death. Nobody had ever really explained it to him.

"Did Dad know?" Max continued to stare at the mark on his hand.

"Yes."

"How did he die?"

"He was killed," Grandpa said solemnly. "He was caught in one of the worlds without laws."

Max tried to speak, but the lump in his throat stifled any words.

"I think Alan killed him."

5

Yelka

Max tossed and turned all night because of the conversation with Grandpa. Larry's father, Alan, had murdered his father. How did he get away with it? In which world did it happen? The night passed slowly and Max wondered how much his mother knew. Was she safe? He had many questions and he wanted answers. He didn't like that he didn't have a choice when it came to saving the world. It was early in the morning when he finally nodded off, but his sleep was fitful and filled with darkness.

He awoke at sunrise. Waking brought back all of his fear and unanswered questions. After an hour of trying to get back to sleep, he decided it was no use and got out of bed.

He went to the kitchen to get a drink of water and found Grandpa reading the morning paper.

"It looks like you had a hard night." Grandpa looked at him over his paper.

"Yeah." Max yawned.

"I expected as much. How about I fix you a big breakfast?" Grandpa put down the paper and went to the cupboards.

Max didn't bother to respond but took a seat. "Grandpa, does Mom know?"

"Yes," he answered as he started preparing breakfast.

"Is she safe?"

"Yes, your mother has some skills. She understands how important this work is."

Grandpa's answer made Max feel better. It only made sense that his mother knew. He wondered if she had magical powers and if so, did she ever use them.

"And my dad? How did he die?" Max swallowed the lump in his throat.

Grandpa's face turned very pale, and his eyes looked sad. "I don't know all the details. I want to find out more before I tell you the story. I don't want to give you wrong information."

"Okay, I understand."

"Let's have some breakfast."

Within minutes, Grandpa Joe had whipped up some pancakes and eggs.

"What are we going to do today?" Max took a bite of pancakes.

"We are going to visit a friend of mine. But since you're up already, perhaps we can get an early start on the morning chores."

"What's today's chore?" It might have been the lack of sleep or the weight of his new responsibility, but Max really wanted to skip the morning tasks. He felt like going back to bed.

"We are going to trim the trees."

Max was surprised when Cindy joined them soon after they had started trimming the trees. He hadn't expected to see her since they were starting their chores earlier than usual.

"Couldn't sleep?" Max asked as she dragged herself through the gate.

"Nope."

Grandpa put them to work but things were going very slowly. Cindy and Max were tired and the morning crawled by. Grandpa trimmed while Cindy and Max carried the branches to the fire pit.

When they were returning to the front yard, they noticed a man dressed all in black walking up the street towards them. He wore a long coat and a big hat. The collar of his coat was turned up making it impossible to see his face. The man limped slightly and kept his hands in his pockets. Max and Cindy stopped and stared as he approached.

"Hey, what's the hold-up?" asked Grandpa as he climbed down the ladder. "It doesn't sound like anyone's working."

They could hear the stranger's raspy breathing as he halted outside the gate.

"Cindy, Max, get inside now!" Grandpa ordered, but they remained motionless. Max felt transfixed by the unknown man. "I said now!" Grandpa's command startled them into submission.

"Whys didss yous sends thes childrenss awaysss." Max heard the man's snake-like voice hiss his question as he and Cindy entered the house. They darted into the front room where they could watch through the window. Max couldn't hear anything but he could tell that Grandpa and the man were engaged in a heated discussion. After several tense moments, the man walked back down the street.

"He sure was creepy," Cindy commented.

"I don't think he's leaving." Max watched the retreating figure.

"What do you mean?"

"Look," Max pointed. The man walked three houses away and stood under the shade of an old Maple tree. He appeared to be watching them from under his dark covering.

Grandpa walked into the house muttering something under his breath. He looked agitated.

"Who was that?" Max asked.

"They're called Night Shades," Grandpa spat. "They are very nasty warlocks. He was sent here to spy on us."

"Is he from another world?" questioned Cindy.

"Yes."

"Well at least he can't stay here forever," Max offered. "He didn't come through the gateway right, so he can't stay permanently?"

"No, but there are enough of them to keep a constant watch," Grandpa added. "We have a lot of work to do. They know who you are, Max, and they will do anything to keep me from training you. I'm afraid things are more desperate than I had thought. I wanted to teach you only a few things this summer, but you will need to learn much more."

"They can't get in here can they?" asked Cindy with an alarmed expression. "And what about my parents and my house?"

"No, they can't get in here. It would take a powerful being years to break my protective spell," Grandpa said. "And as for your house and your parents, I am taking you to a friend who has something to help you protect them. We should get started. Follow me." Grandpa led them up to the third floor.

"Where are we going?" Max asked as they climbed the spiral staircase.

"We're going to see my friend," Grandpa responded as they entered the room. "Step inside the circle. If your entire body isn't inside the force field when it starts, you will be thrown against the wall."

Max and Cindy were surprised. Where the bright light had been, which Grandpa had vanished and reappeared through, stood a revolving mirror about the size of two doors.

Max thought that the unique cherry-carved frame looked like an antique.

Cindy stepped up to Max and took his hand. "Where are we going?"

Max felt the blood rush to his cheeks as he felt her soft skin. He had never held a girl's hand before and he was glad none of his friends back home could see him. "I'm not sure." He tried to sound brave but he was as nervous as she appeared to be.

Grandpa flipped a switch on the console and the humming began. The force field spread from the five metal pillars until it formed a dome. He then turned a couple of dials and the mirror started to revolve. The humming increased as the mirror spun faster. In its center, a light appeared and began to grow. It spread until it enveloped the mirror.

"Max, you take my hand and Cindy, you. . ." Grandpa smiled as he noticed that they were already holding hands.

Max and Cindy both blushed, but didn't release their hold. Grandpa took Max's free hand and led them to the light. "Are you ready? As you enter the gateway, take a big step down."

Grandpa stepped into the gateway pulling them behind him. The light turned into rolling green hills with tall grasses and colorful wildflowers surrounded by snow-capped mountains. The sky was an ocean of blue with a few white fluffy clouds. Max, surprised by the sudden change of sce-

nery, forgot to step down and yanked Cindy with him.
Grandpa caught them before they fell. "Sorry," he apologized, "it's more like two big steps."

Max looked back through the gateway but it had vanished. "How do we get home?"

"With this." From his pocket, Grandpa took out a
small golden medallion with a crystal in the center. He
waved it around in the direction of the gateway and every
time it passed over it, the crystal flashed a bright white light.
"We used safety lines on our first trips through the gateway.
Eventually we figured out that crystals reflect the light of the
gateway. The naked eye can't see it, which is to our advantage."

"It sure is beautiful here," Cindy commented.

"Yes it is," Grandpa replied.

"Ouch." Max cried out and looked at his hand. The
mark burned and was darker then before.

Grandpa examined the mark. "I was afraid of this.
They know you have left and will be coming soon. We have
to hurry."

"What do you mean?" Max asked with panic in his
voice.

"They marked you to track you. It will take them a
while to find where you are, but eventually they will. We
have maybe two hours." Grandpa led them up and down several small hills in a westward direction.

Max became extremely nervous. The thought of
someone hunting him upset him deeply and he constantly
looked over his shoulder. The tall mountain grass swaying
in the wind caused him to see movement everywhere.

"How far is it?" Cindy asked.

"About half a mile from here." Grandpa took long
strides. At the bottom of the fifth hill, they followed a path
running along its base. After a couple hundred yards, they
saw a small cottage nestled between two low hills. It was

surrounded by a copse of trees that had kept it hidden from a distance.

The cottage looked like it belonged in a fairy tale. It had a bright red roof, green shutters, and flower boxes under the windows. Driven by a stream, a water wheel rotated slowly at the right side of the house. In the center of the house was a green door with a shiny brass handle.

As they approached, the door opened, and a woman wearing a colorful dress emerged. With a beautiful face and blonde braided hair, she was only a tiny bit taller than Max. As they drew closer, he saw she had pointed ears. "Hello, Joseph." She smiled. "I've been expecting you."

"Hello, Yelka," Grandpa said.

"I see you've brought some students," Yelka said with a peculiar accent. It sounded like she was almost singing her words and her voice had a perceptible ring to it. She placed a pair of half moon spectacles on her nose and studied them.

Grandpa took her by the hand. "This is my grandson, Max, and our friend, Cindy."

"Hello," Cindy said.

"How do you do?" Max asked politely as he shook her hand. He couldn't help but stare at her beautiful but slightly strange features.

"They do seem curious, don't they?" Yelka said.

"They're kids," Grandpa said.

Yelka eyed them for a moment. "In case you were wondering, I am not a human like you."

"The enemy is closing in on us, Joseph, and we don't have much time." Yelka's tone became suddenly serious. She beckoned them towards the door of the house, "Follow me, children."

"How do you know?" Max asked.

"Oh, don't be surprised, young Max. I sensed the mark on your hand." She winked at him over her glasses.

"Now, I want you two to do whatever Yelka tells you," Grandpa urged.

"You're not staying?" Max asked.

"No, I am going to keep watch outside." Grandpa motioned towards the door. "We don't want to be caught unaware."

Max and Cindy followed Yelka into the living room and she motioned them to sit on a couch with a coffee table in front of it. She sat in a chair opposite them. Max observed that the furniture was smaller than human furniture. Even the ceiling was lower.

"Do you know why you are here?" Yelka asked in her sing-song voice.

Cindy and Max shook their heads. Max felt mesmerized; he couldn't take his eyes off Yelka. Though she did not quite look human, she was very beautiful.

"Well then, I shall briefly explain. It is obvious that you have some questions about me. I am what you would call an elf, although we call ourselves Svetice and our world is called Svet. We are an ancient people, born with the ability to use magic. I will be your magic teacher."

"Did you teach my grandfather?" Max asked.

"Yes, I was one of your Grandfather's teachers."

"Grandpa had other teachers?" Cindy asked.

"Now, children, we can answer such questions later. We really must begin. We don't have much time." Yelka retrieved a tray from an end table beside her and placed it in front of Max and Cindy. Long green plants with twisted black roots lay piled on the tray.

"Almost every creature has the ability to perform magic," Yelka began. "I am sure you have heard that humans only use a portion of their brains. Part of the power that goes untapped is the ability to use magic. These roots contain a compound that will awaken the portion of your mind that is sleeping. I want each of you to take a plant and eat the roots."

Both Max and Cindy took one of the plants and examined them.

"I warn you," Yelka said, "it is not candy."

Cindy gently touched the roots to her tongue and quickly removed it. "*Augh*, it tastes like puke."

Max, after seeing Cindy's reaction, wanted it over quickly. He plugged his nose and bit off the black portion of the plant. The taste was worse than he had imagined. He tried to swallow quickly, but his gag reflex kicked in. It took several tries to get it down.

Cindy was having a harder time. She would take a nibble and then gag multiple times before she could swallow it.

"Can I have some water?" asked Max, the horrible taste clinging to his tongue.

"Give it a minute," Yelka smiled. "If you continue to eat these roots, you will learn magic faster than those who are currently learning it in your world. I want you to take five roots each and eat one a day for the next five days."

By now, Cindy had finished but was still gagging. "I thought I was going to barf. Is there some other way of getting this compound?"

"I am afraid not, dear."

A comforting warmth washed over Max's body. He thought he could sense a connection with everything around him. "I feel weird."

"That is normal; part of your mind is being awakened." Yelka moved to the edge of her chair. "This first spell I am going to teach you will allow you to move objects. You will only be able to move small objects at first and it will be difficult. The more you practice, the easier it will become." She then placed two marble-sized stones in front of Max and Cindy.

The bitter taste was disappearing and Max felt better, stronger. "What do we do now?"

"Concentrate on the rock in front of you. Picture it blowing off the table as if it were a feather. Do you think you can do that?"

They nodded.

"Now, as you picture this, I want you to say the word *premakni*. Let's say it together."

"*Premakni*," they repeated.

"Now you try."

Max stared at the stones and repeated, "*Premakni*." After several minutes with no results, he was starting to feel frustrated and he could tell by Cindy's expression she was feeling the same. He didn't believe it was going to happen.

"I don't think this is going to work," Cindy moaned.

"That is why it isn't working," Yelka's voice rang. "Concentrate, you must see it happen in your mind and say the word, *premakni*."

Max concentrated harder than ever. Blood pounded in his brain like a vein was going to pop out of his forehead. "*Premakni*." He felt his face turn red.

"Relax yourself, Max. Pushing all that blood to your head isn't going to help. Calm down and picture it in your mind." Yelka took a deep breath and held out her hand. "*Premakni*." Both stones flew off the table and landed on the floor. "Like that." She gathered the stones and placed them back on the table.

Max took a deep breath and closed his eyes. He envisioned the stone flying off the table. He opened his eyes and stared at the stone. "*Premakni*." The stone moved a couple of inches.

"It moved." Max said with excitement. "It moved! Did you see it?"

"Yes, I saw. Now try to blow it off the table," Yelka encouraged.

"I will."

Cindy took another turn. "*Premakni*." Her stone slid closer to the edge of the table. Max saw that she had beaten his mark and her expression told him how pleased she was.

Max didn't allow her satisfaction to last long. It took him only two tries before his stone flew off the table, while Cindy's stone didn't budge on her next four attempts. On her fifth try, the stone jumped two inches and when it stopped, she called again, "*Premakni*." This time the stone traveled the remainder of the way off the table.

"Very good, children," Yelka praised them. "I want you to practice every day. Soon you will be able to do it without the help of the roots."

"Now I am going to teach you some more spells to practice. We will not do them here, for our time is short. I will help you with the pronunciation and imagery. Remember imagery is as important as the correct pronunciation. The next spell is to stop an object. If someone has thrown something at you and you want to stop it, you need to picture it stopping dead in the air and falling to the ground. The spell is pronounced *vstani*. Now let's all say it together."

"*Vstani*," they repeated several times.

"Remember these words, children, and their meanings."

"Can we write them down?" Cindy asked.

"No, I am afraid not. We don't want to risk the enemy getting any knowledge of these spells," Yelka warned.

"What do you mean?" Max asked with a surprised look. "They don't use the same spells?"

"No, they use evil spells. There are people who say evil is more powerful than good because they know both good and bad. They try to convince others that good only understands good, and that we don't have the knowledge they do. The truth is the more someone practices evil, the more they lose the ability to do what's right. Soon the very thing they tried to understand enslaves them. Only those who avoid evil are truly free and have the ability to choose and recognize the difference. Do you understand?"

"I think so," Cindy said.

Max nodded.

"Now," Yelka began. "The next spell is to bring an object to you. Remember the stone. Instead of sending it off the table, you need to picture it coming into your hand. The spell is *pridi*. Let's say it together."

"*Pridi*," they repeated over and over.

"The next spell will slow objects down. Again, you will need to visualize the object slowing down. The spell is pronounced *pochasi*. Together."

"*Pochasi*," they said.

"Ouch." Max looked at his hand.

Yelka jumped to her feet and snatched Max's hand. "They have entered Svet." Her pretty face creased with lines of worry.

Just then, Grandpa raced through the door. "We have to go." His face was flushed and his breathing heavy.

"How many, Joseph?" Yelka asked.

"At least seven Night Shades, maybe more." He gasped for breath.

Yelka ran to a cabinet behind Max and Cindy and took out a penny-shaped disc on a chain. "Cindy, take this and hang it in your bedroom window. It will help protect you and your family until you can learn enough magic to protect them." She handed it to Cindy, who put it in her pocket.

Max thought Cindy looked relieved as she accepted the charm. He remembered how worried she had been about her parents since their first discussion with Grandpa. Now she had something to help them.

"You bring up the rear, Joseph." Yelka led them out the front door.

Yelka motioned them to follow her around the side of the house near the stream. She directed them over the water on stepping stones and after everyone crossed, she gathered them under a tree. "I am going to teach you a more advanced spell. It is used to make things invisible, including yourselves." Yelka was up and moving again. She guided them up a narrow ravine between the hills behind her house.

After they crossed over the hill, they crouched in a clump of shrubs. It was their last cover before they headed into open grasslands. They wouldn't reach the tree line until they were farther up into the mountains.

"The spell is pronounced *izginem se,*" Yelka whispered. "I want you to perform this spell on yourselves now. You must visualize yourself disappearing. I know this is a lot to ask of you so soon, but you must try." Yelka poked her head above the shrubs. "Five black-cloaked figures are approaching my house from the opposite hill. Keep low."

She ran, moving down the hill parallel to the gateway. Max muttered the spell under his breath, but the visualization was difficult. Between running and the thought of creatures attempting to kill them, concentration was difficult. Max imagined Cindy was having the same problem.

They went down the hill and up the next before they stopped again. "I forgot. If you manage the invisibility spell, you will need the spell to make yourselves reappear," Yelka whispered between gasps. "*Prikazi se* is the word to discover what has been hidden." Yelka froze, watching the hill behind them.

On the top of the hill, the five Night Shades appeared and were moving quickly. Max gritted his teeth against the throbbing in his palm. Yelka took him by the hand and the pain instantly subsided. "I can help lessen the pain." She pulled him down the hill after her.

They reached the bottom of the hill and were climbing up the next. Max heard the word *Premakni* spoken in a commanding voice.

Max looked up and saw two Night Shades thrown down the hill in front of them. He turned to see Grandpa standing erect with his arms stretched out in front of him. Grandpa had spotted the trap ahead.

On the hill behind them appeared the trailing Night Shades. They were dressed in black and wore hoods to hide their faces. A roar escaped their mouths as they sighted their prey and raced down the hill towards them.

Yelka let go of Max's hand and joined Grandpa. "Joseph, get the children out."

"I won't leave you alone," Grandpa said.

"Max can't hide in this world and you know it. You need to get him home where he will be safe. I will be all right. This is my world not theirs."

"Cindy, Max, come on." Grandpa took the lead.

Max didn't want to leave Yelka, but he knew they couldn't help her. For a moment he stared at her in a silent goodbye.

"Don't worry, children. We will meet again," Yelka promised. "*Izginem se*," she uttered and vanished.

"Come on!" Grandpa reached back and dragged them after him.

Max tried to watch over his shoulder, but he couldn't get a clear look with the pace Grandpa was setting. From somewhere behind, howls of pain filled the air. It comforted him that none of the screams were Yelka's voice.

Grandpa led them up the hill and then turned right along the top. The cries stopped behind them. Suddenly, at the bottom of the hill there was a flash of black in the sea of green.

"Grandpa!" Max yelled.

"I see him. Keep running!"

The Night Shades were gaining on them. A sudden, incredible force struck Max in the back and sent him flying into Cindy and Grandpa. They went down in a pile of tangled arms and legs. Max tried to stand, but his lungs burned and he couldn't breathe.

Cindy extended her hand to help Max up when a Night Shade reached the top of the hill. The Night Shade advanced quickly towards them and Cindy stepped in front of Max as he struggled for air. "*Premakni*," she screamed with no result.

"Premakni," Grandpa said with his hands extended. The spell yanked the Night Shade off the ground and threw it sideways down the hill.

Max regained his breath and was ready to move. Grandpa was next to them in an instant, the crystal in his hand. He waved it through the air, and when he found the gateway, he handed the crystal to Max. "Take Cindy. Remember you have to step up into the gateway."

"You have to come with us," Max argued, his voice full of panic.

"I'll be right behind you. But I need my hands free to fight. Go now. *Izginem se*." Grandpa vanished.

Max took Cindy by the hand and pulled her after him. He could see the gateway about three hundred yards away on the next hill. As they started down the hill Max slipped on the grass and slid down on his butt. Cindy, rather than be dragged down head first, kicked her feet out and landed on her backside to slide after him. At the bottom of the hill, they climbed to their feet and dashed up the last hill.

An occasional scream of pain or shout of anger reached their ears as they ran hard. Max could see the gateway. They were getting close. They scrambled with all the energy they could muster when, on the hill behind the gateway, more Night Shades appeared.

"Run to the gateway," Grandpa yelled from somewhere behind them. "It's our only chance."

Max and Cindy sprinted as fast as they could. The Night Shades rushed towards them and the gap between them closed quickly. Max reached the gateway at full speed and dove through, pulling Cindy behind him.

They landed on the floor and rolled to their feet watching the gateway.

"Come on, Grandpa," Max whispered.

"Max, if he doesn't come, we don't know how to operate the machine!" Cindy gasped for breath.

"He's coming," Max responded. Deep down he was worried, but he didn't want Cindy to know.

The light of the gateway flickered, brightening and dimming a few times. Max could feel his heart in his throat. A couple of minutes had passed and still Grandpa hadn't appeared.

"What are we going to do?" Cindy asked. There was definite fear in her voice.

"He's coming," Max insisted, but with each passing second his anxiety increased. The constant humming of the force field only added to the tension.

Time froze as seconds turned to minutes. All they could do was wait. The light around the gateway suddenly flashed brighter and they covered their eyes. When the light dimmed, a Night Shade stood in front of the gateway.

"Childrensss," it hissed.

6

Larry's Father

The Night Shade stood in front of Max and Cindy. The only visible parts were gnarled hands covered in thick, black hair with long, claw-like fingernails. "Nowheres to runsss." It laughed through its teeth, hissing.

Max pushed Cindy behind him. He didn't know what to do. They had no weapons and they couldn't escape with the force field on.

The Night Shade moved forward. It appeared confused, as if unsure how to proceed. As if it did not know what to do with its prey.

"Duck!" shouted Grandpa. As they dropped to the ground, he called out, "*Premakni.*" The spell drove the Night Shade head first into the force field. The force field repelled it backwards several feet, where it landed in an unconscious heap on the floor.

Grandpa rushed to the console and shut down the system. The light of the gateway began to diminish.

The Night Shade stirred, but Grandpa didn't seem interested. "It's moving," Max said.

"It will soon be too weak to do anything," Grandpa said as the light of the gateway faded and the mirror appeared, revolving slowly. The force field was also gone.

"But it came through the gateway. You said if someone came through the gateway they could stay without becoming weak," Max stressed.

"True, but this creature entered Yelka's world using magic. By entering our world through the gateway, it is now in a very precarious position. Its energy source is trapped in the world we just left."

The Night Shade rose up on its hands and knees, and tried to stand.

"What is your name?" Grandpa asked.

It hissed at Grandpa, "You havesss no powerssss over meeesss."

"You're quite mistaken. The gateway is closed and you are trapped here."

The Night Shade's head twisted and turned as it searched for the gateway. "*Odpris luknjos*," it hissed, and a faint ball of light appeared in the air and then disappeared.

"I asked your name." Grandpa demanded, but still the Night Shade refused to answer. "*Reci*," Grandpa commanded and the Night Shade started to tremble. Whatever was happening to it, it was obviously resisting.

"Noretsss," the Night Shade spat.

"What do we want to know?" Grandpa asked more to himself than anyone in particular. He rubbed his chin in thought. The Night Shade looked cornered, like a snake ready to strike.

"How about, *what's this mark on my hand and how do I get rid of it?*" Max thrust out his hand.

The Night Shade let out a harsh, barking laugh. "It'ss marksss of darknesss. A powerfulsss curse it issss."

Grandpa slowly shook his head. "There are only two ways to get rid of it, Max. One is a counter curse, the other is extremely painful."

"Counter curse?" Max didn't want to discuss any painful method.

"Only you can make it go away," Grandpa stated. "You need to practice what you've learned. You need to gain the power to remove it."

The Night Shade leapt with lightning speed towards Max, a curved blade appeared in its hand. It seized Max from behind and held the blade to his throat. "I canss still finishshsss my jobsss. Youuu still losssssse, old mansssss."

"I beg to differ," Grandpa said calmly and pointed a finger at the Night Shade. "You lose. *Unichi*." The Night Shade let out a scream and then turned to dust. The knife fell to the ground with a clatter.

Max remained frozen. His grandfather had just killed the Night Shade. Before Max could recover, Grandpa collapsed.

Cindy rushed to Grandpa's side. Max felt like he was watching the scene from outside his body. He could see himself kneeling over his grandfather. He stared as his grandfather opened his eyes and managed a weak smile.

"He's bleeding." Cindy lifted Grandpa's shirt to reveal an ugly stab wound.

"We need to get him to a doctor," Max said.

"No." Grandpa's voice was barely audible. "You can't take me to a doctor."

"What?" Max asked, astonished.

"No doctor in this town will help me. Get me to my room. Cindy, there is a first-aid kit in the bathroom closet. Bring it to me."

Max assisted Grandpa down the stairs and into his bedroom. After Cindy brought the medical kit, they helped

Grandpa clean and dress his wound. "Don't look so worried," Grandpa reassured them. "I just need some rest."

Max was not convinced that everything was going to be all right. Somehow, he knew the wound was worse than Grandpa admitted.

"You two need to work on the spells Yelka taught you," Grandpa said. "Today and every day."

Max and Cindy spent several days practicing their spells and taking care of Grandpa. Their concern continued to grow, when Grandpa didn't show any signs of improvement. He actually looked worse. He slept most of the day and barely ate or drank anything. Max helped him make trips to the bathroom and he noticed Grandpa leaning more upon him.

Grandpa got out of bed only once for a non-bathroom visit. It was to let Yelka travel from her world into another via the gateway.

"How's the wound?" Yelka asked.

"I'm not sure. I think I might have been poisoned," Grandpa winced with pain.

"What!" Yelka rushed to him and felt his forehead.

"I think they used strup."

"Strup takes a couple of weeks to manifest itself. Have you told Max or Cindy?"

"No, I don't want them to worry if it's nothing."

"And if it is strup?"

"I will contact you," Grandpa said.

"We might not be able to communicate where we are going."

"Then I will have to send Max and Cindy to find you and Marko," Grandpa assured her.

"Be sure you do."

Every day Max and Cindy improved their magic skills. They were now moving larger objects with the *premakni* spell. They had eaten all the roots and were now casting spells without any help. They could also bring marbles and coins towards them. Max gave himself another black eye when he tried to bring a chair towards him and then couldn't stop it. After that they stuck with smaller objects until they could gain more control.

While playing catch in the yard they practiced the *pochasi* and *vstani* spells. Max now knew how Larry and his friends had cheated during the baseball game. With the *pochasi* spell, they could slow down the ball so that it resembled something out of an animated cartoon. *Vstani*, the spell to stop objects, was more difficult and they had only limited success.

Neither of them had managed the *izginem se* spell yet. Grandpa told them that *izginem se* was used to make themselves invisible and they needed to start small. He taught them to use *izgini* to make objects invisible and *pokazi* to make them visible again.

After two days of practicing the new spells, they could make coins invisible and visible again. Larger objects were more difficult. Max tried to get Grandpa to teach them more, but he told them they needed to master the spells they knew. Only then would he give them additional incantations.

Two weeks after their visit with Yelka, Grandpa grew worse and became very ill. Max and Cindy were scared and didn't know what to do.

"We need to get help," Cindy said with worry as they finished practicing their spells.

"I know, but he won't go to a doctor."

"Let's talk to him," Cindy suggested and before Max could argue, she headed towards Grandpa's room.

Grandpa opened his eyes as they entered. He was pale and quivered with pain. "What have you two been up to?"

"We've been practicing spells," Max answered.

"How's it going?"

"Never mind that," Cindy interrupted. "We're very worried about you. You need help."

Grandpa smiled at Cindy and touched her cheek. "There's something you can do, but you will have to travel to another world."

"Will it help you get better?" Max asked.

"Yes, but can be dangerous. I have a friend who can help you while you're there. Bring me some paper and a pencil. I will write down the instructions and you will need to follow them exactly."

"I'll be right back." Max left the room in a flash and came back with the pencil and paper.

"What are we going to do that is so dangerous?" Cindy asked.

"It's not what you'll be doing, but where you'll be going that worries me."

"Tell me what to write," said Max.

"Give me the paper and pencil." Grandpa held out his hand. "I need to draw several things for these instructions. Why don't you fix lunch while I work out the details."

Max and Cindy raced to the kitchen, Max's spirits rose at the chance to help Grandpa. They had been trying to help him for two weeks but he wouldn't hear of it. Now he finally gave in. They made a quick lunch.

In ten minutes, they were back in Grandpa's room eating lunch. Max could almost see him getting worse. If they didn't do something right away, who knew what would happen? Max was anxious to get going but didn't want to push Grandpa because he didn't want him to change his mind.

Finally, Grandpa broke the silence. "I'm going to send you to another world." He sipped on a glass of water. "I didn't want to have to do this, but I can't reach Yelka."

"How do you reach her?" Max asked.

"With this," Grandpa pulled out an unusual looking pocket watch and opened the cover. There were several strange dials and buttons on its face.

"What's that?" Max asked.

"This is something you must keep secret. There are only about seven of these in existence. They allow Yelka, others, and me to communicate even though we are in different worlds. It gives us a great advantage over our enemies. They rely totally on magic and there is so much more than magic. I know they would love a device like this and it is better they don't know about it."

"Do you speak into it?" Max asked.

"It's more like text messaging you would do with a cellular telephone."

"So, you've been communicating with Yelka?" Cindy asked.

"Yes, but I haven't received a response for two days. Yelka and Marko went to spy on enemy movements. They don't take their communicators with them while doing such investigations. That way, if they are captured, the enemy won't get their hands on it. I will continue to call them, but if I don't get an answer, you will need to go. Don't worry; you'll be safer in this world than you were in Yelka's. It's a neutral world."

"What do you mean *neutral*?" Cindy asked. "Are both sides present?"

"Very perceptive. That's exactly what it means. They will know you are there because of the mark on your hand, but they shouldn't harm you."

"Why not?" Max asked.

"A magical creature controls this world. She sets the rules and she doesn't like disturbances in her kingdom. However, that won't stop the enemy from following or harassing you. They have gotten bolder lately and that's why Marko and Yelka are watching them. I'll bet money they will be waiting for you."

"Why?" asked Cindy.

"I'm sure they know I was stabbed. I'm not getting better because the knife was poisoned. The reason I didn't send you earlier is that I had to make sure I was poisoned. This poison takes a couple of weeks to start working. They designed it to torture before it kills. The pain will continue to increase over time before I die. They know I will need a certain type of medicine and the only way to get it, without sending you into a dangerous place, would be in Reeka City in the world known as Mir." Grandpa winced with pain. He held one arm pressed to his side and handed Max the paper. "Here is a map and instructions for when you get there. The second page contains instructions for operating the gateway."

Max took the paper. His excitement about being able to help was fading. He hadn't expected to travel through the gateway, but rather to the local drug store. He glanced at Cindy and could see she felt the same way. Max wanted to help but he didn't want to go through the gateway without Grandpa. The memory of their last trip and their encounter with the Night Shades was fresh in his mind.

"Don't worry," Grandpa reassured them. "I have faith in you both. I want you to go upstairs and memorize the instructions for operating the gateway. Then I want those instructions destroyed. We can't let anything about the gateway fall into the wrong hands. You can leave tomorrow morning, so you'll be back before Cindy's parents get home from work."

"It will take us all day?" Cindy asked.

"Most of the day, yes."

Max studied the second sheet of paper. It looked like the top of the gateway control console. "Are you sure we'll be all right?"

"No one can be completely sure, but I do believe you can do this. They will be waiting for you, but you won't be alone."

"Come on, Cindy," Max said. "He needs rest and we should learn how to operate the gateway."

They went and hovered over the gateway console spending several hours going over each dial and knob. A main power switch operated the force field and another turned on the gateway. One dial turned three hundred and sixty degrees to control the direction the gateway opened in different worlds and several others controlled the pitch or angle of the gateway. Still other knobs determined the world into which the gateway would open. They turned everything on multiple times to make sure they knew the procedures.

The next morning they ate a hurried breakfast with Grandpa before they set off. He looked worse than the day before, so Max knew they had to get the cure quickly.

"Anything from Yelka?" Cindy asked.

"No, I'm sorry. You will have to go," Grandpa responded.

"Are you going to be all right?" Max asked.

"I'll be fine." Grandpa forced a weak smile. "You're the ones we need to worry about." He reached across to the nightstand and retrieved the small disk with the crystal in the center and a compass. "You will need these." He handed them to Max. "Remember, the crystal is the only way to find the gateway."

Max took the items and put them in his pocket. He then handed the gateway instructions back to his grandfather. "We don't need these anymore."

Grandpa gave the instructions back to Max. "I want you to burn them before you leave."

Max nodded, a lump in his throat. He hadn't realized over the past month how much he had grown to love his grandfather. He needed his Grandpa to get well.

"Remember, find Reeka City, and then go to the address I wrote down. This is where you will meet Marko and Yelka."

"Can we get you anything before we go?" Cindy asked.

"Perhaps some water. And don't forget to burn those instructions." Grandpa answered.

Cindy leaned over and kissed him on the cheek. "We'll see you this afternoon."

After getting Grandpa some water and burning the paper with the gateway instructions, Max and Cindy went up to the third floor. They stood beside the console in silence. Max wasn't certain what they were going to do.

"We should go," Cindy suggested.

"Yeah." Max turned on the force field. "I'm glad you're here." He turned on the gateway and made the necessary adjustments.

The mirror began revolving slowly. The white light appeared and grew brighter and the mirror picked up speed. The humming of the gateway and the force field vibrated the hairs on their heads and arms. They moved in front of the gateway.

"I guess it's now or never." Max walked through the gateway with Cindy right behind him.

They emerged from the gateway and landed with a thud. They forgot to step down and Max fell on his stomach with Cindy atop him.

"Sorry." Cindy climbed off his back and brushed herself off.

"I forgot to step down too."   Max grinned and glanced around. "Well, I didn't expect this."

They were in the middle of a dense forest with trees and shrubs larger than any they had ever seen. They did, however, drop out of the gateway right onto a path.

"These trees look a bit like pines.   Larger-than-average pines." Max tried to see the tops of them.

"What kind of people do you think live here?"

"If they are anything like the trees, they're giants. But Grandpa didn't mention anything like that."

"Which way is Reeka City?"

Max took a compass from his pocket and watched the dial point north.   "Grandpa's instructions say to head West on the trail, so that way." He pointed in the opposite direction.

They followed the trail for almost an hour when they noticed something following them. Several dark shapes maneuvered in and out of the trees. At first, they thought they were only imagining them, but now they could make out their shapes. They were creatures dressed in black. It reminded Max of the people on his first night at Grandpa's.

"Do you think they'll attack us?" Cindy kept looking over her shoulder.

"Grandpa said they might harass us," Max tried to sound confident, but the way they kept getting closer made him nervous. "Look," Max pointed. "There's the fork we're looking for." He felt better knowing they were going the right way but he knew the creatures would continue to follow.

A post stood right in the middle of the fork. It had two arms, one pointing left with the words 'Marebor' the other pointing right 'Reeka'. The road to Reeka appeared well traveled; it was wide with wagon ruts, and fairly busy with travelers.

Max and Cindy turned to the right, but the shadowy figures following them made no attempt to keep out of sight. They walked on the open road not far behind and a soft chanting floated on the breeze. The followers disappeared from view only when they passed close to travelers heading in the opposite direction.

Finally, they crested the top of a hill and saw Reeka City. It was a lot larger than Max had imagined. It sat in an extensive valley surrounded by the giant trees. Most of the buildings were one to two stories high with clay tile roofs.

Max and Cindy walked all morning before they found the street they were looking for. They turned right on Ulica 3 and followed it until they reached Number 223. It was a white, two-story building with brown trim and it looked like an inn, though a bit decrepit.

They paused to check the address and then walked into a dimly lit entryway with a wooden counter in the middle. An old man with angular features slept on a stool behind the counter. Max wondered whether or not he should wake him.

"Should we ring the bell?" Cindy motioned with her head towards a bell sitting on the desk.

Max moved towards the desk, but before he could ring the bell the man stirred. Max stepped backwards with a start.

"Wha, What yew doin?" the man asked in a grouchy voice. "Ye look a wee bit teu young ta be needin' a' roum."

"We're looking for someone," Max explained. "Marko."

"I see," the old man said, the gruffness wearing off. "Yoseff sent ya."

"Yes, he's my grandfather."

"Wait here." The man disappeared through a door behind the desk and returned with Yelka.

"Max, Cindy, I am so glad to see you," Yelka sang. "I have been so worried about Joseph. Marko and I just returned and got his message that you were on your way. He said he might have been poisoned with strup." Her face reflected great concern.

"How serious is it?" Max asked. "Grandpa tried to tell us that he was fine."

"Strup is a slow-working poison that takes about two weeks to really take effect. If your grandfather is not treated right away, he may die. But now that you are here, I am certain everything is going to be fine."

From the same door Yelka had used, a tall dark man emerged. He was dressed all in black with boots and a coarsely woven poncho. He walked directly up to them, smiling, and shook their hands. "I'm Marko." Even his hair was black, but his smile revealed a set of pearly-white teeth.

"Max," Max responded and Cindy introduced herself.

"I was hoping to see Joseph but I guess the wound is worse than we thought. He was supposed to bring you two here sooner. I am going to train you in weaponry."

"Weaponry?" Max asked with some enthusiasm.

"Yes, but unfortunately that will have to wait," Marko said. "We need to help your grandfather first."

"He told us we could buy medicine here that would make him better," Cindy said.

"Yes," Yelka said. "We can buy the cure here but we need to go into some, how would you say, unpleasant places."

"There isn't a drug store?" Cindy asked.

"Unfortunately, it was an evil poison that infected him. It means we need to go to an evil source to find the cure," Marko explained. "Let me get my things." He exited through the door.

"How has your spell practice been going?" Yelka asked while they waited for Marko.

"It's going good," Max volunteered. He was pleased with the progress he and Cindy had made over the last two weeks. "Grandpa taught us more about the vanishing spell."

"It must be going pretty well, if you are working on the invisibility spell."

"Yes, but it is the hardest by far," Cindy said. "We have only managed it with small coins."

"Well, that is still something," Yelka smiled. "I think I will have to come for a visit once Joseph is better."

Marko returned with a pack slung over his shoulder. "We better get going so these two can get back as quickly as possible to help Max's grandfather." Marko went to the door and held it open.

"Come, children." Yelka led them outside, where Marko guided them down the street.

Marko set a quick pace with his long legs and they struggled to keep up. He zigzagged up and down streets and alleyways. In a matter of minutes, Max and Cindy were completely lost. Reeka was a gigantic city and Max wondered if Marko knew where he was going.

As they walked, everyone watched them and another group of dark beings followed. It appeared to be the same crowd from the forest. The relief Max felt when they found Marko and Yelka faded fast.

"I take it we are not in a friendly neighborhood?" Max commented.

"No." Yelka shielded her mouth with her hand. "It is controlled by the enemy."

They continued in silence as they navigated the crowded streets. Finally, Marko turned into a dead-end alley and huddled them together. "That store on the corner." He pointed. "It will have what we need."

"Are we all going in?" Max didn't think he and Cindy should be left alone. He couldn't explain why, but he felt safer with Marko. It might be that he was a big man, but it was more than that. He could tell by the way Marko moved that he knew how to handle himself.

"Yes, we all go in." Marko looked around the corner. "There are enemies everywhere now and I don't know what they'll do."

"I thought they wouldn't attack us here," said Max.

"Who told you that?" Marko asked.

"They're not supposed to attack here, but that doesn't always stop them," Yelka explained. "They can usually get away before Helaina shows up. She is powerful, but she can't be everywhere at once."

"That means guerrilla tactics. Hit and run," Marko informed them. "So we stick together. Follow me and don't touch anything." Marko escorted them out into the street and towards the corner store.

They were almost to the store when a bulky, monstrous man approached and stopped directly in their path. He was dressed in shabby pants and a torn shirt. A mop of black hair sat on the top of his square head and his face had chiseled rough features. The man smiled revealing a row of rotten teeth. "Where you go?" he asked in a deep voice.

"I go where I want." Marko headed straight for him.

"Not here. You no go here!" The man's muscular arm reached out to stop Marko.

Marko displayed a sudden burst of speed that surprised Max. He caught the man's arm in a sweeping motion. Instantly, Marko had him on his knees with his arm bent in what Max thought looked like a terribly painful position behind his back. "Now my big friend," Marko spoke kindly. "My friends and I have some business here. We won't be long and we don't want any trouble."

The man winced as Marko wrenched his arm even farther behind his back. "You no get trouble," he gasped.

"Thank you." Marko released him with a slight bow. "I knew I could count on you."

The man remained on his knees clutching his arm until they passed. Marko escorted them to the store and ushered them in. Max glanced over his shoulder and saw a fierce-looking crowd closing in on the building.

The size of the store's interior shocked Max; it took up the whole block. An old, ugly witch-like woman stood behind the counter gasping at the sight of them as they entered. Rows of shelves lined with a variety of weird, creepy things formed narrow aisles. One aisle looked entirely like dissected animal parts in glass jars. Another had what appeared to be bottles of potions and/or poisons. Still others had scrolls, dried goods, and clothing.

Marko walked up to the witch, who looked as if she were on the verge of having a seizure. "Aren't you going to ask if we need any help?" He smiled disarmingly.

"Aggghhhh," she spat.

"I know, I know, you don't want us here and we don't want to be here. So, let's make this as painless as possible and we will leave."

"What ya need?" she barked.

"The cure for strup."

Almost on queue, the front door opened and in stepped a man. Not just any man but Larry's father, Alan. He wore a black cape over a business suit. He had a smug look on his face and appeared to be enjoying himself. Alan glanced at each of them in turn and then finally at the witch behind the counter. When their eyes met, he shook his head.

"Ahh. Have a friend who is dying, eh?" The witch's lips curled up into an evil grin. "Good riddance to 'em. You won't find the cure here."

"You don't mind if we look around then?" Marko asked pleasantly.

"Of course I mind, but I s'pose I can't stop ya." She waved her hand in the direction of the aisles.

The others followed Marko down one of the aisles and Alan joined the woman at the counter.

"What *are* we looking for?" Marko asked when they were alone.

"It will be a dark red mixture," Yelka informed them. "Almost like blood."

"Narrow it down a bit," Marko said. "That could be a thousand bottles in here."

"The label should say Zdrava. I think we should split up while we are in here. If anyone finds it, call out."

"I agree," Marko added.

"How do you spell it?" asked Cindy.

"Z-D-R-A-V-A," Yelka spelled.

"Whoever finds it call out," Marko ordered. "I will wait by the door to keep an eye on everyone who enters." He walked towards the entrance.

"Why don't you two stick together," Yelka suggested. "I will take the farthest aisle and you take the one next to it."

Max and Cindy nodded and followed her to the back of the store.

"You look at the stuff on the right and I'll take the left," Max suggested and Cindy agreed.

"Some of this stuff is really disgusting," Cindy shuddered.

They made their way down the end of one row and were about to round the corner to the next when they nearly bumped into Alan, who had appeared directly in front of them.

"Sorry." Max took a step back.

Alan quickly grabbed Max around the neck, clasped a hand over Max's mouth, and uttered a strange spell that immobilized Cindy. He pulled Max to him and moved his mouth right next to Max's ear. "Hello Max," he whispered. "I am going to release you. I only want to talk." He eased his grip on Max and took a step backwards.

Max wanted to shout for help but he didn't want to show he was afraid. "What do you want?"

"To keep you from making the same mistake your father made." Alan's face twisted into a sadistic grin.

Max could feel his anger and fear rising. Grandpa suspected Alan killed his father. He loathed the man in front of him.

"Didn't your grandfather tell you about your father's unfortunate accident? Why, if your father hadn't been poking his nose in other people's affairs, he would be alive today."

"He told me enough." Max's fear subsided and his anger increased.

"Well, I hope you don't make the same mistake. You see it was rather enjoy. . ." Alan paused, "painful the way it happened. I wouldn't want you to meet the same fate."

"My grandfather told me enough."

"Then you must realize you are no match for us. It only took one of us to do him in."

"You killed him, didn't you?" Max spat. He hated Alan even more than Larry.

"There is no proof of that." Alan's expression changed to one of wrath. "You don't know what kind of trouble you're in. That old fool should just give us the gateway. It will be ours eventually. It would be better to join us instead of fighting us."

"He's not a fool for keeping it out of your hands."

Alan's hand shot out like a coiled snake and clasped around Max's throat. "Listen here, boy. We've come too far to worry about you or your family. We *will* kill you, all of you."

Max tried to speak but Alan's grip was like iron. His attempt to pry Alan's hand away was pointless.

"You stupid boy."

Cindy couldn't believe what was happening. She wanted to scream but nothing would come. She couldn't even move. It was like she had been frozen in place. Then, on the shelf behind Alan, she noticed a jar with some grotesque animal's head floating in a clear liquid. She pictured the jar moving towards her and she thought, *Pridi.*

The jar moved slightly. The scraping of the jar against the shelf startled Alan. He shot a careful glance up and down the aisle.

Again Cindy thought, *Pridi.*

This time the jar shot forward off the shelf. It crashed onto Alan's head and shattered, covering him in a messy, foul-looking liquid. He released his grip in surprise and Max jerked away.

"Why you little. . ." Alan raised his fist as slimy gunk ran down his face.

"Marko," Max yelled but Alan had disappeared.

"Are you all right?" Cindy asked. Not only had Alan released Max but she was free as well.

Marko rushed up the aisle and Yelka ran from the other direction. They arrived in seconds and looked at the puddle of slimy broken glass and the animal's head.

"What happened?" Marko asked.

"Larry's father," Cindy shuddered.

"Who?" Yelka asked.

"His name is Alan," Max said. "He came into the store just before we started looking for the Zdrava."

"Ah," said Yelka with recognition on her face.

Marko's expression was unreadable. "We need to get the cure and get out of here. Are you two all right?"

"Yes, I think so," Max replied glancing at Cindy who nodded in agreement.

"Good, keep looking so we can leave." He returned to the front of the store to keep watch. This time, however, he stood at the end of the aisle Max and Cindy occupied. Max could see that he was keeping an eye both on the door and on them. It wasn't long until Yelka found what they needed. They quickly paid the clerk, who was happy to see them leave.

Out in the street, the crowd had doubled in size. Max didn't think Marko even noticed the crowd as they parted before him. Max wondered what powers Marko possessed. He was greatly outnumbered yet no one stood in his way.

The crowd shouted and harassed them. "Let the old man die," some said. "You'll be next, boy," others shouted. Max wondered how long this hostility would last, but after a few blocks the crowd dispersed.

It wasn't much longer until they were back at the inn eating lunch. Marko and Yelka planned to accompany Max and Cindy back to the gateway. They felt it wasn't safe for them to be out there alone. After lunch, they packed some supplies along with the Zdrava and left for the gateway.

They were surprised to find very few travelers on the road and that no one followed them. After they passed the fork in the road, there were no more travelers.

"I don't like the look of this. Something's wrong," Max uttered.

"I, too, have a bad feeling," Yelka said. "I thought they would continue to harass us, if not attack us, on the way out."

Max was worried. Yelka's voice, which always had a singing sound, had changed. He could sense her nervousness. Marko, on the other hand, didn't give any indication about how he felt. He looked like a cat always ready to pounce.

"We should be coming up on the gateway," Marko said. "Do you have your crystal?"

"Yes." Max knew he would feel much better once they were through the gateway. Then they could give Grandpa the curing potion. Max held the crystal out in front of him across the trail. Nothing happened.

"Do you see it?" Cindy stood behind Max. She watched the crystal over Max's shoulder, but was unable to see any flash of light.

"No," Max responded. "We must not be close enough yet."

Marko stopped. "We are here."

"Where?" Max waved the crystal around with no result.

"It should be right here." Marko wrinkled his forehead.

Yelka produced a similar crystal from her pocket and held it in front of her face. "Max's right. The gateway," she paused, "It must be closed."

7

Waiting and Training

Marko took his own crystal from his pocket and tried in vain to see a flash. He then attempted to use his communicator. "What's this? My communicator isn't working, and who could have closed the gateway? Or worse, what's happened to Joseph?"

"Mine is not working either!" Yelka exclaimed, holding her communicator.

"We need to get through," Max said frantically. "Grandpa needs the Zdrava or something terrible might happen!" He couldn't bear to think about the possibility of his grandfather dying.

"Yes," agreed Marko. "Someone is going to have to enter your world another way. It might be the only way to find out what has happened."

"I hope Joseph is all right," Yelka said.

"I think we should move off the road." Marko scanned their surroundings. "There," he pointed to a group of trees. "You three wait behind those trees while I scout around."

They hustled towards the thick patch of trees as Marko searched the trail where the gateway should have been, stopping every few seconds to examine the ground.

"Behind the trees," Yelka ordered as they reached a dense cluster. They found gaps through the branches from which to watch Marko. Max hoped Marko would figure out what had happened to the gateway.

Marko spent a good deal of time roaming up and down the path. Finally, he broke off a tree branch and then followed the trail back towards Reeka until he disappeared.

"Where's he going?" Cindy asked.

"He's going to cover our tracks." Yelka sat on an old log looking thoughtful.

"Are you sure he's coming back?" Max asked, his attention on the trail.

"Don't worry," Yelka sang. "Marko will never abandon us."

"What are we going to do about Grandpa?" Cindy sat next to Yelka. "We need to give him the medicine right away."

"Yes, I know." Yelka put a comforting arm around Cindy. "We'll let Marko finish and then we will decide what to do."

Max continued watching the trail. A short time later, Marko reappeared. He brushed the trail with the branch but not in a manner Max had ever seen. He flicked it with his wrist in a way that left no footprints, but left no brush strokes from the branch either. "Marko's coming."

Marko erased all signs of their passage. He used his strange sweeping style until he was twenty yards off the trail. He turned and joined them behind the trees.

"What did you find?" Yelka asked.

"It doesn't appear anyone has entered or come through the gateway since Max and Cindy emerged this morning," Marko began. "There are a few other tracks on the road, but they seem to be the tracks of everyday travelers."

"What does that mean?" Max asked.

"It means no one has entered the gateway from this side. I think the gateway was closed from the other side," Marko explained.

"You think something has happened to Grandpa?" Max felt an empty, sinking, feeling in his stomach.

"I don't know," Yelka said. "There is a powerful spell guarding your grandfather's house. I don't think anyone could have shut down the gateway but him."

"It must have been someone from this side," Max insisted.

"It's possible," Marko stated. "I am only telling you what I can see. There are dark forces working against us, and they, too, can cover their tracks. I've never seen anyone do it perfectly, however."

"What will we do now?" Cindy asked. Max could tell by her tone that she didn't care who closed the gateway. She was only concerned with the fact that Grandpa needed their help.

"Someone is going to have to go to him." Marko looked at Yelka as he spoke.

"I've only used magic to enter another world once," Yelka said. "It was difficult and took some time. I usually travel through the gateway with Joseph."

"You have the strongest magical talent here," Marko pointed out. "And you have done it before. There is no other way. Yelka, Joseph needs you."

"I know," she agreed. "I will need to be alone."

"Very well, but stay in sight," Marko insisted. "I will keep watch."

Yelka stood up and walked deeper into the woods. She found a spot of grass where the sun penetrated the forest canopy. She pulled a cloak out of her pack, spread it over the grass, and then she lowered herself onto it and closed her eyes.

"What are we going to do?" Cindy asked.

"We're going to make a blind."

"A what?" both Cindy and Max asked.

"We're going to make a good hiding place for us right here." Marko motioned to the area behind the trees.

Suddenly, Max's hand started to tickle as if someone touched it lightly with a feather. He looked at it and watched the mark grow darker than usual. "I don't think that's going to help us."

"Why not?" Marko asked.

"I'm marked." Max held out his hand for Marko to see.

Marko took Max's hand and examined it closely. "I see." He removed his pack from his back. "Then we need to build two blinds." He pulled out a pocket-sized pouch tied shut by two drawstrings. "Hold out your hand in a cupping position," he ordered Max, who extended his hand. Marko opened the pouch and took a pinch of a powdery substance and sprinkled it into Max's palm. Then he took out a water skin and poured a few drops on top of the powder. "Rub that around, it will help."

Max mixed the water and powder together in the palm of his hand which formed a clear gel. Immediately, the tickling stopped and the mark began to fade.

"Keep rubbing until the gel disappears," Marko ordered. "Cindy, I want you to cut some tree branches." He handed her a knife.

After Max finished massaging his hand, he gathered branches with Cindy. They spent most of the afternoon constructing their blind. Marko made it look like a natural part of the forest from the front while hiding everything behind it. Yelka continued to sit unmoving a short distance away. She was far enough off the road and short enough that no one would notice her from the trail.

"Here." Marko handed Max and Cindy something that looked like granola bars. "Eat them. It's not much but it should ease the hunger pains."

Max and Cindy devoured the small snack. It had been several hours since they had eaten lunch. They sat on a log behind the blind while Marko kept an eye on the trail. No travelers had passed their position since their arrival.

"How long do you think this is going to take?" Max asked.

"I don't know." Marko continued watching the trail. "Yelka is talented, but you two know how it is when performing a difficult spell. It doesn't always work as planned."

Max exchanged an understanding look with Cindy. He remembered how hard the disappearing spell was and he was sure the spell to transport oneself into another world was even more difficult.

The rest of the evening was the same, no one passed by their location. Marko hadn't budged in hours. He stood and stared like some kind of statue. Max and Cindy would occasionally join him or they would sit on the log to watch Yelka. The sky grew dark as the sun began to set.

"If you get cold, there's a cloak in my pack that you can share," Marko informed them.

"Who do you think will be coming?" Max wondered why Marko insisted on watching the road so intently.

"I'm not sure, but I don't think the gateway is closed because they got to Joseph," Marko said, looking away from the trail to glance at them. "I figure it's a trap for. . ."

"For me," Max finished. He could tell by Marko's expression that he was worried.

"Yes," Marko said.

"Why?" Cindy asked.

"Because, for a long time, Joseph has kept them from gaining control." Marko gave his attention back to the trail.

"Control of what?" Max asked. He had wanted answers to the many questions brought about by this strange summer for so long and now he hoped to get some.

"Of everything," Marko said. "Joseph holds the key. They want the gateway. If they can get rid of you and your grandfather, they can control the gateway."

"I don't understand." Cindy shook her head.

"Joseph, with the help of others, placed a powerful spell on his house. As long as he or one of his heirs live, evil cannot enter," Marko explained. "They can't break the spell as long as you or your grandfather breathes."

"Is that why you think Grandpa is safe? The spell is protecting him?" Cindy asked.

"Yes."

After the sun went down, the air cooled considerably. Max took Marko's cloak from the pack to share with Cindy. Marko gave them another bar to eat, but they were still hungry. Max couldn't see Yelka in the darkness and he wondered if anything had happened. Marko wouldn't let them build a fire because he said it would give away their position. The forest, which had been quiet all day, came alive with night sounds. Something that sounded like crickets chirped, night birds cried, and nighttime predators growled.

Marko opened his pack and got the bag of powder. "Hold out your hand again," he whispered urgently. He put another pinch of powder in Max's hand and then added water. "Rub that in. Stay here and be quiet I'll be back shortly." He slung his pack over his back and darted away into the darkness.

"Was the mark hurting?" Cindy whispered.

"No, I haven't felt anything since this afternoon."

Max waited with Cindy, listening, but he could only hear the crickets and other night sounds. Although he couldn't hear anything unusual, he could feel it. Marko wouldn't have had him rub more powder on his hand and then disappear for nothing. Something was coming and he knew it.

After several minutes, Marko appeared. He was next to them before Max knew he was there. "They're coming," he cautioned.

"Who?" Max asked. "I thought they couldn't attack us in this place."

"They're not supposed to, but if they think they can hit us quickly and run before they are caught, then they will risk it," Marko explained. "I want you to huddle up at the back of the blind and don't move unless I tell you."

"What about Yelka?" Cindy asked.

"She's already gone," Marko answered.

They hunkered at the back of the blind and wrapped themselves in Marko's cloak. Marko threw his pack on the ground next to them. He was a dark shadow in the night. They saw the flash of a sword in Marko's hand. It glowed, and an inner light, like fire, moved up and down its surface.

"*Izginem se*," Marko uttered and disappeared. Only a hint of the blade floated through the air like a transparent ghost as he sped through the woods.

Minutes passed without anything or anyone traveling on or around the path. Finally, torches appeared in the distance, winking on and off as those who carried them moved among the trees. There were only a few at first, but then more came into view. An ominous chanting was noticeable above the insects and night birds. The torch carriers marched up the path to the spot where the gateway should be.

Max huddled nervously with Cindy and watched the crowd through gaps between the branches. Several carts creaked and groaned as they rolled up the path. They carried a cargo of nightmarish beasts. When the crowd reached the place where the gateway had been, they stopped and formed a circle.

"I don't think they're all human," Max whispered. Several cloaked figures were much larger than the others.

"And those aren't animals from our world," Cindy added.

Max stared at the beasts in the cart. What he saw terrified him. They looked like grotesque crossbreeds. Their heads resembled black lizards with rows of sharp teeth and cat eyes that shone in the torchlight. Their bodies were similar to a black panther except for their front paws, which looked like black hands with long sharp talons on each finger.

The chanting grew to a high-pitched fever that made Max want to take Cindy and flee deeper into the forest. "No matter what happens do not move," Marko's voice came from next to them. Max couldn't see him but felt better knowing he was there.

"What are those things in the cart?" Cindy whispered but the chanting almost muffled her voice.

"They're called zvers," Marko said. "You must remain silent now."

The chanting lasted for what seemed like an hour and the beings in the circle didn't move; they just stood there. Each member of the circle held a torch, which cast twisted, horrifying shadows everywhere. Max was wondering how long the chanting would go on when it stopped abruptly. The beings began to move around and appeared to be discussing something. The distance between the beings and the blind made their conversations sound like gibberish.

The figures moved to the wagons parked a short distance away. They lowered the backs of the wagons and released the zvers.

The monstrous beasts hit the ground with ferocious grunts and groans. The hairs on the back of Max's neck stood on end. Some fought amongst themselves, biting and tearing at each other with claws and teeth. One even attacked its handler. Then a cloaked figure stepped into their midst and the zvers snapped to attention. He let out a horrifying cry and they tore off in all directions searching the forest. They were swift and gave off frightening growls as they raced back and forth.

Max wondered how long it would take the zvers to find them. They covered a wide area as they sniffed everywhere with their grotesque noses. It didn't appear they could pick up their scent, but Max didn't think that would help them stay hidden for very long.

Off to their left, a zver let out an earsplitting yawl and fell to the ground dead. The other zvers and the black-cloaked figures rushed towards the fallen beast. Max couldn't tell what had happened, but he guessed Marko had something to do with it.

"Keep the zvers searching," a voice ordered.

With that, a creature barked a command and they resumed their search.

A group of black-clad beings converged on the dead zver's body.

"Its throat's been cut."

"That means there is something out here."

"Yes, but why didn't the chant locate the boy?"

"I'm not sure, but it wasn't a tree that killed this zver."

"I think we should spread out from here," one suggested and the group split up to continue the search.

A cloaked figure moved closer to Max and Cindy; its harsh breathing could be heard as it drew near in a swaying walk. Max's heart pounded in his ears. He didn't know how long they could stay hidden. Exchanging a quick look with

Cindy, Max could see that she was thinking the same thing. He really wanted to run, but he remembered Marko's warning.

Whatever the cloaked figure was, it wasn't human. It was seven feet tall and had eyes that glowed like fireflies under its hood. It approached until it stood on the other side of the blind. The gurgling sound of air going in and out of its body turned Max's blood cold. It examined the outside of the blind as if it had discovered something.

Max could feel Cindy shaking as she clutched him. His mind screamed at him to run but his legs wouldn't move. Both he and Cindy held their breath.

The creature sauntered along the front of the blind. When it was about to round the corner, another zver let out a death howl. This time it was from the other side of the road. The hooded creature jerked around in the direction of the cry. It watched, as if debating what to do when another one yelped not far from the second. The cloaked creature took off like a shot in the direction of the cries.

Max let out a sigh of relief and heard Cindy do the same. He was convinced the figure would have found them. They watched as several cloaked figures raced to the other side of the road, their torches swinging through the air like evil searching eyes zooming through bushes and around trees.

One of the cloaked figures climbed onto a cart and raised his hands high above his head. He yelled a foul spell and Marko was suddenly visible, revealed in the midst of their carts. The air erupted with the sounds of wicked spells. Fire burst around Marko but he was too quick. He dodged left and right as balls of fire and other debris whizzed past his head.

A zver charged Marko but his blade slashed through the air like lightning. It flashed white-hot as it struck down the attacking beast, which let out a frightening scream as it fell.

Marko fled into the woods in the opposite direction from the blind. Foul spells filled the air as they shot from the lips of their evil masters.

Max's muscles tensed as he watched Marko dodge spells and zvers as if he were a rabbit escaping a wolf. Then Max gasped for air as the cloaked figure on the top of the wagon looked straight at him. The zvers and other cloaked figures pursued Marko with vigor, but not this one. He leapt from the wagon and hastened towards them. He took long strides and closed the gap quickly.

"Max," Cindy whispered.

"I know," Max breathed in fear.

As the creature approached, he lowered his hood. Max was shocked to see that it was Alan.

Suddenly, several bolts of lighting lit up the sky. When they faded, a striking woman in long, flowing robes stood in the middle of the path. She held a scepter in her hand. "*Nehaj*," she cried out in a voice filled with power.

Max looked for Alan but he had disappeared. In fact, everyone was gone except Marko and the zvers. The zvers fled deeper into the woods while Marko headed towards the woman.

"What's going on here?" the woman inquired as Marko approached her. "Marko, is that you?"

"Yes," he responded as he reached her.

The scepter she held gave off a tremendous amount of light. Long red hair flowed behind her like a horse's mane and her robes shimmered in the light from her scepter.

"What has been going on here?" she asked.

"Only a friendly little trap."

Max was baffled that Marko didn't even look tired. He wasn't breathing hard or sweating but looked freshly groomed.

"For you?" the woman pressed.

"No," Marko responded. "Max, Cindy, come out." He motioned towards the blind. "I'm protecting them. The trap was for Max."

"Why would they want to catch this boy?" she asked as Cindy and Max emerged.

"Oh, yes, you haven't been told yet. Max is Joseph's grandson," Marko said.

"I see. Why didn't you use the gateway to get out?"

"That is part of the trap. A Night Shade stabbed Joseph with a poisoned blade some time ago, so Max and Cindy came here to get the cure. I think the Night Shades purposely used a slow poison in order to lure Max here. We returned from the market to find the gateway closed. We don't know why, but we suspect it had to do with our visitors." Marko nodded towards the wagons.

"Max, Cindy, this is Helaina," Marko introduced them. "She is the ruler of Mir."

The group exchanged greetings. Max was astonished that this young woman, although large in stature, ruled this world. The way the cloaked figures disappeared, he determined she must possess great power.

"What is being done about Joseph?" Helaina asked.

"Yelka is trying to reach him," Marko said. "I'm glad you showed up. I don't know how much longer I was going to last."

"Well, trying to maintain order in my kingdom requires a lot of time. It is always those who work in dark magic that cause disturbances. They are getting bolder," Helaina stated.

"Yes, I have come to expect that from them," Marko added.

"Do you think you will be all right until Yelka returns?"

"Yes. I don't think they'll come back now that you know we are here," Marko said.

"Yes, I believe you can even build a fire now. I will keep my senses tuned into this place for the next few days. Do not worry, everything will be all right." She looked at Max and Cindy.

"Thank you, Helaina," Marko said and Max and Cindy nodded their gratitude.

"Till we meet again," she smiled and then held the scepter above her head. A white light flowed from the scepter to envelope her. When the light faded, she was gone.

"Wow, she rules this world?" Cindy asked.

"Yes, she does," Marko said with admiration. "Why don't you go back to the blind for safety while I look around." He started inspecting the abandoned wagons. In one, he found blankets, food and water, all of which he brought back to the blind. After he finished his search, Marko moved the wooden vehicles deep into the forest, and then cleaned up the area. When he was finished, the trail in the forest and the surrounding area looked just like it had earlier that afternoon, well-traveled, but with no sign of anything out of the ordinary.

Max and Cindy wrapped themselves in the blankets Marko had found in the wagons. "I hope Grandpa is okay," Max said.

"Me too," Cindy agreed. "What are we going to tell my parents?"

"I don't know." Max could tell by the inflections in her voice she was worried. He hadn't thought how Cindy's parents might feel with their daughter missing.

"They are going to kill me." Cindy sniffed.

It took them a while to fall asleep because of their concerns for Grandpa and Cindy's parents, and the excitement with the creatures, the zvers, and Helaina. When they awoke the next morning, they found themselves cuddled up in front of a fading fire. Marko slept in a sitting position with his back against a tree. He awoke the minute Max and Cindy started moving.

The air was chilly and Max was glad for the fire. "When did you start the fire?" Max moved closer to it.

"Shortly after you fell asleep." Marko stretched his arms and legs.

"What do we have to eat? I'm starving," Cindy asked with a wide yawn. "I didn't realize how tired I was. I didn't think I could sleep after all that excitement."

Marko gave them each a half loaf of bread. "I found these on one of the wagons. I made sure it wasn't poisoned."

Max climbed to his feet and stretched. He remembered Yelka and noted she hadn't returned. Her cloak still lay on the small patch of grass. "How long do you think it will take Yelka?"

"I don't know. It could take her days to find your world," Marko said.

"How do you know she is in another world?" Cindy inquired.

"Max, do you still have your crystal?" Marko asked.

"Yes."

"Take it out and point it at Yelka's cloak."

Max took out the crystal and did as Marko suggested. He was surprised when it flashed every time it crossed in front of the cloak. The blink wasn't as bright as when it pointed at the gateway, but there was a definite flicker.

"The crystal shows you an opening between worlds. I want you to remember this because it is very important. The enemy always travels this way. You can find them and surprise them when they come back."

"Will it also show you the spot where they entered another world?" Max asked eagerly.

"No, that light is with the person wherever he or she is. You can know who actually belongs in the world you are in and who does not. The crystal will flash on those who don't belong. You must keep this information secret. The enemy doesn't know this and we don't want them to."

They finished their breakfast of bread and water, and another of Marko's granola-type bars while sitting around the fire. Marko then led them deeper into the forest where he found a sizeable patch of grass.

"Are you ready for some training?" Marko stepped onto the grass.

"What kind of training?" Max asked with excitement. He remembered how Marko had brought that bigger man to his knees in Reeka and how he had sliced up the zvers.

"Self-defense."

"All right," Max smiled.

"First, I'll teach you some moves to help you escape the grasp of an attacker. Even if he is bigger than you."

"Like Alan?" Max could still feel Alan's grip around his throat.

Marko spent the morning teaching Max and Cindy techniques to use if someone grabbed them around the neck, from behind, or in front. They also learned how and where to kick or punch, once they escaped their captor's grip. Marko taught them that the attack was as important as the escape. "You need to create time to get away," Marko stressed. "Most of the kicks and punches attack the groin or the knee." At first, Max and Cindy practiced on each other, but then Marko made them practice escaping from him.

After their practice session, both Max and Cindy could escape from most of Marko's holds. Max suspected Marko was taking it easy on them but Marko assured them he wasn't.

Marko decided that they should rest during the heat of the day so they returned to the blind for lunch. Max and Cindy wanted to relax, but Marko said that they should practice their magic lessons. Max and Cindy began a short review as they ate.

"Can you teach us another spell?" Cindy asked after they had practiced all of their spells.

"I'm not supposed to teach you any spells. That's Yelka's task," Marko said as he ate some roots he found in the forest.

"Oh, come on," Max pleaded. He had wanted to learn a new spell for two weeks. "Yelka might have taught us a new spell if Grandpa hadn't been wounded?" Max felt a lump in his throat as he remembered Grandpa.

"He will be fine," Cindy said. "I'm more worried about my parents."

Max could tell Cindy was as worried as he was about Grandpa.

"I will make you a deal," Marko said. "If we're still here tomorrow I will teach you another spell. It will be a simple one."

Max wasn't sure how he felt about that deal. He really wanted to learn a new spell, but he didn't want to be here another hour, let alone another day. He knew they needed to get back to Grandpa quickly.

That afternoon they worked on ways to bring down a larger opponent. Once they had these techniques down, Marko had them review everything they learned that morning.

"Repetition is the key," Marko taught. "The more you do something, the better you can do it and the more it becomes instinct."

It was tiring work but Max was glad to have something to do besides sitting around and waiting. Whenever they took a break, his mind always wandered to Grandpa and

Yelka. Finally, when it was too dark to practice, they gathered more firewood and settled down behind the blind.

"How long have you known my grandfather?" Max asked Marko as they ate their meager dinner.

"About fifteen years," Marko responded, but he didn't seem like he wanted to elaborate.

"Is this place your home?" Cindy inquired.

"No, I come from a much more dangerous place where you need a lot of skills to survive. There are evil, frightening creatures there that can rip you to shreds or eat you alive, and the people who control them use dark magic."

"Whoa." Max shivered and the hairs on the back of his neck stood on end. "Did you use magic to get here?"

"No, Joseph brought me here through the gateway. I rescued him from some nasty beasts before they could kill him. In my world, evil is stronger than good. I was always hunted there."

They fell quiet for the rest of the evening. Max couldn't stop being concerned for his grandfather. He hoped they wouldn't be here much longer. He tried turning his mind to other things, such as the moves Marko taught them. Anything to keep his mind from worrying.

Sleep was hard to come by that night. When Max did manage to fall asleep, it was only for short intervals. Several times, he woke up in a cold sweat after dreaming about dark shadows and sinister places. One time he noticed the fire had died out and the air was cool. He looked over at Cindy who was sleeping peacefully and decided to curl up next to her. Another time he noticed Marko was gone. The moon gave off plenty of light, causing the trees to cast frightening shadows.

Sometime in the early morning, Max awoke again. Marko was back and sleeping in his usual position against a tree. Cindy lay curled up in a fetal position with her back against his. Max thought he heard something and wondered if that was what had woken him. He lay still, straining his ears against the early morning sounds. He didn't fall asleep again for some time.

Max woke with a start to Cindy shaking him. His eyes were puffy and his head throbbed with exhaustion. It felt like he had been awake all night.

"Wake up sleepy head." Cindy shook him again. "You look dead."

"I feel dead. I didn't sleep very well last night." Max yawned.

Marko stirred the fire. "Yes, I heard it." Marko looked at Max. "They were signaling each other. They know we are still here."

Cindy looked from Max to Marko with her brow wrinkled.

"A strange noise woke me last night," Max said before Cindy could ask.

"They're watching us," Marko said. "But, so is Helaina and they dare not cross her."

Max wasn't convinced. At breakfast he kept his eyes on the forest expecting to see more zvers emerge from the trees at any moment.

After breakfast, they reviewed all of the self-defense techniques Marko taught them the day before. Max felt that his estimation, of Marko not trying his hardest yesterday, had been correct. Marko's grip was a lot stronger and he had to work harder to get away. Cindy had the same problem.

They practiced all morning and then took a break to eat more bread and water. Max was tired of bread and water but he and the others did not complain, at least not out loud. Marko disappeared again and returned carrying a bundle of sticks. He separated them into two piles.

Max and Cindy looked at each other curiously and then at Marko.

"I told you I would teach you a new spell if we were still here today."

"Oh, that's right," Max said eagerly. His spirit had been low and the thought of learning a new spell was going to brighten his day.

"What does this spell do?" Cindy asked.

"It creates fire. Remember you must visualize it happening and then say the word *prizgaj*."

Max and Cindy spent the rest of the afternoon practicing the spell. They tried to ignite the piles of wood Marko gathered, but they managed only sparks or puffs of smoke. Marko assured them they would eventually be able to start a fire and even use it as a weapon.

It was late afternoon and they were eating their sixth straight meal of bread and water when Yelka appeared.

8

Solo Lessons

"The gateway is now open." Yelka looked exhausted.

Max and Cindy jumped to their feet eagerly and started preparing to leave.

"How's Grandpa?" Max asked.

"He will begin to get well once we give him the Zdrava," Yelka said. "But we have another problem to worry about."

"What? What happened?" they all asked at the same time.

"Cindy's parents are furious." Yelka turned to Cindy. "You have been gone for almost three days. They believe that Max talked you into running away with him."

Cindy grew silent and the color drained out of her face. Max knew she had been worried about her parents and how upset they must be, but everyone's main concern was helping Grandpa.

"What am I going to do?" Cindy asked.

"Joseph and I have an idea, but first let's get through the gateway." Yelka beckoned them to follow.

Marko cast a spell and the fire went out. They gathered up their things and made their way towards the path. Max waved the crystal through the air and on the first try he located the gateway.

"Why was the gateway closed? And why didn't the communicators work?" Max asked Yelka.

"There was a fierce storm in your world that knocked out the electricity," she replied. "Without electricity the gateway closes. The gateway control panel also controls the communicators. It opens up holes for the signals to travel through, but without power nothing could function. Your grandfather has a generator. Under normal circumstances the generator keeps the gateway operational. This time he was too weak to start it."

"The power has been out for three days?" Max raised his eyebrows skeptically.

"Well," Yelka began, "it has been off at your house for three days. The remarkable thing is that the minute I started the generator, the regular electrical power began to function again. There was a storm and dark forces caused a power outage. We think it was part of a plan to trap you here."

They reached the gateway and everyone stepped through. Max waited impatiently for Yelka to turn off the force field. The second it was off they hurried to Grandpa's room.

Max was surprised at how much worse Grandpa's condition had grown since they left. Grandpa managed a weak smile as they entered.

"Max, go and heat up some water," Yelka ordered but Max stood staring at his grandfather. "Max, please."

Max jerked as Yelka's words registered. "Uh, sure." He rushed to the kitchen.

He returned as fast as he could with a teakettle full of hot water, which Yelka took. She sprinkled a pinch of

Zdrava into the teakettle. A decaying animal stench filled the air like rotten sewer gas.

"That's going to make him better?" Max held his nose and even Cindy and Marko pinched their noses.

"You didn't expect something from the enemy to smell like roses, did you?" Yelka asked. "I need a cup." She glanced at Max but he was already halfway out the door.

Grandpa choked down two cups of tea, with Yelka pestering him the whole time. She reminded Max of a bossy nurse forcing a child to take its medicine.

After Grandpa finished the tea, Yelka led Max and Cindy out into the hall. Marko remained by Grandpa's side.

"Cindy." Yelka closed the door behind them. "Your parents are extremely worried."

"What am I going to tell them?" Cindy asked. "They're probably freaking out."

"Your parents must not know what you have been doing. We can use the storm as an explanation for your disappearance," Yelka said.

"How?" Cindy and Max asked.

"We want you to say that you and Max were hiking in the hills when the storm hit. Tell them the path was washed out and you were lost. Eventually you found your way back." Yelka looked uncomfortable. Max could tell by her expression that she didn't like the idea of lying.

"I should go now." Cindy started for the door.

"No wait." Yelka ran after her. She caught Cindy by the arm before she could reach the front door. "You must not be seen leaving this house. Believe me, the enemy wants your parents to believe a different story about your disappearance."

"What? But I have to get home now." Cindy tried to pull free.

"Marko will sneak you both out the back and then you and Max will go to your house as if just returning to town. Max should be there to back up your story."

Cindy paused as if thinking it over.

"Otherwise, your parents might not let you see Max again," Yelka added. "We cannot allow this."

Max hadn't thought about the prospect of never being allowed to see Cindy, and it hit him like a brick. Cindy was his only friend, and this summer, despite the danger, was turning out to be the best of his life.

"All right," Cindy relented. "But can we please hurry?"

"Wait here." Yelka disappeared into Grandpa's room. When she returned, Marko was with her.

"This way." Marko went into the kitchen and turned off the lights.

A knock on the front door stopped all of them dead. They listened quietly from the kitchen.

"Joe, Joe?" a woman called out as she entered the house.

"It's my mom," Cindy whispered.

By the sound of all the footsteps, it wasn't only Cindy's mom at the door. "Joe," Alan called.

Max felt a surge of anger burn through him. He was furious that Alan was in his grandfather's house.

"I'm here," Grandpa's shaky voice called from the hallway. He was out of bed and moving towards the front room.

"We thought we saw shadows through the lighted windows," Alan said.

"That was me," Grandpa said. "I was making myself some tea."

"We hoped the children had returned." Cindy's mother started sobbing.

"Everything is going to be all right, Mrs. Carlson." Alan tried to comfort her. "We will find her. I'm sorry she got tangled up with that troublemaker Max."

"Now, hold on there," Grandpa objected.

"Come on, Joe. We all know his mother sent him here in hopes you could straighten him out. First, he broke my son's nose and now he's run off taking Cindy with him. I don't think we need to hear any more," Alan sneered.

Max couldn't believe his ears. He wanted to rush out there and tell Cindy's mother who the real troublemakers were.

Marko placed a hand on both of their shoulders and steered them to the back door.

"I will remain here in case Joseph needs help," Yelka whispered. "Cindy, remember to practice your exercises." She patted Cindy's hand.

Marko looked out the kitchen window as he kept in the shadows. "There are two people by the back gate." He surveyed the backyard for a moment longer and then crossed the kitchen to a window on the side of the house. Again, he checked the yard. "It's darker here. We'll go out this window."

He slid the window open and popped off the screen. He placed the screen on the floor and climbed out. "Come on," he whispered. He helped them outside.

They dodged from shadow to shadow until they reached a large tree next to the fence. Marko climbed the tree and crept out onto a limb that hung over the fence. He gestured for them to follow. Max and Cindy helped each other up the tree. Marko signaled them to wait as they reached the branch he was on.

Marko looked like a panther observing its prey, as he crouched motionless on the branch. People were watching the street in front of the house and Marko waited for them to move. After a short wait, Marko swung down from the limb and over the fence. He stepped into the shadows and picked up a rock. Marko threw the stone all the way over Grandpa's house. It landed with a loud clatter drawing the attention of the watchers, who moved towards the sound. A few seconds later, he waved Max and Cindy to follow him and assisted them down over the fence.

Once on the ground, they scurried into the shadows. They kept low to the ground as Marko guided them out into the field. They followed him to the end of the street. They raced through a field towards the mountains behind Grandpa's house. When they were finally out of sight of the house, Marko brought them to a halt.

Max and Cindy watched while Marko scouted the area.

"What are you looking for?" Max whispered.

"Loose dirt," Marko replied.

Max exchanged a confused look with Cindy, who shrugged her shoulders. After a few moments, Marko waved them over to a spot of ground that looked like a sand pit.

"This will do," Marko said. "I want you to practice all the moves I taught you."

"What?" they asked with surprise.

"Trust me. Just do it."

They spent some time practicing their escapes. Marko even had them try a few takedowns.

"That's good," Marko said. "Now, you look like you've been lost for a few days. Okay, go to Cindy's house, and remember the story. The storm washed out the trail, you were lost and had to find another way home."

Max and Cindy hurried back to town. They even discussed further elaborations to their story so they knew exactly what to say. When they reached Cindy's house, police cars and a crowd of people surrounded it. Cindy's mother, Alan, and the chief of police were coming out of Grandpa's yard.

Cindy's mother rushed to Cindy, scooped her up in her arms and kissed her face several times. "Where have you been? Are you all right?"

"We were lost," Cindy exclaimed as her mother hugged her.

Just then, Cindy's father ran out of her house. He wrapped his arms around his wife and daughter. He asked the same questions Cindy's mother had.

Max noticed the demonic glares from everyone but Cindy's parents. He could feel their hatred like ants crawling over his skin.

"Max!" Grandpa called out from the porch. "Max, thank goodness you're safe."

Max didn't want to be stuck in the street by himself and darted for his grandfather. Grandpa Joe hugged him and Max didn't want him to let go. He felt safe there, like everything would be all right.

"Are they watching?" Max asked with his face in his grandpa's side.

"Yes, I am sure they will question you. They will try to twist the story so Cindy's parents think you took off and forced her to go with you."

"I know. I heard them from the kitchen," Max said softly. "I hope Cindy's parents don't believe it."

"Me too." Grandpa patted him on the back.

Max didn't realize exactly how much they were going to twist things. They wanted to take him downtown on kidnapping charges. Even though Cindy stuck to the story, they argued that Max had threatened her to say that. Alan and the Sheriff did their best to destroy Max's character in front of Cindy's parents.

Max tried to read Cindy's parents but he couldn't tell how they felt. The one thing that was certain is they believed Cindy. In the end, their trust in Cindy saved Max. The story appeared to have worked and Cindy's parents weren't interested in pressing charges.

The story had a different affect on the enemy. The hatred in their faces was so intense it scared Max. He would never forget those looks as long as he lived.

Max soon found out, that everything hadn't quite worked out as planned. Cindy's parents accepted Cindy's story, but they still forbade her to spend time with him. They even took time off from work to stay home and make sure she didn't see him. When he tried to call, someone other than Cindy would answer the phone.

Grandpa told him to give them time, but Max was sad and frustrated that his only friend wasn't allowed to play with him. Max wondered how much influence the other people in town had over Cindy's parents. Did they believe he was a juvenile delinquent?

Even worse, Larry and his misfits started showing up every day again. They weren't yelling rude remarks at Max, they were going to Cindy's house. They would ask if Cindy could play or if they could do things for her family. Cindy's parents were happy to let her hang out with them. Max's mood went from bad to worse. Cindy would give him a look of, *I can't believe this*, as they rode away on their bikes.

When Grandpa offered to speak with Cindy's parents, Max declined. He thought it better to ride out the storm. He didn't want his grandfather to fight his battles. Eventually, he felt Larry and his friends would do something to screw it up.

The next few days were better because Max had plenty to do. First, Yelka showed up and worked with him on his spells. By the end of the second day, he could start a fire in the fireplace. She wasn't thrilled that Marko had taught him a spell, but because Max was so anxious to master it, Yelka helped him.

Max could also make larger objects disappear and reappear, but the spell Yelka really pushed him on was *premakni*. He was soon moving chairs across the room with much more control. Although Yelka told him he needed more work, he could tell she was pleased with his progress.

"How's Cindy?" Yelka asked.

"I'm not sure. I haven't seen her since we came back," he added with frustration.

"Do you know anything?"

"Larry and his friends come to pick her up almost every day, and her parents won't let her see me."

"I see. They're working on her and her family. I think it's time to do something."

"What are you going to do?" Max raised his eyebrows.

Yelka beckoned for him to follow. They went down to the front room.

"I want you to go outside and sit on the porch swing."

"What for?"

"I need to get outside and it might look funny if the door opened and closed by itself." Yelka smiled.

"What are you two up to?" Grandpa asked, coming into the room. He had improved a great deal since he started taking the Zdrava, and was now able to get around and do simple chores.

"Yelka's going on a mission to Cindy's house," Max blurted out.

"I want to have a look around," Yelka smiled mischievously. "*Izginem se*," she uttered and disappeared. "Open the door please."

Max and Grandpa went outside and sat on the swing. It was a beautiful day and the gentle rocking of the swing made it seem like they didn't have a care in the world.

"Grandpa," Max began. "I was wondering something."

"What?"

"I thought your house was protected from evil by a spell."

"And you were wondering how Alan was able to enter. There is a condition that allows our enemy to enter. If the gate is open, they can come in the yard. If the door to the house is open, they can enter the house. My guess is that he had Cindy's mom enter first and once the gate and front door were open they followed."

"That makes sense." Max continued to rock. "I wonder what Yelka will find?"

"I'm sure she'll learn everything. Yelka is very talented."

They rocked peacefully and Grandpa went to sleep. Although he had improved, he still needed a lot of rest. Max swung quietly and soon drifted off himself.

The next thing Max knew, someone was gently shaking him.

"Max, Max," Yelka whispered.

Max opened his eyes expecting to see Yelka. He was confused for a moment, waking up on the porch.

Grandpa was still sleeping next to him but Yelka was nowhere to be seen.

"Max," Yelka whispered again. "I need you to open the front door."

"What about Grandpa?"

"Let him sleep. He needs the rest."

Max climbed to his feet and stretched. He looked around to see if anyone was watching. A Night Shade stood down the street under a tree. He had forgotten about them and its presence bothered him. He went to the door and opened it. He gave Yelka a few seconds to enter, before he stepped inside and closed the door.

"How did you get out of the yard?" Max realized he had to open the front door for her and the yard had a fence with a gate.

"I went over the fence. I am unable to enter a house through a closed door when I am invisible," she said as if it was common knowledge.

"How did you get into Cindy's house?"

"I used a spell to open her backdoor."

Max went up the stairs and into the room where they did their training. He sat down in the chair he used to practice the *premakni* spell.

"*Pokazi se.*" Yelka reappeared. "That was interesting."

"What was?" Max bounced his legs impatiently.

"There is an evil spell trying to take over Cindy's house. It is a good thing Cindy placed that charm in her window. It is the reason I was able to undo the damage."

"What's going on?"

"Our enemy entered Cindy's house while you two were gone. They put a powerful spell on it to gain control of Cindy and her parents. If I hadn't given her that charm, we would be powerless to do anything."

"Why didn't they remove the charm when they were in her house?"

"It is small and hard to detect, and because of it I was able to use a counter spell that will remove their hold," Yelka looked very pleased. "It will take a couple of days. I don't want the enemy to know what is happening. I want Cindy's parents to see them for who they really are. Light always angers darkness. It will eventually cause Larry and any of the others to show their true colors. You will have to wait, be patient."

Max felt better after Yelka explained the counter spell and the effect it would have, although the good feeling only lasted until the next morning. Once again, he watched Cindy ride away with Larry and his friends.

Cindy seemed different though and the look on her face begged for help. Max smiled sympathetically and gave a wave. He felt depressed about not being able to help her. He kept telling himself it would only take a couple of days.

Later that morning, Marko showed up and put Max to work. "I think you will enjoy today's lesson. I'm going to teach you how to use a sword."

"Do you ever use guns?" Max asked, still gloomy about Cindy. He felt low about Cindy and didn't really want to do anything.

"Yes and no. If we are in worlds with guns, we use them. But, when we are in worlds without guns, we do not wish to change their destiny by introducing them. Swords and knives exist almost everywhere. Therefore, they are our weapons of choice."

"That makes sense. Can magic stop bullets?"

"I suppose theoretically it could, but you would not be able to cast a spell before the bullet struck."

Marko spent the morning teaching Max how to stand and hold a sword. Then, he demonstrated how to block an opponent's strikes and the positioning of one's feet. Marko stressed how balance and footwork were the keys to being a good swordsman.

They ate lunch together with Grandpa, and Marko told Grandpa how pleased he was with Max's progress. After lunch, they reviewed escapes and takedowns. Marko emphasized, as always, the importance of practice to master these skills.

"Repetition is the key," Marko said. "Soon they will become second nature and you won't have to think about how to do them. You'll just react."

After Marko left, Max thought he would spend the rest of the day being lazy. Grandpa, however, made him practice his spells and this time he supervised his practice. He made Max stretch himself by moving bigger objects and then stopping them. By the end of the lesson, Max was starving and exhausted.

The next two days were more of the same. Cindy would appear desperate and Marko would work Max twice as hard. Strangely, Larry and his friends did seem on edge. Max couldn't quite put his finger on it, but they acted tense.

The next day, Grandpa decided they needed to get back to their morning chores. The yard was looking a bit shabby again and weeds were growing everywhere.

Grandpa led Max into the yard with work gloves and shovels in hand. He told Max to dig up the weeds on the side of the house while he went to fetch some garbage bags. Max had barely started digging when Larry and his crew showed up. Max could see them clearly from this side of the house. They were in a foul mood. Max didn't know if they had shown up in a bad mood or if Yelka's spell was affecting them. Their use of foul language, which they had cleaned up around Cindy's parents, returned. They were back to their usual ways.

The Night Shade down the street was paying close attention to the boys as well.

Larry strolled towards Cindy's front door and his expression changed with each step. His fake smile transformed into an ugly scowl. Before he reached the top step, he stopped and shook his head as if a fly was harassing him.

"Cindy, get your *!#@#**, *!#@#**out here," Larry roared. He then looked at his friends as if to say, I can't believe I said that. "I mean get your *!#@#**, *!#@#**, *!#@#** out here," he yelled again. This time he clamped his hands over his mouth to stop anything else from coming out.

Cindy's mom burst out of the house, her face flushed with anger. She tore into Larry for his foul mouth. Larry and his friends screamed back at her. Cindy came outside with eyes as big as saucers and mouth agape.

Grandpa appeared with a handful of garbage bags. He walked to Max and dropped the bags. "I see Yelka's spell is working."

The yelling match lasted several minutes before Larry and his friends rode away. Max and Grandpa went back to work and Cindy threw them a confused look before her mom dragged her back into the house.

That wasn't the end of the commotion. Not more than an hour later, Alan drove up to Cindy's house. He looked happy until he stepped into Cindy's yard. Max felt like he was experiencing déjà vu. The closer Larry's father got to Cindy's house the angrier he looked. When he opened his mouth, a flood of obscenities rolled off his tongue. Alan acted like he couldn't believe what was happening. Before Cindy's mom could open the door, Alan retreated hastily to his car. She flew out of the house in time to see him speed away.

Max's day was brighter and more cheerful than it had been all week. Granted, Cindy wasn't with him, but she wasn't with Larry and his friends either. Somehow, he didn't know why, but everything felt like it was going to be all right.

That afternoon, Yelka came to give Max a lesson. Max wondered if Yelka scheduled this session as a normal one or if she knew the exact day her spell would work.

"You should have seen it, Yelka. It was incredible." Max beamed. "Larry and his dad didn't have a clue as to what was happening. It was like they couldn't control themselves."

"Really?" Yelka smiled.

"Yes, I only hope Cindy's mom will let her hang out with me now."

"Oh, I think she will. It might take some time, but she will."

"I hope you're right."

"Give it a few more days. The lies they spread are over and will disappear with time. Cindy's parents can now hear and see the truth. The anger of today's events might hold them back a day or so, but they will come around."

His practice with Yelka was half-hearted and his mind was wandering, which didn't seem to bother Yelka. Usually, she would be adamant that he concentrate fully; but today she seemed to know that he needed the relaxation, and let him take it easy.

The next morning, Max and Grandpa started painting the house. Max stood on the top of a ladder making wide brush strokes when he heard a familiar voice.

"Can I help?" Cindy asked.

9

The Disappearance

Max was so excited to see her he almost fell off the ladder.

"Well, Cindy, how are you?" Grandpa stopped painting for a moment.

"Much better, now that I don't have to spend the day with Larry and those losers. I don't know what happened the other day, but I am glad it did. I couldn't have taken that torture much longer."

Grandpa chuckled. "Yelka happened, that's what."

"You kind of helped," Max said as he climbed down. "If you hadn't put Yelka's charm in your house, your family would have been doomed." Max sat on the bottom step of the ladder and told her everything Yelka had done.

"Now, I know why I felt angry and confused," Cindy said. "I'm sorry to admit I directed those emotions at you two even though I knew it wasn't your fault."

"It is the nature of their spell. It is designed to make you hate," Grandpa explained.

"I'm glad you're back," Max said.

"Me too," Grandpa agreed.

"As mad as my parents were with you, it's nothing like what they are now towards Larry and his dad. Anyway, do you need some help?"

"Always." Grandpa handed her a paint can and a brush.

They spent the morning painting the house and then took their usual break. Cindy sipped her lemonade with a mischievous grin.

"I've never seen anyone smile like that after two hours of hard work," Grandpa noted, as he looked at Cindy.

"This beats hanging out with Larry and his chumps." Cindy's smile grew wider. "They are totally full of them-selves, and constantly trash you guys."

"Really." Max rolled his eyes. "I thought they would profess their undying love."

Cindy laughed. "I don't know. If I had stayed with them another week, they might have."

"What did you do?" Max raised his eyebrows.

"Oh, for fun, I would throw out something to get them riled up."

"Like what?" Max asked.

"How Larry cried when you broke his nose," Cindy said. "They hated that and it kept me in stitches all day."

Max started to laugh at the thought of Cindy teasing Larry.

"Or I would say how wonderful Grandpa is," Cindy continued. "That always did it too."

"I bet they are glad to be rid of you."

They all laughed even harder.

"What have you been doing since I've been gone?" Cindy struggled for breath. "I can see you are better Grand-pa."

"Yelka and Marko have been working me to death." Max wiped the tears from his eyes. "I haven't learned any new spells, although Yelka helped with the fire spell. Marko taught me how to use a sword."

"Cool," Cindy said. "When will he be back?"

"Not until tomorrow," Grandpa said. "Yelka will be here after lunch. She will be pleased that her handiwork was a success."

"Not as pleased as I am," Cindy stated. "I will definitely thank her. My life was becoming so dark and gloomy. Not to mention how much my parents were changing. The scary thing is I was starting to believe the lies too."

Max tried to understand, but it was hard to understand how she could ever think like Larry. Max knew he never would and it was hard to imagine Cindy could either.

"I'm so glad to be back," Cindy said. "I couldn't bring myself to practice anything we were taught. I wonder if it was because of their spell."

When Yelka arrived, she made them review every spell. It was obvious who had been practicing and who had not. Cindy had a hard time manipulating a penny and the other spells were worse.

"I don't understand," Cindy moaned.

"It will take time," Yelka comforted her. "Not only did they try to convert you, they tried to remove your goodness. That includes your ability to cast good spells. Don't worry. You will get it all back and more. It will take practice. In time you will know how to combat their hatred.

"Now, I want to teach you the spell to extinguish fire before I go," Yelka said. "I don't like leaving my students with only half of an equation."

Max was excited to learn a new spell, but Cindy appeared more depressed. Max wondered if she saw it as another opportunity to fail.

"Remember, visualization is the key," Yelka said. "Oh, I almost forgot." She ran and grabbed her bag. She then retrieved one of the roots that helped Max and Cindy learn their first spells. "Cindy, this is for you. I wish I had remembered sooner." She handed it to Cindy. "Max doesn't need any but it will help you."

Cindy took the root and devoured it like candy.

"The spell is pronounced *ugasni*," Yelka said. "Repeat after me."

"Ugasni," they repeated.

"Max, start a fire in the fireplace for us."

Max concentrated on the wood in the fireplace and uttered, *"Prizgaj."* A ball of fire appeared in his hands and flew into the fireplace. The pile of wood burst into flames.

"Now, Cindy, I want you to put it out. Remember, picture it in your mind."

Cindy closed her eyes and paused. Then she extended her hands and said, *"ugasni."* The fire flickered and then went out.

"Well done." Yelka clapped her hands.

"Good job," Max encouraged.

Cindy beamed, but she looked surprised that it worked the first time. "Must be the root. I wish we could do the lesson again."

"I'm sorry but I have to leave soon," Yelka said. "You can practice with Max after I'm gone."

They continued to start and extinguish fires until Yelka left. Max picked it up easily but with Cindy it was hit and miss. Sometimes she put out the fire, other times it would flicker but keep burning.

Max offered to help Cindy practice other spells but she said she felt exhausted.

"I don't know if it is because I haven't practiced in a while, or the lingering affects of the enemy's spell," Cindy said.

Just before dinnertime, Grandpa suggested that Cindy should probably go home. He explained that they didn't want to upset her parents after what happened. Cindy agreed and hurried off.

During dinner, Grandpa sprang a surprise. "I was inspecting the gateway today and I noticed a worn part."

Max put down his fork.

"We need to replace it ASAP. In time you will need to understand every aspect of the gateway, including how to maintain it."

"How do we fix it?" Max asked.

"We have to travel to the city where I get my supplies. I'll buy our tickets tomorrow."

"Can I invite Cindy to come with us?"

"I don't think so, it's best we don't push Cindy's parents. I'm surprised they allowed her to come back so soon. We should take it slow for now."

"Oh," Max understood his grandfather's concern. He didn't want to upset Cindy's parents but he didn't want to leave her either. "How long are we going to be gone?"

"Only for the weekend. We'll be back Monday afternoon."

Max couldn't sleep that night. He felt nervous about leaving Cindy behind and worried the enemy might try something when she was alone. She had been through a lot. *It's only for a couple of days*, he told himself as he drifted off to sleep.

The next day, Max wanted to tell Cindy about their trip but couldn't find the words. She seemed much happier than the day before. Max's mind raced with possible ways to bring up the topic while they continued painting the house.

"Cindy, will you do me a favor?" Grandpa asked.

"What?" Cindy asked with a puzzled look.

"Max and I need to go and purchase some parts for the gateway this weekend and I need someone to water the lawn. Will you do it? I'll pay you."

Max continued to paint. He didn't want to meet her gaze because he expected her to be unhappy they were leaving her behind.

"You don't have to pay me," Cindy said with a worry-free tone. "I'd be happy to do it."

Max felt disheartened because she didn't sound like she would miss them at all.

"I will pay you anyway." Grandpa went back to painting the house.

"Are you excited to get out of this town for a couple of days?" Cindy asked.

"Sure, I guess," Max tried to hide his feelings. He didn't want Cindy to know he was upset and he didn't understand why. Maybe it was because he had missed her more than she had missed him over the past week, but he dismissed that idea.

That afternoon, Marko showed up and put them through a workout. They reviewed everything Cindy had learned and then he taught Cindy what he had taught Max. Max practiced his footwork by himself while Marko worked with Cindy.

Before Cindy went home, Grandpa gave her instructions for watering the lawn. Then they accompanied Cindy home to speak with her parents. Grandpa explained to them that he and Max were leaving for the weekend and wanted Cindy to take care of the lawn while they were away. Cindy's parents agreed.

The next morning, Grandpa put them to work painting the house while he went to buy their tickets.

"I asked Grandpa if you could come with us," Max said.

"Really?" Cindy looked surprised.

"Yes, but he didn't think it was a good idea, with all that has happened."

"He's probably right. My parents are kind of touchy right now. They don't think you're a juvenile delinquent, but they don't think you're an angel either. Our disappearance shook them up pretty bad."

"I can understand that."

"But thanks," Cindy smiled.

"For what?"

"For thinking about me."

Max could feel his face turning red and he went back to work. "It sure is hot today."

Grandpa returned with the tickets. They would leave the next day at 8:00 a.m. Then, he joined them for the rest of the chores.

"I'll see if I can go with you to the bus station," Cindy said, as she prepared to leave.

"That will be fine," Grandpa said. "But if they don't agree, don't worry about it. We don't want to put any unnecessary pressure on them."

Cindy waved good-bye as she walked towards the front gate.

The next day they ate a light breakfast and cleaned up the kitchen. They collected their things and headed for the door.

Cindy waited on her porch. As Grandpa and Max exited the front gate, she went to meet them. "I can't go to the station, so I figured I would say good-bye here."

"That's all right." Grandpa took a key from his pocket and handed it to her. "This is to the house, in case you need to get in."

Cindy took the key. "Good-bye Grandpa."

"It's only three days," he said with a smile.

"Later, Max." She kissed him on the cheek and rushed home before he could reply.

"Well," Grandpa raised his eyebrows with a smile.

Max felt himself blush. He didn't mind that Cindy had kissed him. He actually liked it, but he wished she hadn't done it in front of Grandpa.

"Come on," Grandpa chuckled. Then he started down the street.

Max saw Cindy watching through her living room window. He waved and then caught up with Grandpa.

The ever-present Night Shade stood under the usual tree glaring at them. "Goingss on a tripssss?"

"None of your business." Grandpa brushed him off.

The Night Shade glared at them as they passed and then followed. "Youss don'ts wantsss to beee coming backss, Maxxssss."

Max wanted to cast a spell on the horrible creature, but he didn't think it would be smart to pick a fight. Still, he wasn't comfortable with a Night Shade behind him.

When they were within sight of the bus station, Larry and his gang rode by on their bikes. They looked surprised to see Max and Grandpa, but that didn't stop them from shouting a parade of nasty comments. They hung around until the bus carried Grandpa and Max away.

On Monday, Cindy was ready to tend Grandpa's yard for the last time. As she walked down her porch steps, she noticed the Night Shade standing next to Grandpa's front gate. Its presence at this new location made her nervous enough to decide to go in through Grandpa's back gate.

From the street, she turned right into the field that separated the two houses. She kept watching the Night Shade as he stood motionless by the front until the house blocked her view. When she reached the dirt road behind their houses, she turned onto the trail that led to Grandpa's house.

She felt better with the gate in front of her, but then another Night Shade appeared and advanced towards her.

"Ccccindysss," it hissed.

Cindy opened the gate, rushed into the yard and slammed the gate shut behind her. She let out a sigh of relief once she was behind the fence, knowing a spell protected her. The second Night Shade really bothered her though, or was it the same one that had been by the front gate? Now her curiosity was aroused. She moved backwards towards the house eyeing the Night Shade staring at her through the back fence. She then walked to the side of the house at an angle where she could still see the Night Shade in the back. When she reached a point where she was about to lose sight of the Night Shade at the back gate, she ran towards the front yard. She only sprinted a few yards when she saw the one still by the front gate. There were definitely two of them.

What could they want? She was frightened. A single Night Shade had been hanging around for weeks, but it was always down the street. Now, there were two of them and she was alone. *At least I am safe here and Max and Grandpa will be home tonight.*

She tried to busy herself with the yard. *Maybe they will go away while I work.* She placed the sprinkler where Grandpa had instructed, when her nervousness turned to annoyance: Larry and his friends were riding their bikes up the street towards her.

"Well, well, well." Larry stopped his bike next to the Night Shade by the front gate. "Little Mindy, all alone and trapped like a rat." He laughed and his friends joined in.

"If it isn't Catcher's Mitt Larry," Cindy said with a grin.

"What does that mean?" Larry looked confused.

"The way your face caught Max's fist, I thought it looked like a catcher's mitt."

"We'll see how smart you are when we catch you out and about sometime." Larry turned his bike around and he and his friends rode away.

Cindy was glad to see them leave, but was surprised at how quickly it happened. She went to sit on the porch swing.

The Night Shade remained by the front gate and didn't appear to be paying any attention to her. He only stared out into the street.

Cindy was amazed at how long Night Shades could stand perfectly still. She rocked gently, letting the sway of the swing take her worries away. She could feel herself getting drowsy but she didn't mind. Slowly, she drifted off to sleep.

She awoke to see water everywhere. Puddles were all over the lawn like a small swamp. She jumped to her feet and all the blood rushed to her head, making her dizzy and momentarily causing black spots to appear in front of her eyes. When she regained her balance, she rushed to the faucet and turned off the sprinkler. She moved it to a section of lawn that was still very dry and turned the water on again.

When she went back to the porch, she remembered the Night Shades. One stood back at his usual spot down the street. This time she watched the water to make sure she didn't drown the lawn.

When she was satisfied, she turned off the spigot and rolled up the hose. She then used a water jug to water a few plants Grandpa had asked her to look after. Once she was done, she headed home.

When she rounded the house, she could tell the Night Shade down the street was watching her. She didn't want to have another incident like the one earlier and ran for the gate.

Cindy opened the gate before she noticed the Night Shade standing in the center of the street. Its hands shot out from under its cloak and Cindy heard it hiss a strange word. The spell lifted her and threw her backwards into the yard. She landed with a hard thud, which knocked the wind out of her. Dazed, she saw that the gate was wide open. Larry, his friends, and the Night Shade stormed in.

Cindy jumped to her feet and raced towards Grandpa's house. She fished the key out of her pocket as she scrambled up the steps. She didn't know what else to do except go inside. As Larry reached the top step, she stepped inside and slammed the door in his face.

"You can't hide from us," Larry called.

Cindy backed away from the door. Her heart pounded in her chest as she listened to Larry and his gang outside. At first, she could hear only yelling and footsteps, but then the sound of glass breaking reached her ears.

"We's coming for youss, Cccindyssss," the Night Shade hissed through a broken window.

She wondered where she could hide. They would be in the house any minute. She knew she couldn't fight them all and she needed help. Suddenly, she knew what to do.

Max and Grandpa arrived in town later that evening. Max had learned a lot about the gateway, but he was happy to be back.

They strolled home breathing in the fresh dusk air but when they reached Grandpa's street they could tell something was wrong. There were police cars everywhere and it was apparent that someone had vandalized Grandpa's house. Windows were broken and graffiti had been spray painted on the walls.

Cindy's mother rushed up to them, "Cindy is missing and I think someone tried to break into your house." Her words tumbled out of her mouth as she tried to catch her breath. Tears streamed down her cheeks and fell from her chin.

"What happened?" Max felt a tingle run down his spine.

"I don't know." Cindy's mother continued to cry. "When I came home from work, I noticed the damage to your house and then looked for Cindy. I know she watered your lawn, but I can't find her anywhere."

"Did you check my house?" Grandpa asked with a worried look.

"Yes, the doors are locked. It looks like they broke your windows but didn't go in. And there is a very slight humming noise coming from inside," Cindy's mom said in a quivering voice.

"Max, you stay here while I go check things out." Grandpa bolted towards the house.

"I'm sure everything will be all right." Max tried to comfort Cindy's mom but he felt awkward because he wasn't sure where he stood with her.

"Mrs. Carlson, when was the last time you saw Cindy?" the sheriff asked as he joined them. It was the same officer who came with Alan when they accused Max of being a juvenile delinquent.

"This morning before I went to work." She wiped her eyes.

"And where were you Max?" he asked in an accusing tone.

"I was on a bus heading back from shopping with my grandfather." Max fought to stay calm. He didn't want Cindy's mom to see him angry or arguing with a police officer.

The sheriff acted concerned, but Max thought he could detect a slight smirk on his face. *He knows where Cindy is and what has happened to her.*

When Grandpa returned, he looked worried. "She isn't in the house. You were right; it doesn't appear that whoever vandalized my house went inside."

The police officer didn't ask Grandpa any questions about his house nor did it look like he wanted to. Grandpa didn't seem to care about the police. Max knew in this town, they were the enemy along with most of the other inhabitants. When the sheriff spoke with him, it was more like an interrogation. All of the questions were in reference to where he was and what he had been doing all day. Since Grandpa still had his ticket stub to prove where they had been, he backed off.

Max walked to the house and examined the damage. On one side of the house, was graffiti that read, *This is what you get for breaking my nose.* He rushed to his grandfather, who still stood by the police officer.

"I know who did this," Max reported.

"Who?" the police officer sneered.

Grandpa looked at Max with raised eyebrows.

"It was Larry and his friends," Max declared.

"That's quite an accusation," the officer responded. "Where's your evidence?"

"On the other side of the house." Max pointed. "It reads, *This is what you get for breaking my nose.*"

"I thought Cindy broke Larry's nose," the officer responded.

"She did," Max said. "Cindy was taking care of our yard. I bet that is when they did this. So you agree it was Larry because of the mention of a broken nose?"

Grandpa's look of curiosity changed to a grin of pride. Max could tell he had caught the officer off guard with that last remark.

The officer's face turned a bright red. "That's not proof," he spat. He looked like he wanted to tear Max's head right off his shoulders. Instead, he went to question Cindy's mother and father again.

Grandpa chuckled softly.

"What's so funny?" Max asked.

"That was. He knows who did it. And, boy, did he hate being caught."

"What are we going to do?"

Grandpa's grin disappeared. "I have an idea what has happened and I know where to start."

"Where?"

"Well," Grandpa said, "The gateway is open."

10

Destroying the Mark

"Why is the gateway open?" Max felt a sinking feeling in the pit of his stomach.

"I'll explain later," Grandpa whispered. "Right now act like you haven't got a clue. I suspect they know she's gone, but I'm not totally sure."

They explained where they had been all day. Since they still had their ticket stubs and the bus driver vouched for them, they were eliminated as suspects. They tried to offer some comfort to Cindy's parents after the police had grilled them.

Finally, when everyone was gone, they returned home and raced up the stairs. Broken glass was everywhere but otherwise the inside was untouched. The light of the gateway and the steady hum of the force field filled the room.

"How did they get into the yard but not the house?" Max asked, surprised that they hadn't destroyed the house.

"I figure they got through the gate while Cindy was coming or going, but she shut the door to the house. Even with broken windows as possible entrances, if the door is shut they can't enter."

"Okay, but now what do we do?" Max realized they couldn't get past the force field.

"Unfortunately, we have a real dilemma." Grandpa moved around the force field. "I purposely positioned the console so no one could read it from outside the force field. I'm guessing she tried to find Marko, since Mir is the only world she knew how to get to."

"How do we get past it?"

"Oh, that's easy. I'll kill the power and the force field will go off. The real problem is another feature I added to protect the console. If the system loses power, all the settings are reset to a default. That way they wouldn't know how to follow me into any particular world."

"So, if we turn off the power, we'll lose Cindy's settings. And if she didn't get the settings right we'll have no idea where she is?"

"Exactly," Grandpa exclaimed with a worried look. "Well," he took a deep breath. "I'll go kill the power. The more time we waste, the longer it might take to find Cindy. Believe me; the enemy is already looking for her. We have to find her before they do."

Grandpa hurried down the stairs while Max stared at the gateway. A few moments later, the room went dark and the humming stopped. When the lights came back on, the revolving mirror had come to a halt.

Grandpa rushed back to the console. He pulled out the communicator and started adjusting the dials.

"Who are you calling?"

"Marko." Grandpa pushed several more buttons. "If Cindy did get the correct coordinates, we need to start there."

"How long will it take him to respond?"

"Not long. And here's something else you didn't know. We can open the gateway with almost any coordinates we want. We can open it right in downtown Reeka but we usually try to open it in an isolated area, so no one sees us coming or going. But when the need is great we open it wherever we want. Now, the first thing I want you to do is to pick up all the broken glass in the house."

"What?" Max asked with frustration. "I want to help find Cindy."

"You will. First, we need to get organized and Marko can start searching his world."

Max reluctantly went downstairs and began cleaning up the glass from the broken windows. He wondered why Cindy went through the gateway. Didn't she know they couldn't come in the house? If they got into the yard, she must have thought they could get in the house.

He had cleaned several rooms when a lightning strike in the distance caught his attention. A storm approached, but that wasn't all. Outside, the people dressed in black surrounded the fence just like they did on his first night. There were only a few but others were joining them. Max could hear them chanting and his hand started to tingle.

The sudden hum from upstairs caught his attention. He dropped what he was doing, ran upstairs and entered the third floor as Marko came through the bright light.

Max wanted to hear their conversation, but Grandpa didn't turn off the force field. Max watched them for several minutes and then Marko returned into the gateway before Grandpa shut it down.

"What did he say?" Max asked as soon as the force field was off.

"He said he would start looking. I told him that if she is there, she probably came through in the forest and that would be the best place to start looking."

"Ouch!" Max's hand felt like someone had touched it with a hot iron. He held it out and saw the symbol had turned a bright red.

Grandpa took his hand and examined it. "What's happening?"

"The people from the town are outside, the same as my first night here."

"They must be trying to strengthen the curse. Let's see what we can do." Grandpa headed to one of the bed-rooms. "I need to hurry. The others will be arriving short-ly."

"Others? What others?" Max followed his grandfa-ther.

"Not the people outside. The others to help us find Cindy."

They entered a room that overlooked the front yard. Grandpa moved to the window and Max followed. His hand throbbed.

"I see that almost all of our neighbors are around the fence." Grandpa peered down at the gathering crowd. "I think another ten minutes should be enough time for every-one in town to arrive."

They patiently observed the scene as more people arrived. The chanting grew louder and Max's hand was burning. Even in the growing darkness of the storm, Max could see the mark clearly. It glowed like the embers of a fire.

Max couldn't help wishing for Grandpa to do some-thing terrible to the people outside. They were causing him pain and he wanted vengeance.

"Well, they want you, so I'm going to give you to them." Grandpa winked and grinned mischievously.

"What?"

"An illusion of you. They are so focused on you right now it might work."

They waited until the crowd stopped growing. Max wanted his grandfather to act quickly because the pain was almost unbearable.

"The beauty of them breaking our windows is they won't know a spell is coming. I can cast it without going outside." Grandpa then moved farther back into the room where he couldn't be seen from outside. He took a deep breath and closed his eyes. He raised his hands to his chest and thrust them forward, "*Poglej Maksa v drug drugem!*"

"What did you do?" Max stared down at the people.

"Wait and see." Grandpa moved back to the window.

Fire erupted around one of the people. Another burst into flames then another. Others scrambled to avoid the flying fireballs and debris. Some were tossed through the air with their arms and legs flailing like rag dolls before crashing to the ground. The people screamed and attacked each other all over the place. Several groups fought with swords while others engaged in hand-to-hand combat.

In a matter of minutes, the perimeter of the fence was a combat zone. People fought and yelled at each other as if they were mortal enemies. Some fled while others pursued them.

"Wow!" The spectacle shocked Max. "What did you do to cause that?"

"I gave them what they wished," Grandpa chuckled. "They wanted you so badly. I caused them to see you in each other. Normally this only works on lesser magical creatures, but they weren't expecting it."

"That has to be the best way to battle your enemies. Get them to fight themselves." Max smiled.

Grandpa's communicator flashed a soft white light. "Right on time. Finish cleaning up the glass. I will call you when everyone has arrived." He went back upstairs.

Max continued watching until the crowd dispersed. An occasional fireball popped up farther down the street. His hand still tingled but the pain was gone and the mark was not as dark as earlier.

Rain started falling in steady sheets and came through the broken windows. Max hurried and found some duct tape and garbage bags. He rushed from room to room covering up the broken windows. Every now and then, the hum of the gateway would fill the house and then go silent. Max figured it was more help arriving and he wondered how they were going to find Cindy.

In no time he had sealed all the windows and picked up the broken glass. Finally, Grandpa called him upstairs. Normally he would have been exhausted, but the need to find Cindy propelled him up the stairs.

When he entered the third floor there were five others besides Grandpa. Yelka was the only one he knew.

"Max." Yelka ran over to him. "Let me see your hand."

Max held it out and Yelka examined it.

"Joseph told me what happened. The enemy must already be hunting her. We need to do something about this mark on your hand or wherever you go they will find you," Yelka said.

"Yes, but what?" Max asked. He didn't like the idea of his enemies knowing where he was at all times.

"I will teach you the spell to remove the mark." Yelka smiled. "After the meeting. First, let me introduce you to everyone." She led him to a tall man with black hair and a trimmed beard.

"Max, I presume," the man said in a deep voice and extended his hand. "I'm Finster."

"Nice to meet you." Max shook Finster's massive hand.

Max then met a man who looked like he was the same age as Grandpa. His name was William and he said that he had helped Grandpa build the gateway. Yelka explained how he retired to another world but continued to work on new technologies to aid them in their cause.

"I have something for you, Max," William said before Yelka drug him away. He handed Max a communicator similar to his grandfather's. "I'm sure your grandfather will teach you how to use it later."

The next person Yelka presented resembled a character right out of a space movie. He had green skin with round black eyes and a narrow mouth. He wore a shiny silver jump suit. "I am Olik," he said in a gentle voice, taking Max by the hand. "I will be one of your teachers."

"Finally, this is Saria." Yelka led him to a dark haired woman. She was beautiful with the lines of age starting to show. Max shook her hand and noticed her skin felt strangely cold to the touch.

"I've called this meeting to inform you of a very serious problem that could affect all our work," Grandpa began. "You all know that this summer I began training my grandson, Max. What some of you don't know is that I have also been training his friend Cindy."

There were a few grumbles about Grandpa training an outsider and involving more people than necessary.

"We know what happened to Max's father," Yelka interrupted. "Joseph thought it was better for Max to have someone to lean on."

Max's ears perked up at the mention of his father. He had never heard what really happened to him. Grandpa told him he suspected Alan killed his father. He thought he was finally going to get some answers, but the conversation went back to Cindy.

"It is too late to argue about my decision. What's done is done. The problem is that she is lost in another world and we aren't the only ones looking for her. If our enemy finds her first, we may be in serious danger."

"What do you want us to do?" Finster asked.

"We need to find her quickly," Grandpa said. "I taught her and Max how to enter Mir. I'm hoping that is where she is. Marko is already looking. However, if she didn't set the correct coordinates she could be anywhere. I have made a list of possible worlds based on slight miscalculations from Mir. I think that is where we should start."

"Good idea," Yelka agreed.

"What do you see as our worst scenario?" Olik asked.

"That they find her first and want to make a trade," Grandpa replied, "for Hudich."

Everyone's face reflected a great deal of concern at the mention of the name.

"Then we had better not let it come to that," Finster uttered.

"I wish I had a picture of her to pass around but I don't. Hopefully, Marko will find her before this gets out of hand," Grandpa said.

"Our luck has never been that good," William commented.

"I know," Grandpa agreed. "We need to get started."

Grandpa went to the console. Yelka led Max down the stairs and into a side room where she examined his hand again. "We need all the help we can get. This mark could be a problem. The spell to remove it is pronounced *izbrisi znamenje*."

"*Izbrisi znamenje*," Max repeated several times.

"This is not your normal visualization. This mark is under your skin and woven into your tissue," Yelka explained. "You must visualize it leaving your blood, cells, flesh, and bone."

"I understand."

"I wish I had more time to work with you on it. I would have taught you sooner, but this is way above the beginner level and unfortunately, I've other work to do right now."

The hum of the gateway filled the house. Yelka and Max went and joined the others. When they reached the third floor, Finster disappeared in a flash of light.

Max concentrated on his hand and kept repeating, "*Izbrisi znamenje.*" He had been working on it with no results until everyone but Yelka had left.

"Don't worry, Max. It will happen. You just need time," Yelka said as Grandpa started the gateway again.

Max watched Yelka leave and then Grandpa switched off the gateway once again.

"Now what are we going to do?" Max asked.

"I'll wait here for Marko. You keep working on your hand."

Max wasn't excited about waiting. He was having trouble concentrating while others searched for Cindy. Sitting around doing nothing wasn't his way. He wanted to do something.

"Am I going to be able to help?" Max didn't want to be left behind.

"Yes, I wish I could leave you here nice and safe, but our need is too great and people we can trust are too few. If Marko hasn't found her, I am going to send you with him. I will have to stay here and work the gateway. It is going to have a lot of traffic. There are many worlds out there. Some of which haven't been explored."

"I thought you had been to them all." Max cocked his head with a puzzled look.

"There are some I have only poked my head into. Others are extremely dangerous places and have never been explored."

"Why are they so dangerous?"

"Some are going through an ice age or volcanic activity. Others have dangerous creatures living there. But our enemies control the most dangerous places. If Cindy accidentally went into one of those worlds, we are in big trouble."

While they waited, Max worked on removing the mark. This was harder than he thought. The mark had not changed nor did he think it would. "How am I going to help?" he asked with frustration.

"Don't worry, Marko will help." Grandpa lowered his eyes and avoided Max's gaze.

That look bothered him. It suggested something bad was going to happen. Max dismissed it as worry for Cindy. "Marko has that powder."

"What?"

"Marko, he gave me a powder before that helped hide me and my mark from the enemy."

"What powder?" Grandpa raised his eyebrows. Before Max could answer, Grandpa's communicator began flashing again. "That was quicker than I thought." He turned on the gateway.

Max shuffled his feet impatiently as he waited for Marko to step through the gateway. He didn't appear to have good news as he emerged.

"If she's in Mir," Marko said, "she didn't come in through the forest."

"I want you and Max to go back and search together," Grandpa said. "You won't have much time because of his mark."

"Do you feel up to it?" Marko asked Max. "We will be moving fast. This isn't going to be a picnic like our last trip."

Max would hardly call his last trip with Marko a picnic, but he understood the danger. He was sure they were going to run into trouble and he might have to fight. "Yes, I'm up to it."

"Max, I want you to follow Marko's orders exactly." Grandpa's face was grim.

"Don't worry, I will," Max promised, trying to boost his grandfather's confidence. "Is there any other news about Cindy or the enemy?"

"I have some friends keeping an eye on our enemy's movements. Other than that, nothing," Marko reported.

"You should get going." Grandpa said.

Marko nodded goodbye and stepped through.

"Be careful," Grandpa cautioned before Max entered.

"I will," Max reassured him and walked through the gateway into the forest where they had stayed before.

It was night and the trees blocked moonlight and starlight. Immediately, Max's hand started to tingle. He tried to examine it in the darkness, but couldn't see anything.

"You already feel it don't you?" Marko asked.

"Yes."

"They will be coming soon. I don't think Helaina will be able to help us this time." Marko looked up and down the path. "They won't be coming by torch light like before. This attack will be quick and silent."

"What are we going to do?" Max felt like he should have remained with Grandpa. Then he thought about Cindy and he found his courage.

"We're going to fight." Marko pulled something out of his coat. What moonlight filtered down through the trees reflected off its surface. It looked like a broken sword. Then Marko put the pieces together and they formed a beautiful blade with an ivory handle. He handed it to Max. "This is yours. I will teach you how to break it down later."

Max took the sword. "How long do we have?"

"You tell me." Marko motioned towards Max's hand.

"This stupid mark," Max spat. "I wish I could get rid of it."

"How bad do you want it gone?"

"What do you mean?" Max asked suspiciously.

"There is another way besides the spell, but it is extremely painful."

"How painful?" Max's suspicion turned to worry. Just then, his hand throbbed with each beat of his heart. "Can it be done before they arrive?"

"Yes, but the pain will be greater than anything you have ever felt."

Max's heart rate increased. He wanted the mark gone but he wasn't sure he could endure excruciating pain. He knew he was a hindrance and would be as long as he had the mark. "Let's do it." Max tried to control his breathing.

Marko led Max off the path. "Gather some wood," he ordered and they began picking up fallen tree branches. In moments, they had a sizeable pile.

"You want to do the honors?" Marko nodded towards the pile.

Max moved next to the pile and took a deep breath. He pictured the wood bursting into flames, and then he called out, "*Prizgaj*," and thrust his hands towards the wood. A ball of fire appeared and smashed into the woodpile, igniting it.

"Give me your sword," Marko said and Max handed over the blade. Marko took it and shoved the tip into the fire.

Max thought his heart was beating fast before, but when he realized what Marko was going to do, every beat pounded through his brain like a drum.

"Did my grandfather ask you to help me remove the mark?" Max remembered the look on his grandfather's face from earlier in the evening, when Grandpa appeared worried.

"He did." Marko adjusted the sword in the fire. "He said it was to be your choice."

"And if I didn't want to do it?"

"I was to take you back before our friends arrived. Because you would be of no use to us."

"So, if I don't do this I will be stuck at Grandpa's doing nothing?" Max felt his resolve harden at the thought of being useless.

"That is the case," Marko admitted, and pulled the blade out of the fire.

The tip of the sword glowed white hot, and Max became more fearful. His mouth was dry and his heart raced. "Is there no other way?"

"Not unless you can get Yelka's spell to work in the next five minutes."

"What do you want me to do?"

"Sit with your back against the tree." Marko picked up a short branch and wiped it off on his pants. "Bite on this." He handed the stick to Max.

Max put the branch in his mouth, and then stuck out his hand. Max couldn't remember ever being this scared. Marko knelt in front of him and placed Max's hand on his knee. "Close your eyes."

Max did as Marko ordered. He wanted to pull his hand away. He didn't want to do this. Then, he felt an excruciating rush of pain in his palm and it felt like his hand was on fire. He started to shake as the pain reached an unbearable level. The smell of burning flesh reached his nose. He screamed and then everything went black.

11

Stalked

When Cindy stepped through the gateway, a sense of dread washed over her. Instead of being in the forest of Mir, she stood in a dense jungle. The sound of heavy footfalls close by caused her to duck behind a tree. She didn't know what it was, but it was big and moving in her direction.

A small-elephant-sized creature trotted through the jungle, but the dense trees made it difficult for Cindy to see the creature clearly from her current position. It was unlike anything she had ever seen before. At least six feet tall, it walked on four legs with shaggy black hair covering its bulky body. Just when she thought it was going to pass by, it came to an abrupt halt. Cindy froze, heart pounding, her mouth dry.

The creature sniffed the air with loud grunting noises. It turned in every direction as if trying to get a better grasp on a scent it couldn't identify. Finally, the massive head turned in her direction and she covered her mouth to keep from screaming.

The monster's head was grotesque. It had a long snout with a black nose and several rows of razor-sharp teeth. Long gray whiskers the size of knitting needles surrounded its mouth and from behind the coarse black hair that hung from its head, Cindy could see its yellow blood-shot eyes.

Cindy wanted to run but she knew this would draw its attention. If she remained still it might find her by her scent. Sure enough, the creature moved in her direction, sniffing with disgusting huffs of air.

Remain calm. Cindy scanned her surroundings for a way out. She noticed an old log lying on the ground, took a deep breath, and pictured the log flying into the tree behind it. *Premakni.* The log moved slightly making a rustling sound.

The beast turned towards the noise.

Premakni. This time the log slid several feet.

The creature roared and tore into the log with such ferocity it terrified Cindy. She was astounded at the creature's speed. It had the log in its jaws in seconds. Its head thrashed about and its knifelike teeth shredded the log into mere sticks.

It could run her down and bite her in half. *Don't run.* Maybe, if she had a head start she could hide, but at this short distance she couldn't risk it. Then something more frightening entered her mind, she no longer knew where the gateway was and she didn't have the crystal to find it.

The creature shook its head shedding bits of wood and saliva everywhere. For a moment, it appeared it was going to leave, but then it started sniffing again. Slowly, it crept towards her once more.

Cindy looked around for another distraction but couldn't see anything. She had to do something quickly or the creature would find her. *Premakni.* She threw a blast of pressure into the animal. It twisted and turned, biting wildly, as if trying to catch whatever struck it in the face.

Cindy wondered if she was doing the right thing because the creature appeared more agitated than before. *Pridi.* A pile of sticks and leaves flew into the air and onto the creature's back.

Again it thrashed around biting air. Its roar was almost a scream that could terrify anything living or dead. It stopped with its back to her.

Prizgaj. A ball of fire flew across the jungle and struck the creature's rear. The fur ignited, sending the creature into a rage. It raced around frantically trying to extinguish the flames.

Cindy seized the opportunity to put some distance between her and the beast. She backed away, keeping trees between them.

The creature howled with rage as it rolled on the ground to extinguish the fire. After several minutes, it was back on its feet. A burn mark the size of a doormat covered its backside.

Cindy had created a sizable gap between her and the monster. She could only catch glimpses of it through the trees as she continued to back away until she could no longer see it. Finally, she reached a point where she felt safe enough to turn around and run. Grunts and growls from the creature still reached her ears.

"I need a plan," Cindy mumbled. She didn't know where she was or how long she was going to be here. She needed to get back to the general area of the gateway. She might be able to find it if she tried.

Then she realized she didn't have any food or water. "What if I am here for a while? Why did I turn on the gateway?" She realized she had to do it. She needed help and to keep the gateway safe.

Max and Grandpa are coming home today. They will find me.

She decided to climb a tree and wait for the creature to leave. Then she would head back to the gateway. Picking up some white-colored stones, she marked her path by dropping them on the forest floor because she didn't want to forget the direction she needed to go. Then she found a tree that was high enough to place her out of her stalker's reach.

She started climbing, and went to the top to see her surroundings. From there she realized her situation was worse then she feared. The only things in sight, except for the jungle, were mountains jutting skyward here and there.

"I'm not going to find a way out of this." She swallowed the lump in her throat. The reality of her situation started to sink in.

Her blood froze as she saw the creature a short distance away. It was moving in her direction, sniffing the ground as it approached. She realized she had a serious decision to make. She could get out of the tree and keep away from the creature or let it trap her in the tree without food or water.

The persistence of this creature told her she shouldn't wait it out in a tree. She figured she would starve to death before it would give up. As quickly as she could, Cindy scrambled out of the tree. She managed to reach the ground and rushed behind some trees before the creature caught sight of her.

The creature had its nose pressed against the ground like a bloodhound. It was close so she backed away slowly. The humid climate played to Cindy's advantage, as the damp jungle floor silenced her footsteps.

The creature continued to track her scent. It looked up only once to check out the tree she had climbed. It stood on its hind legs to scan the tree, and only after it was satisfied that its prey wasn't there, did it resume its hunt.

Cindy's mind raced. She had to get rid of this creature fast, because if this continued she wouldn't be able to find her way back to the gateway. Her stomach growled with hunger. She hadn't eaten since breakfast and she was famished. She paused, afraid the creature might have heard her stomach, but it continued sniffing the ground.

To her horror, the beast was closing the distance between them. She needed to pick up her pace or it would catch her. Finally, she turned and walked at a brisk but cautious pace, moving so that trees would shield her from the creature's view.

After a while of fleeing, she could no longer hear or see the creature. She began circling around to find the gateway. It was going to be impossible but she had to try.

She needed to make a wide circle and head back the way she had come. She wanted to create enough distance so the creature wouldn't see her pass by. When or if she found the gateway, she didn't know what she would do, because deep down she knew the creature wouldn't stop until it caught her.

After making her first turn, Cindy counted almost five hundred steps. She was about at the five hundred mark when she heard the sound of rushing water. *There must be a river nearby.* Her spirits rose at the thought of a cool drink and at the idea of using the river to lose her stalker. Her gait quickened as the roar grew louder but the river's noise would keep her from hearing the creature's approach.

She reached the edge of a clearing and came to a halt. The size of the clearing caused her to pause before stepping out into the open. The river flowed about a hundred feet away.

The problem wasn't the width of the clearing but the length. It was only about a hundred yards wide but its length appeared to be as long as the river. Once she reached the river, there would be no place to hide. She wanted to wade in the water so that the creature couldn't follow her scent and since the gateway was upstream, she needed to go that way.

Nothing moved in the clearing except for a few strange birds flying overhead, but they weren't big enough to worry about. The need for water drove her from the shelter of the trees. She kept low to the ground to make herself as small as possible.

The river was a large, fast-moving sea of rapids. She searched along the bank for a spot to drink. When she found a small calm pool, she dropped to her knees and put her face down to the water, sucking in several mouthfuls. The cold water felt good as it went down her throat.

After getting her fill, she climbed to her feet and looked around. She couldn't see anything unusual. Her next task was to wade upstream a few hundred yards. This was going to be more difficult than she had anticipated.

She stepped into the shallow water near the bank and lost her footing, landing with a splash at the river's edge. A slick mossy growth covered the bottom of the river. Slowly and cautiously, she managed to stand. She remained there for a moment figuring out her next move. *This is going to take awhile.*

Movement in the trees caught her attention. She dropped to a crouch and peeped over the top of the bank. The creature stood at the edge of the clearing.

It acted different than before. It no longer had its nose to the ground, but moved with caution towards the clearing with its head held high. It appeared to be scanning for something. The creature sniffed the air as its head stretched forward.

Fear rushed over Cindy like a wind, as she remained hunched in ankle deep water. Her pursuer was afraid of something and it had her trapped by the river. Time froze as the creature continued to test the clearing. Cindy looked around for something besides the beast, but there was nothing.

The creature finally returned to smelling the ground and it slowly stepped into the clearing. Cindy's heart pounded like never before. She took a deep breath. *Prizgaj.* A ball of flame flew across the clearing. Right before it hit, her pursuer looked up and the flame went out. Its eyes locked on Cindy.

It let out a thunderous roar and charged her. Cindy could feel the ground shake each time its monstrous feet hit the soil. She looked for help but found none. Summoning what courage she could, she dove into the raging river.

The icy river's touch took her breath away and its power pulled her swiftly down stream. She clawed her way to the surface and took a gulp of air. She caught sight of the creature as it reached the water's edge and plunged in after her. The wave from its splash propelled her out of its reach. Luckily, the water was deep enough that the creature couldn't stand so it didn't have an advantage.

The rapids carried them downriver. Cindy could tell by the creature's thrashing, that it didn't like being in the water any more than she did. It looked like it was trying to get out. Cindy let the river carry her away and she could see she was gaining distance from the creature.

She rode the river until she could no longer stand the cold. She didn't know if the creature was still in the water, but she hadn't seen it for a while. Her teeth were chattering, and her muscles ached from the frigid temperature. She needed to get out with enough time to dry off before dark.

She figured it would be easier to reach the shore by swimming with the current. She also wanted to stay on the same side of the river as the gateway, even though she felt she might never find it.

Cindy was surprised at how easily she made it to shore. As she climbed out of the water, she watched for the creature. After a few moments of waiting, she assumed it had already gotten out.

She found a massive boulder and lay down on its smooth, black surface. The heat of the rock felt good, but her teeth continued to chatter. It reminded her of playing in the water in an outdoor swimming pool last summer and lying on the warm cement after.

"I hope Max and Grandpa are home." She imagined them searching for her. She closed her eyes with her face against the warm rock and fell asleep.

An animal's call woke Cindy and brought her back to the horror of her situation. The sun had set and stars littered the sky. She shivered against the chill, because her clothes were still damp.

The moon gave off enough light for her to see fairly well. She looked in all directions for any sign of movement but found none.

Another animal's cry started her heart jumping. It wasn't the creature but it sounded close. "I wonder if there are any people here." While trying to decide what her next move should be, she realized she was out in the open.

She hadn't notice before, but the river was exactly in the center of the clearing and appeared to be the same width here as it was before. It looked like a strange road. She didn't know why, but she felt it was a road and the things that used it were not friendly. Maybe it was the creature's behavior before it entered the clearing that influenced this thought.

She ran to the edge of the trees and scanned for life. She could use the clearing to move in the general direction of the gateway. If she stayed close to the jungle, she could take cover quickly at any hint of danger.

Her stomach let out another growl, reminding her that she hadn't eaten in hours. She returned to the river to drink again, just in case it was a while before she could get another one. After quenching her thirst, she moved back to the edge of the jungle and began walking up stream.

The moonlight made it easy to see her footing, and the clearing was surprisingly smooth. A layer of knee-high grass covered the ground and there were no rocks or tree stumps to worry about. All of her senses were working at a high level. Her ears were constantly straining for any noise, so much so that she jumped whenever the breeze rustled the trees.

Then a familiar growl caused goose bumps to spread all over her body. It came from down by the river and brought her to stop. The creature stared at her from the other side of the river with its yellow eyes glowing in the moonlight.

It paced back and forth at the water's edge as if searching for a way to cross. It wanted her but didn't want to cross the river to get her. *Run.* She sprinted along the edge of the jungle.

The creature let out a roar as she fled.

Cindy ran as fast as she could. She heard a splash and knew the creature was crossing the river. She hoped the current would move it down stream before it could get out. She wanted to put some distance between the two of them before she entered the jungle.

She fled until her legs were about to give out and sweat formed along her forehead. She stopped to listen and then realized that sprinting wildly in a strange world might not be a good idea. The noise she made could draw unwanted attention from other unknown, horrible monsters.

She couldn't hear anything over her gasps for air. A smirk crossed her face at the thought of how the creature had struggled before to get out of the river, and when it finally got out, it was on the wrong side of the river. *It would be hilarious if it happened again.*

A rumbling sound filled the air and vibrated the ground. It was coming from upstream, so Cindy took refuge in the jungle. Peering between the trees she waited.

The shaking grew as the object approached. Suddenly, the entire clearing was alive with light.

A city-sized ship hovering above the ground roared into view. It was as wide as the clearing and hundreds of yards in length. It reminded Cindy of an aircraft carrier with decks and towers. Black men-like creatures swarmed all over it; they had arms and legs like a man but with black, rubbery skin. At first, she thought they were Night Shades but their skin reminded her of a killer whale's. They were too far away to make out much more.

The craft slowly glided by and the strange language spoken by these rubbery-skinned men reached her ears. They passed by without appearing to notice her.

Cindy was about to let out a sigh of relief when the craft slowed down. Raised voices rang out from the ship's decks and they sounded excited. Then she heard something she did recognize. The growl of her stalker. The beings on the ship had spotted the beast.

Cindy moved closer to the edge of the clearing for a better look. The ship hovered above the ground about a half mile down river. Several of the men were lowered to the ground and started pursuing the creature. The creature raced under the floating platform in her direction, but it wasn't running towards her as much as it was fleeing the strange-looking men.

Cindy realized the creature was going to bring these men past her. She ducked into a tangle of plants and from there watched the chase.

Spotlights from the ship's decks descended on the creature like a waterfall, and shouts from the pursuers filled the air as more of them joined in the chase.

The creature sprinted past Cindy's hiding place at full speed. Its eyes darted back and forth looking for a place to hide. It stayed in the clearing for another fifty yards and then dove into the jungle. The men were in wild pursuit. They were running and screaming, but didn't appear to have any weapons.

Then, three smaller hovercrafts, the size of compact cars, flew overhead. These smaller crafts used powerful spotlights to scan the ground. As they followed the creature into the jungle, they rose above the trees.

What's this all about? Cindy sat uncomfortably in her hiding place. Branches and roots poked her everywhere but she didn't dare move. *At least they got that thing off my back.*

The ground began to vibrate again as the hovercraft floated back up the clearing. Cindy watched it pass, hoping it wouldn't come back. After sitting in the same position for a long time she was about to leave when something moved out in the clearing. More men were walking towards her hiding place and they were studying the ground close to the edge of the jungle.

Cindy knew they were examining her trail. Every few feet one of them would stoop down and study the ground, as they drew closer. Her heart started racing. She had rid herself of one stalker only to have gained a whole city's worth of new ones. The bad feeling about these men-like beings continued to gnaw at her.

Without the noise of the hovercraft, Cindy didn't know how to escape without making any sound. The river wasn't close enough to help. The problem was that she sat in the middle of a bush with hundreds of branches. Although everything was moist, if she broke one branch, the sound of it would give her away.

Her indecision eventually kept her from moving at all. The men were only twenty yards away and now appeared to be armed with weird looking spears.

When they were close to where Cindy entered the jungle, Cindy caught a break. A bolt of lightning flashed across the sky followed by an earsplitting roar of thunder. A downpour immediately followed the thunder. It rained so hard that the men moved into the shelter of the jungle. They stared quietly into the rain.

Cindy stayed where she was. The rain made enough noise to cover any sound she might make, but they were still close enough that they might see her. She could barely hear them speaking above the rain.

She realized how lucky she had been, another few feet and they would have found her. She hoped they would think she had moved farther up the clearing. If so, the storm would cover her tracks and they wouldn't be able to find her.

The rain was good for keeping Cindy hidden but it wasn't good for her comfort. Soon rainwater penetrated the jungle canopy as it made its way down the leaves and trees. She was soaked again.

The men stood as if they were waiting for something. They hadn't moved for quite a while and they were getting on Cindy's nerves. At one point she wanted to scream at them, but she knew that was a very bad idea.

The downpour slowed to a steady rain and the temperature dropped several degrees. Cindy worried that her teeth might start chattering and give her away, so she wrapped her arms tight around her body for warmth.

After what seemed like an eternity, Cindy felt the ground vibrating and she knew the floating city was returning. The men stepped out into the open area and moments later the hovercraft flooded the clearing with light. It stopped and a cylinder-type structure descended from it. The men entered the tube. It then ascended into the main section of the craft and the hovercraft departed. Cindy waited where she was until she was certain she was alone.

Cindy could no longer sit in her current position. She hadn't seen anything for a while so she climbed cautiously to her feet watching for movement. It felt good to stretch because some of her limbs were numb. After verifying she was alone, Cindy went to find better shelter.

She wanted to stay close to the clearing, since it was her only source of water. It took her a few minutes to find a dry spot under the branches of an umbrella-like tree. The bottom layer of its branches drooped over and touched the jungle floor, creating a miniature-like room.

Once inside she sat with her back against the tree and wrapped her arms around her legs. Despite being soaked, hungry and worried, the warm air under the tree helped her drift off to sleep. It was not a restful sleep. Her dreams were full of frightening images and of fleeing tireless pursuers. Right before a creature bit into her, she jerked awake.

Her breathing was deep and her heart was pounding. She could tell by the light that it was sometime in the early morning. The rain had stopped and the sun was about to rise. She still felt tired and wanted to go back to sleep but the reality of her situation kept her awake.

"My parents are probably freaking out," she uttered. She hoped they wouldn't blame her disappearance on Max and Grandpa. She wondered if they were searching for her. Then a terrifying thought dawned on her, she could be stuck in this place forever. She quickly pushed that idea out of her mind.

She finally accepted she wasn't going to get any more sleep, and decided to resume her search for the gateway. Yesterday, she'd hoped to find her old tracks and use them to trace her way back, but the rain wiped everything clean.

She cautiously poked her head out of her shelter and paused several minutes to survey the area. When she was positive that it was safe, she ventured out into the jungle. She stayed close to the edge of the clearing but remained inside the jungle.

A broad leaf with a puddle of water on top provided her with a drink. The cool water and the fact that she didn't have to walk to the river made her feel better. She was still hungry and needed to find something to eat.

Moving close enough to see the clearing, she started weaving her way up stream. The sun peeked over the horizon and it looked like it was going to be a beautiful day. Not a single cloud floated in the sky and only a gentle breeze blew.

Cindy walked for a long time and started wondering if she should venture into the jungle and look for the gateway. She resolved to continue along the clearing a while longer and then go into the jungle. If nothing looked familiar, she would come back to the clearing.

Suddenly, a scream-like roar hit her ears like a car horn which terrified her. She stopped to listen. After a few moments the noise came again. It was definitely the snouted creature from the day before, except it sounded different. It took Cindy several minutes to figure out from which direction the noise traveled. She decided it was coming from the jungle to her right.

The creature's roar sounded like something was wrong. It wasn't the same sound as the previous day. This noise resembled some kind of struggle. Cindy's heart raced and she couldn't believe what she was contemplating. She wanted to take a look. Her curiosity got the better of her, so cautiously; she made her way in the direction of the sound. With every step the sounds grew louder. She continued to scan the area as she crept along.

As she rounded a group of trees she saw the creature. It was on its side with its legs bound. Mud completely covered its fury body, giving evidence of a fight. Tufts of fur lay all around. Then Cindy noticed a strange pole sticking up from the ground. It was a shiny silver metal with a narrow gray box on the top with flashing lights.

Cindy realized the creature had stopped struggling, which drew her attention away from the pole. The beast stared at her, but it wasn't a look of rage. It almost appeared to have a pleading look in its eyes.

She didn't know why, but she found herself moving closer to it. For some reason, she wasn't frightened anymore. She stepped close enough to touch one of the creature's massive feet. The creature hadn't moved for quite sometime and Cindy no longer felt threatened.

The next thing Cindy did, she couldn't explain. She reached out and actually touched the creature's foot. She jerked her hand away as if she received a shock. "What the—"

She paused a moment and then put her hand back on the creature's foot. The result was the same as before. She heard a strong, clear voice inside her head. *Please help me.*

12

Behind Enemy Lines

When Max awoke, he was surprised to be in his own room. It was night and it took his eyes a moment to adjust to the darkness. His hand ached and had a bandage wrapped around it. He remembered going with Marko, the sword and then eliminating the mark. He sat up and his hand throbbed. He found if he kept his hand elevated the pain lessened.

He climbed out of bed and walked to the door. He kept his hand above his shoulder to make the wound bearable. When he opened the door, he could hear the gateway humming. The clock on his nightstand read 1:08 a.m. and Grandpa was still working.

He was headed towards the tower when Marko appeared. "You're up."

"Yes. How long have we been here?"

"About an hour. Is it painful?" Marko gestured to Max's hand.

"Extremely. Is the mark gone?"

"Yes, they won't be able to track you anymore."

"That's good." Max tried to look pleased but the pain was excruciating. "And Cindy?"

"No news. Come on, let's do something about the pain." Marko led Max down to the kitchen where Olik waited with medical equipment.

"Max," Olik smiled. "I hear you've had a busy night."

"Painful, but not really busy."

"Yes." Olik nodded to the chair across the table. "Let me have a look at it."

Max sat and lowered his arm and a burning sensation rushed through his hand. His face twisted and contorted as he tried to hide his discomfort.

"Very painful night, I see." Olik chuckled. "I'm not laughing at your suffering. I'm laughing at the face you're making trying to hide it."

Marko snorted as he looked at Max's face. Max cracked a smile as he pictured how he must look.

Olik removed the bandages. The wound was worse than Max expected. Marko had laid the blade across his palm several times and from different angles. Multiple lines shaped like the tip of the sword were visible and his palm was multicolored and swollen. In a couple of places the skin was broken and oozing a bloody white mixture.

"My, you were thorough, Marko," Olik commented. "You did get ointment on it right away, which was good."

"I wanted him to be free," Marko said.

"I am sure he will be." Olik examined the wound. "Let's ease the pain." Olik took a syringe with a long needle from the table and gave Max several shots around the damaged area.

The aching subsided. In seconds, the throbbing was gone and only a slight tingle remained. Max relaxed as the pain vanished.

"This will only last a couple of hours," Olik said. "I will give you some pills to take when the pain returns." He then gave Max another shot. "This will prevent infection and will help it heal in a quarter of the time it would normally take. We have access to better medicines in my world." Olik then wrapped Max's hand with a clean bandage and gave him a small bottle of tablets.

Max counted five capsules in the bottle.

"Don't worry, Max," Olik said. "Take one a day and by the time you finish you won't need any more."

They arrived upstairs in time to see Finster leave through the gateway. Grandpa shut the system down so they could talk.

"What's the latest?" Max asked impatiently. Somehow Max knew what the answer was going to be. He understood that this was going to be a long slow process.

"Nothing new," Grandpa frowned. "No one knows anything."

"Marko, Max." Olik drew their attention. "I have something for you." He held out two jellybean-sized devices.

"What are they?" Marko took them and gave one to Max.

"Place it in your ear and it will translate any civilized language and several primitive ones," Olik said.

"Where are we going?" Max asked.

"You are going someplace very dangerous," Grandpa said, "but the enemy will not be looking for you, there; so it might be the safest place for you." Grandpa made some adjustments to the control panel.

Max could tell that Grandpa was worried. "Where is it?"

"It's called Tabor," Grandpa said.

"It's the main enemy camp," Marko explained. "We need to know if they found Cindy. If they have, we may be able to learn where she is and help her."

"Wow," Max swallowed nervously.

"Max, normally I wouldn't send you into such an evil place," Grandpa said. "But, I have my reasons. I want you to know where the enemy congregates and to comprehend the strength of our enemy."

Marko took two packs off the floor. He passed one to Max and also handed him a black cloak with a hood. "Put this on so you will blend in."

Max fastened the cloak and slung the pack over his shoulder.

"Oh, I almost forgot." Marko returned the sword he had given Max earlier. "You've earned it."

Max hooked the sword onto his belt. He was barely tall enough to keep it from dragging on the floor. He then placed the translation device in his ear.

After turning on the gateway and the force field, Grandpa walked to Max and placed a hand on his shoulder. "Remember, do whatever Marko says."

"Don't worry Grandpa." Max held up his bandaged hand. "I will."

"I know. Tabor is a dangerous place." Grandpa then took a crystal on a chain from his pocket and handed it to him. "This one is yours to keep. If you are caught, you need to lose it before they find it."

"I understand." Max gave his grandfather a hug.

"It's time to go," Marko said.

Max joined Marko. "We will signal you if we need help or if we have any information." Marko then stepped through the gateway and Max followed.

It was night when they entered Tabor, but Max could tell they were not in a forest or grassland. The ground beneath his feet felt like stone. He could make out high ridges and the area was devoid of trees; they were in a rocky desert.

"We need to find a place to hide," Marko whispered. "The sun will be coming up soon."

No life forms moved around them and no light indicated there were any towns or villages nearby. "Do they control this entire world?"

"Yes, there are eyes always watching here. Once it's light, I can determine where we are and how to proceed."

"How do you know where we are?"

"This used to be my home." Marko started down the slope.

Max followed, imitating Marko's hunched-over stance as they made their way into a canyon running between the hills. A scattering of plants grew at the bottom of the canyon.

The temperature stifled them and caused Max to perspire. The pungent air stung his nose and he could taste a hint of sulfur on his tongue. Sweat trickled down his forehead and burned his eyes. "It's hot here." he whispered as he wiped his face with his sleeve.

"Yes."

They continued in the same direction for quite some time. The sky grew lighter, but it was a different sky. It had a grey tint that gave it an overcast look.

Max wondered if there were any good people in Tabor. Marko had lived here and he was good. Had the evil people killed them or driven them into remote areas?

Marko pointed to a cave in a rocky outcropping. "We can hide there." Marko led Max towards the opening.

When they were a short distance from the cave, Marko stopped. "You wait here," he whispered. "I want to make sure it's empty." He disappeared into the hole.

Max tried to imagine the kinds of creatures that lived here. Now that it was somewhat light out, he could see that the ground and rocks were black, as if a fire had burned the whole area.

A shriek startled Max and he looked around. In the distance, a strange black bird circled high in the air.

A hand clasped over his mouth and pulled him inside the cave. "It's me," Marko whispered. "I didn't want that skaff to see or hear you."

"What kind of bird is it?" Max asked after Marko had released him.

"A vicious bird. The enemy uses them as scouts and as weapons."

"Are there any good people here?"

"Probably. Only, I don't know who or where they are."

"What are we going to do?"

"I want you to get some sleep. You need to be rested before tonight."

"I'm all right." Max stood erect.

"Still, try to get some sleep. I'm going to look around. I will be back shortly. If anything tries to enter the cave without identifying itself, use your sword only. If you cast a spell, our enemy will know we are here."

Marko slid off his pack and took out a water skin. He took a long drink and then tucked the skin under his cloak. "Get some sleep." He left.

Max took Marko's advice. He looked around for a comfortable spot but with the rocks and animal bones littering the floor, it wasn't easy. He used both packs so he could lean against the wall and closed his eyes. Sleep didn't come easily because he was concerned about Cindy. He wondered where she was and if she was all right. After a short period of worrying, weariness overcame him and he fell asleep.

Marko nudged Max awake a little after sunset. Max's hand throbbed terribly, so he took one of the pills Olik gave him to ease the pain.

"Their main camp is a couple miles south," Marko reported.

"Camp?" Max expected there to be a city not a camp.

"Yes, there aren't many permanent inhabitants in this world. Whenever the enemy gets together, they use magic to come here. There are no cities so they set up camps."

"Did you get any news?"

"No, I only observed the camp's layout and where we might find information. There is a hierarchy and the closer we can get to the top, the better the information we might obtain."

They ate a quick meal and then hid their packs inside the cave. Marko said they needed to move fast and they couldn't accomplish this while carrying a thirty-pound pack. "I know you couldn't show the enemy how to use your communicator because you don't know how, but leave it here. If we are captured we don't want them to have it."

Marko led Max south through a winding canyon. No starlight penetrated the blackness and only a little moonlight. The darkness made it difficult for Max to see but Marko glided along as if streetlights lined their path.

They emerged from the canyon and Max noticed an orange glow across the skyline. He gave Marko's cloak a tug and pointed.

"Fires from their camp." He pulled his hood over his head concealing his face and told Max to do the same.

Max covered his head with his hood and tied it tight.

"Don't talk to anyone. Remember we will under-stand them with these earpieces, but that doesn't mean they will understand us. We don't need any unnecessary atten-tion. If anyone speaks to you, give a nod or a grunt."

"Okay." Max pulled his cloak tighter.

When they cleared the next ridge, the camp spread out across the valley in front of them. Thousands of tents dotted the landscape, each with a fire out front. Black bird-like creatures flew everywhere. They reminded Max of gar-goyles on old churches.

No guards patrolled the perimeter. Max figured the enemy controlled this world and they didn't expect trouble. He also noticed the hierarchy Marko mentioned. The tents were larger and more ornate towards the center of the camp.

Max followed Marko into the camp where no one paid them any attention. Strange and horrifying creatures moved around the place and many of them resembled zombies in a horror movie. Max was amazed at how well he understood what they said. There was a definite buzz in the camp. Most talked about a missing human that could give them an edge in the war.

To Max's relief, it didn't sound like they had found Cindy yet. With all this loose talk, he and Marko would know everything right away. He wondered why they were still moving deeper into the camp when they could find out everything right here.

Max thought the camp looked big from the outside but from the inside he fully comprehended the enormity of it. The hills around the camp were no longer visible. It was as if they were in a city.

After walking for a while, the size of the tents started to increase. Fewer creatures stood around talking, and whenever one passed it moved as if it had a purpose. He imagined the differences came from power, not wealth, although the two often coincided.

The creatures in this area had a certain air about them, as if they possessed greater abilities and their patterns of speech suggested a higher level of intelligence. There was, however, less gossip about Cindy.

He wanted to ask Marko how much farther but he didn't want to draw attention to them. They continued to walk until the tents gave way to a well-lit open field with a raised platform in the center. Torches burned around the area giving off plenty of light.

A crowd of creatures gathered around the platform with several small groups on it. Marko led him right into the crowd and towards the stage.

On stage, a black winged creature spoke to the crowd about finding the lost human and how it was vital for their effort to free Hudich. He said once Hudich was free they would destroy their enemies and finally rule everything.

After the winged creature finished speaking, a hooded figure moved to the front of the stage. "Friends of Hudich," the man began, for he was a man.

There was something familiar about him.

"We have been given a great opportunity to free Hudich," he continued.

The man lowered his hood and it hit Max. It was Alan! The crowd was eating up every word he said. After every sentence, he would pause to a roar of approval. He wondered if Alan was speaking in English or some other language.

"Thousands have been dispatched to search for the human, Cindy," Alan said. "We must find her before that old fool Joe and his friends. Then we will have the advantage." These last statements brought cheers.

The bit about Grandpa infuriated Max and he wanted to launch a spell at Alan.

"This is the girl." Alan cast a spell that didn't translate into English. A smoky hologram of Cindy appeared suspended in the air. "Look close and remember. We need her alive but that doesn't mean you can't rough her up a little. Go and spread the news." The roar of the crowd grew to a deafening level and Alan joined the others behind him on the stage.

The part about being rough with Cindy troubled Max. He looked around and realized he had lost Marko. He had been too busy listening to Alan. The crowd began to disperse and Max figured it was best to stay put and let Marko find him. A few creatures told Max to get moving but he just nodded. He was happy they hadn't found Cindy yet.

Max expected Marko to show up but there was no sign of him. The entire crowd hadn't left yet and small pockets of creatures still huddled together in conversation. To Max's real surprise, creatures vanished with a flash even as he was looking at them. He figured they were moving either to their own worlds or another to conduct their search.

He walked around and eavesdropped on those that remained. He wanted to find out all he could about their plans. After passing various groups and not learning anything new, he moved closer to the platform.

The crowd on the stage was the same as when he and Marko arrived. They kept in groups and Max wanted to hear their conversations. He stayed away from Alan, because Alan could recognize him.

Max watched the platform as he crept closer. He didn't hurry because he didn't want to draw attention to himself. Twice, creatures gave him looks warning him to stay away, but he continued his advance.

When he reached the platform, he could hear some of them speaking. They weren't talking about Cindy but about him. They were discussing how, up till a night ago, they were able to track him and now couldn't. They debated whether or not he possessed more magical power then they had guessed. They wondered how he had removed the curse and sounded upset by this change of events.

"Do you think we underestimated Joe?" a dark creature asked.

"No," Alan interrupted angrily. "That old fool found another way."

Again, Max wanted to protest, but remained silent.

"I'll find that little brat," Alan continued, "and when I do I'll finish him just like I did his father."

This comment hit Max like a punch and he stumbled backwards into a goliath-sized creature eight feet tall with puny yellow eyes. He grabbed Max by the cloak and yanked him off the ground.

"Watch where you're going, maggot." The creature's bellow drew everyone's attention.

Max didn't know what to do. He couldn't break free without undoing his cloak and that would give him away.

"Well," the creature barked. "Speak." He then took off Max's hood.

The creatures stared and Max thought they were going to attack. Then his blood froze. He could feel Alan's eyes boring into him. Max glanced towards the stage and his eyes met Alan's.

13

The Zeenosees

Cindy studied the bands around the creature's legs while the beast lay still. She looked around for something to cut him free but found nothing. Then she discovered if she could pull one of the loops over the creature's back foot it would create enough slack to remove the whole thing. It looked like it would pinch the creature's back leg in the process.

Cindy placed her hand on his foot. *How long do we have?*

Not sure.

I think I can untie you but it might hurt. She looked into the creature's eyes and they were full of fear.

If you can't free me, my fate will be filled with pain and then death.

Cindy tugged on the rope to check for slack. It moved to within an inch of clearing the foot but then grew tight.

She touched his foot again. *Are you ready?*
Yes.

Cindy yanked the rope hard and it almost cleared his heel. She let the rope fall back to its original position and then she pulled again. It was close but she couldn't quite get it all the way over.

In the distance, she heard a humming sound. Cindy's eyes met the creature's and she could tell it was thinking the same thing she was. The hovercraft was coming. She placed her hand on the creature's foot. *I'll be right back. I promise.* She ran into the trees.

The humming increased in intensity as Cindy reappeared. She dragged an old tree branch, which she set behind the creature's hind legs. She stood on the branch so that she could lift the rope upward giving her the leverage she hoped would loosen the rope. She then took hold of the rope and pulled as hard as she could. The rope barely slid over the creature's heel and tightened on its foot.

The jungle floor vibrated as the hovercraft approached. It sounded like it would appear at any moment.

Cindy jumped to the ground and moved to the creature's front legs. Then taking the rope with both hands she tugged with all her might. The rope was inching along.

The humming was so strong Cindy expected them to catch her as well. Then the buzz of several smaller crafts filled the air.

Cindy leaned back to use her weight and lost her footing. To keep herself from landing on her back she held on to the rope. The sudden snap of her body weight generated enough force to pull the rope off the creature's foot. The rope came free, and Cindy hit the ground with a thud.

There were voices nearby. Cindy got to her feet and untangled the creature's legs.

Once free, the creature rolled onto its feet and then knelt in front of her. It leaned its head into Cindy's shoulder. *Get on!*

Cindy clutched two fistfuls of fur and scrambled onto its back. The beast sprang to his feet and darted through the jungle. Cindy held tight to keep the creature's movements from throwing her off. Every now and then she ducked to avoid low hanging tree branches.

Do you have a name? Cindy asked, as she lay low on the creature's back.

I'm called Ell. What's your name?

Cindy.

It's nice to meet you, Cindy.

It's nice to meet you, Ell. Cindy smiled in spite of the situation.

Ell ran for a long time before he took a break by a small stream. He leaned his head into the river to drink.

Cindy slid off his back and knelt to quench her thirst. She splashed cold water on her face. She hadn't slept much in the last twenty-four hours and worse, she hadn't eaten. She looked around wondering where they were in relation to the gateway.

Ell was staring at her so she moved closer and put her hand on his neck.

Thank you. Ell thought.

You're welcome. Are they following us?

Yes.

Cindy removed her hand as a dark thought entered her mind. Why was she placing so much trust in a creature that had been stalking her? Had he been hunting her for food or trying to warn her? She summed up enough courage and placed her hand on Ell's back. *Were you chasing me for food?*

Yes.

She jerked her hand away as if she had touched a hot stove. Ell looked at her with sad eyes as if imploring her to touch him again. Cindy placed her hand back.

I didn't know what you were. I was curious because I had never smelled your kind before. And, yes, I considered you food.

Cindy kept her nerve and didn't remove her hand. *And now?*

Nothing will touch you without going through me.

Thank you. Cindy let her hand slip down to her side.

Ell then placed a foot on Cindy's shoulder and almost knocked her over. *We cannot linger. They'll be coming.* He lowered his foot and they started moving along the stream.

Cindy moved up along side of Ell so that she could touch his neck. *Are there any fruits to eat in this jungle?* She hoped that Ell was an omnivore.

Yes. Ell continued following the stream. They walked for a while when they came to an area that had some strange plants. They reminded Cindy of watermelon plants but the strange round objects growing on the vines were hard as rocks.

Ell picked up one of the orbs in his teeth and bit down, cracking the outer shell. He dropped it in front of Cindy and then scooped up another. This time, he rolled the ball around in his mouth and spit out the shell fragments before eating the rest.

Cindy peeled away the cracked shell to find a soft inner fruit. She broke off a small piece and put it in her mouth. The texture was that of a hard peach and very sweet. It reminded her of something, but she couldn't decide what. She devoured the whole thing.

Ell moved to her after eating several of the fruits and held up his foot like a dog wanting to shake paws. Cindy realized Ell had something to say and touched his foot.

We must go. I can hear them. They aren't far. He knelt and Cindy climbed onto his back. Once Cindy was secure, he took off at a good pace. It was hard for Cindy to tell directions, but she figured Ell knew which way to go.

Who are these things following us?

They are the Zeenosees. A brutal race who delight in the torture and suffering of others.

What did they want with you? Cindy desired to learn more about their pursuers.

For sport. I would have to fight another animal or a group of Zeenosees. They are always capturing animals to use in their games. In the end, all are destroyed.

That's horrible. Cindy was shocked. *Where are we going to hide?*

We're just running until they give up.

How long will that take?

I'm not sure. Ell responded and Cindy noticed a different feeling with this thought.

Even though she was communicating with Ell through her thoughts, Cindy could also sense a tone. She wondered if her feelings were also transmitted to him.

What do you mean? Ell interrupted her thoughts.

When people speak in my language, you can sometimes tell how they feel by the sound of their voice. I can tell your emotions much the same way by your thoughts.

I understand.

Even though Ell was a hideous looking creature, Cindy felt safe with him. *Ell, if we lose these Zeenosees, can you take me to the spot where you first picked up my scent?*

Yes.

They headed in the same direction for quite some time. Ell set a good pace. He ran for a while and then trotted for an interval. Cindy assumed he did this for rest because she couldn't tell if he was tired. He never thought about it.

Ell took a short break after another long sprint. He kneeled to let Cindy get off. She stroked his back affectionately and felt he appreciated it.

Have we lost them? Cindy asked.

I don't know. I haven't heard or smelled them for a while. That's why I decided to rest.

Cindy sat with her back against a tree and wondered how her parents were doing. At least this time they couldn't blame Max or Grandpa, because they were out of town. She looked up at a patch of sky through the jungle canopy, and the position of the sun suggested it was late afternoon.

Ell moved to Cindy, his eyes darting back and forth. She could tell that he was anxious about something so she reached out and put her hand on his leg.

They're near. Ell knelt so Cindy could get on. Then Ell bolted in the direction they had come from.

Why are we going this way?

They're coming from the other direction. Ell increased his speed.

We could be heading into a trap.

I know. I'll turn again in a little bit.

Have they chased you before? And, if so, how long did it take to lose them?

Yes, and they gave up quickly. This is the hardest I've ever seen them hunt for anything. I think they're after you.

What? Why?

I think they're curious. Like I was. I'm sure they saw your tracks where you released me.

Cindy remembered her experience of the previous night when the rain saved her. She was sure she had sparked their curiosity then. She related the story to Ell as they fled through the jungle. He told her they would want to catch her.

After a long hard run, Ell changed his speed to an all-out sprint. Trees and plants turned into a blur of color as Ell moved faster than Cindy thought possible.

What's wrong? Cindy gripped Ell's fur as tight as she could.

They're gaining on us. And they're closing from several directions.

What are we going to do? She was frightened. Ell's description of the Zeenosees scared her.

I know a hiding place but I'm not sure it will save us this time.

He continued running at full speed until they came to another river. A flood of water fell over Cindy as Ell leapt into the river and started running up stream. The river was only a couple of feet deep but Ell's pace slowed. His bulky body threw water everywhere as his mammoth feet slammed in and out of the river.

Cindy could hear hovercrafts behind them. She looked for Zeenosee craft but it was difficult to see anything the way she was being bounced up and down on Ell's back.

The roar of raging water grew with each passing moment and soon drowned out the sound of the approaching hovercrafts. As Cindy and Ell rounded a bend, a waterfall thundered. Ell sprinted straight towards the falls. The explosion of water smashing into rocks swallowed up every other noise. Cindy gripped Ell's back tighter as he leapt through the falls and a wave of icy water soaked her. A moment later, Ell lay in a small cave behind the falls.

Cindy slid off Ell's wet back. She twisted the ends of her shirt and hair to wring out the water. She could see distorted images out of the waterfall. If the Zeenosees were out there, they hadn't seen where she and Ell had gone.

Ell was breathing heavily as he rested on the cool cavern floor. Cindy walked to him and placed her hand on his neck. *Maybe you should go. If they're after me, you might be able to get away.*

Ell looked at her with sad eyes. *No, I won't let them capture you.*

How far behind us were th. . . Cindy didn't finish her thought. Beyond the waterfall something flew by and she knew they were out there. They wanted her and they weren't giving up. The only way out of this was through the gateway.

Suddenly, there was a lot of activity in the area. Through the waterfall, distorted ships flew by and blurry Zeenosees moved up the river. In a matter of minutes, a squad began scouring the area.

Ell got up and walked to Cindy. She put her hand on his neck. *Can you understand them?*

A little. But I have to hear them. The loud rumbling of the waterfall makes it hard to hear.

Hovercrafts buzzed by every few minutes. Zeenosees studied the ground around the river but didn't pay any attention to the waterfall.

The old trick of hiding our tracks in the river might have worked. Ell thought.

I thought everyone knew that trick.

So did I.

The squad moved closer to the waterfall but the waterfall didn't seem to concern them. When they were within a few yards of the falls, Cindy could almost hear them speaking.

Remove your hand for a second, Ell ordered and Cindy lowered her hand.

Cindy watched Ell listen to the Zeenosees. They continued to move closer and their voices grew loud enough for Cindy to hear. Then their conversations faded as they searched upstream.

Ell looked at Cindy so she touched his neck.

They were talking about us. They're interested in you, I would be a bonus.

Did they say what they want with me?

They see you as a rare animal and are excited about watching you fight in their arena. We better wait here until night. Later I'll take you to where I first picked up your scent.

When the Zeenosees had left, Ell asked, *How did you get here?*

Cindy explained all about the gateway, Grandpa, and Max. She told him about the other worlds and how they could travel to them through the gateway. She also told him about magic and how she was learning to use it, and about the fight between good and evil. She then apologized for burning his backside.

The Zeenosees practice dark magic, Ell informed her.

Beyond the waterfall the sun was setting and the sky was a deep purple-gray color. They hadn't seen anything since the Zeenosees left.

Cindy, do *you think you could take me to another world? Here the Zeenosees hunt my kind.*

I'm not sure. Cindy could feel Ell's disappointment. *But I will try. I know Grandpa has moved others.*

We will wait a while longer, Ell thought. He lay down and Cindy sat with her back against the wall.

Cindy was cold and the damp air behind the water- fall kept her from drying out. Her stomach rumbled and she wondered if Ell was hungry too. Why hadn't Grandpa and Max shown up yet? She was angry with them. She had been running for her life for two days and they didn't seem to care.

Cindy was exhausted but she was too cold to sleep. She was shivering and had her arms wrapped around her legs.

Ell walked to her and lowered his head. *It's too cold for you here, you're freezing. I'll be right back. I'm going to check things out.*

Cindy nodded and watched Ell leave. His gigantic body caused the water to splash everywhere as he went through the waterfall, and the spray added to Cindy's misery. She hoped everything was quiet so they could go somewhere warmer. She didn't want to spend two nights in a row drying out.

After a short wait, the waterfall parted and Ell reappeared. Cindy was happy he didn't shake like a dog and douse her with water. He acted strange, so she climbed to her feet and put a hand on his back.

What's wrong? Cindy asked.

I'm not sure. I can't see any sign of them, but something doesn't feel right. I think the area is being watched.

What should we do?

We need to get you dry and warm. You're going to get soaked again when we leave, the sooner we get it over with the better.

Cindy agreed. She had forgotten that she was going to get drenched on the way out and she was dreading it. Ell lowered his belly to the floor and Cindy climbed on.

The air is warm tonight. It should help you feel better.

Cindy didn't reply but settled into a comfortable position. Ell rose to his feet and leapt through the waterfall with an incredible burst of speed. Cold water swept over them and in a second was gone. It felt like a shower of nails hit her. She was so cold the warm night air offered little comfort.

Can we find some of those fruits we ate earlier? Cindy thought some food might warm her up.

If it's safe. Ell stepped out of the river onto the shore. He crept along, sniffing the air. Cindy was happy to have Ell, because she couldn't tell if there was anything out there.

They moved only a short distance when Ell stopped. He looked in all directions.

What is it? Cindy's heart pounded in her chest like a base drum.

I sense something.

Ell stopped in his tracks as if waiting for something to happen. When he started to move again it was with slow cautious steps. Every few feet he would pause to listen. Cindy tightened her jaw to prevent her teeth from chattering.

Something is out there. I don't know which direction to go.

Ell let out a vicious roar, as something lifted Cindy from his back and propelled her through the air. She couldn't move her arms as the object lifted her higher. The buzzing of hovercrafts filled the air around her but she was rising so rapidly she couldn't tell how many there were. She glanced down to see her arms fastened to her body by cords.

She came to an abrupt stop that jarred her whole body. She lay on top of a hovercraft. There was an area for a driver and railings around the edge. A Zeenosee took hold of her shoulder and dragged her across the deck. There was a hole in the center of the deck, like a bilge of a ship which she was dropped through. She fell several feet and landed with another hard crash into a cage. With her arms tied, she couldn't break her fall and she landed face first. Unlike a bilge, the walls were not solid but rather steel bars. She was able to see the world around her.

Hovercrafts zoomed everywhere but what caught Cindy's attention were Ell's roars. It wasn't the call of a proud beast but the cry of an animal in pain. She struggled to her feet and moved to the bars. Down on the jungle floor the Zeenosees surrounded Ell. They held weapons that resembled spears. Every time they struck Ell, he howled in pain and a bright blue spark crackled in the air.

The Zeenosees appeared to be enjoying his pain. Ell tried to fight but he was outnumbered. Every time he lunged at a Zeenosee, two or three would shock him with their staffs.

"Leave him alone!" she screamed but this seemed to excite the Zeenosees. More joined the game with different weapons. Whenever they hit Ell with one of these weapons, Ell screamed and a large patch of hair would disappear.

Cindy felt a rage building inside of her like never before. She wanted this horrible scene to end. Ell had become her friend and she didn't want him to suffer. As she looked at the happy faces of the Zeenosees, they were twisted and wicked and this infuriated her even more.

A flood of anger erupted from her lips, "*PREMAK-NITE*," she screamed with all her might. The spell slammed into Ell's attackers, throwing them like rag dolls in every direction. A few crashed into trees while others slammed to the ground. "Run Ell." Ell gave her a last look before he fled into the jungle.

The Zeenosees were so stunned they let Ell go and all eyes turned to Cindy. She hated the way they looked at her. Those stares frightened her. She could sense evil that she never knew existed.

Cindy looked away after Ell had escaped. The fact that she had helped him get away brought her some satisfaction, although she worried about her situation. She sat with her back against the bars and stared at the floor. She was cold and alone.

A ladder was lowered into her cage and two Zeenosees descended. Cindy hadn't seen them up close before. The ordeal with Ell had distracted her, but now she got a good picture.

They wore black uniforms over skin that was rubbery. Their eyes were black marble, void of any expression and a nose that was more like a bump than a nose. Their mouths had rows of round cone shaped teeth.

One grabbed her and slammed her face down on the floor, digging his knee into her back. He seized her ponytail and pulled her head back. The second fastened a device around her head that made it impossible for her to speak. Then they released her and disappeared up the ladder.

They think my power is in my voice. This could be to her advantage. Suddenly she had a strange thought. She couldn't explain it. No one had taught her the variation of the spell that she used on the Zeenosees. It just came. She knew it was the plural form of the spell. Maybe the magic itself taught her.

Cindy moved back to the bars as the hovercraft took off over the treetops. It appeared they were going to let Ell go and she wondered if she would ever see him again. The wind caused by the speeding hovercraft was drying her out but it wasn't warming her.

A few minutes later, the lights from the main craft appeared in the distance. It floated in the clearing and looked bigger from the air than from the ground, twice the size of a cruise ship. There were towers and buildings all across its surface. Cindy guessed that several thousand Zeenosees lived on it.

They were heading for a landing strip that sat on pillars running the entire length of the larger hovercraft. The ship that held her captive moved over the runway and released her cage. It hit the runway with a thud.

Cindy remained sitting against the bars. She could feel eyes watching her. Their curiosity was probably due to her display of magic but the more obvious thing was they hadn't seen a human before. She didn't want to give them the satisfaction of seeing her do anything. She remembered visiting the zoo and how boring it was when the animals didn't move. That was how Cindy wanted them to feel.

A crane lifted her cage. Cindy quickly adjusted her feet to keep from falling over. It was obvious by how they handled her they didn't care if their prisoners were hurt during transport.

Finally, the crane dropped her cage and again Cindy's bottom took the brunt of the impact. Several cages sat a short distance from hers. They held all kinds of creatures, some even more horrifying than Ell. They stared at her. She noticed the cages sat in a larger circular glass enclosure. Zeenosees crowded around her side of the glass and stared at her.

Cindy drew her legs up close to her chest and lowered her face to her knees. Their insistent knocking on the glass begged for her attention but she ignored them. It wasn't until the ship started moving that the engines drowned out the knocking.

Tears began rolling down her cheeks. She started to think the nightmare would never end. The thought that she couldn't escape wasn't as bad as the thought that Max and Grandpa would never find her. Even though she had been angry with them earlier, she knew they'd be looking for her. The only bright side was that it was a warm night and her clothes had dried out. She was warming up but her stomach was growling.

The ship increased its speed. She raised her head occasionally to see a mountaintop go by. Eventually, an orange tint appeared in the sky ahead of them. The orange color continued to grow and Cindy guessed they were heading towards a city.

"You will be the main event," a voice spoke out of the darkness.

What? Cindy wanted to speak but the device around her head stopped her voice. She looked at the creatures across from her as they continued to stare at her.

"So, you understand English."

Cindy looked for the speaker. Zeenosees continued to stare at her through the glass. She decided to continue making herself uninteresting and ducked her head down to her knees again.

"Don't worry, Cindy."

Cindy's head jerked up. *How does it know my name?*

"It is Cindy, isn't it?"

Cindy nodded hoping the speaker was part of a rescue party.

"Alan and the others will be very happy I found you." The voice turned cold.

That wasn't the answer Cindy wanted to hear. She hadn't realized the enemy was also searching for her. *The enemy must want me for something. That's why they drove me into the gateway.*

"Don't worry. We won't let the Zeenosees have you, at least not until we're through with you."

A black, winged gargoyle with sharp glowing eyes approached her from between the other cages. "See you soon." It leapt into the air and flew away.

Cindy watched it fly into the orange glow until she could no longer see it. She was even more frightened now. She thought her chances of fighting some horrible creature in an arena would be better than fighting the enemy.

Soon the orange glow engulfed the hovercraft. She figured they were inside the city. Every now and then, instead of mountains going by, there appeared to be skyscrapers. Flying craft of all shapes and sizes whizzed by in all directions.

When the gigantic ship came to a halt, the crane moved Cindy back up to the landing strip where another hovercraft picked her up and sped away. They flew towards a mountain in the center of the city and entered a wide opening in the mountainside. Cindy was just happy to be set down more gently. She saw the winged creature standing close by. He was speaking to another creature in a dark cloak. Several fully armed Zeenosees stood around them.

The winged creature suddenly disappeared with a flash. The cloaked creature approached her and lowered his hood. Cindy was shocked to see the sheriff.

"Well, well, well, Cindy." The Sheriff smiled with enthusiastic delight.

14

The Escape

A scream from across the park distracted the beast holding Max. Max took advantage of the moment to bend back his captor's fingers, and kicked it in the chest. The enormous beast dropped him and hurried to join the crowd gathered around the fallen creature on the far side of the park. While attention was drawn away from him, Max crawled towards the stage and slid under the wooden structure.

"My comrades." Alan drew everyone's attention. "Our enemy is among us."

This statement brought a silence Max didn't think possible from such a gathering. He scooted farther under the stage between two support beams.

"Look," Alan shouted and added the words that didn't translate. From what Max could see through the cracks in the stage floor above him, everyone was staring at something in front of the stage. Max assumed it was an image of him.

"This is what he looks like. He is here. Find him. Find him now," Alan ordered.

A roar broke the silence as Night Shades surrounded the park and began searching the crowd. They pulled hoods off everyone. A few creatures protested but they seemed frightened by the Night Shades and complied.

Max looked for a way out of the park. When he glanced up he glimpsed Alan standing a few feet to his left. He was speaking to some Night Shades and pointing to where Max had been.

Max scanned the park for Marko. He hadn't seen him since they arrived, but he was sure Marko was the one who had killed that creature in order to help him get away. So far, no one had searched under the stage, but Max knew it was only a matter of time. He had to get out of there.

A flash of light from the stage caught Max's attention. He looked through a crack to see a gargoyle-type monster standing next to Alan. Max figured it had just arrived in Tabor. He crawled directly under them but he couldn't hear what they were saying. He spotted the stage's stairs off to his left.

He couldn't believe what he was thinking, but he wanted to get closer to hear what the monster was telling Alan. After crawling a short distance, he reached the edge of the stage. He hoped they wouldn't catch him once he climbed the stairs, but they wouldn't expect him to be on the stage. He took a deep breath then left his shelter and climbed the stairs.

He moved across the wooden structure towards Alan and the winged monster. Other groups huddled together but no one noticed him. The Night Shades were still searching the crowd and didn't seem interested in anyone on the stage.

Max walked to where he could hear the conversation between Alan and the monster. He kept his back to them so Alan wouldn't recognize him.

"The Zeenosees caught her and we moved her to a safe place," the gargoyle said.

"That's excellent news."   Alan sounded pleased. "You're sure it's Cindy?"

"Yes. She told me herself."

Max's blood turned cold. The enemy had captured Cindy! He was relieved to know she was safe for the moment. He repeated the word *Zeenosees* over and over in his mind so he wouldn't forget it.

"Go back and keep an eye on things," Alan said. "We have a situation here and I will come after I'm done."

The creature bowed and then disappeared in a flash of light. Alan went back to discussing Max with a Night Shade.

Max glanced around trying to figure out his next move. He needed to find Marko and get out of there. The Night Shades had almost searched the entire crowd and had set up checkpoints around the park. He stayed put, waiting for them to finish their search. He moved some distance away from Alan to place a group of creatures between Alan and himself.

He watched the Night Shades work the crowd. What his grandfather had said was true. The closer you are to your enemies sometimes, the safer you are.

Max heard his name mentioned and his heart began racing. It was time for him to leave the stage. He stepped backwards and bumped into something.

"It's me," Marko whispered. "Very clever of you, to come up here."

"How do we get out of here?"

"Put your hand behind your back."

Max did as Marko asked and Marko dropped something cool and damp into his hand.

"Rub that on your hands and face."

Max smeared the black substance on his hands and a horrible stench reached his nose. "Woo, what is it?" Max didn't want to touch his face with the stuff.

"I'll tell you later, but put it on. It will hide your skin."

Max wiped his hands over his face. He thought the smell was bad before, but with it on his face it was nearly unbearable. His eyes watered, his nose ran, and he felt nauseous. "Okay," his voice was a harsh whisper. Breathing through his mouth was worse. The nasty vapors soured his taste buds when he opened his mouth.

"Follow me and don't speak." Marko led Max off the stage.

Max's hand started burning. The stuff was seeping through the bandage, and his painkillers were back in the cave.

"Marko," he whispered at the bottom of the steps.

"What did I tell you?"

"I know, but they have Cindy."

"Are you sure?"

"Yes."

Marko didn't respond but continued through the crowd. He moved in a pattern that kept them away from the Night Shades.

Max's hand was now throbbing. He knew it was from the stuff Marko had given him and he wondered if he was going to be able to make it back to the cave.

They got behind the searching Night Shades and headed towards a checkpoint. "Don't speak," Marko whispered out of the side of his mouth.

Max wanted to tell him about his hand but remained silent. The pain had grown to where he felt lightheaded. He waved his hand around at his side hoping some air would help, but it felt like he'd dipped his hand into boiling water.

As they reached the checkpoint, a Night Shade blocked their path. "All who passsss musst showss themsselvesss."

"Of course." Marko lowered his hood and nodded for Max to do the same.

Max's heart pounded as he lowered his hood.

"Aachsss, you stinksss," the Night Shade hissed, stepping backwards. Every Night Shade at the checkpoint looked at Max and covered their noses.

"He has been cursed," Marko said.

"Getss him out of heress." The Night Shade whipped his hand in the air.

Max replaced his hood and glanced around to see if anyone was watching. Alan was observing them from the stage. He didn't seem to recognize Max but he looked curious.

Marko coughed drawing Max's attention and they walked through the checkpoint. Max couldn't stand the pain any longer and he removed the bandage in an effort to get the stuff off his wound. Max didn't notice that his hand, which had been black, was now his normal color. Sure enough, the instant the bandage was off, the pain decreased.

Suddenly, a shout came from the stage. Max turned to see Alan pointing at them. "There he is," Alan shouted and a roar erupted from the crowd.

Marko tugged Max so hard he almost lost his footing. Fireballs exploded around them as they fled and two Night Shades appeared ahead of them. Max barely registered their presence before Marko knocked them flat. They didn't even slow Marko down.

By the shouts of their pursuers, Max thought everybody in the camp was chasing them. High-pitched shrieks pierced the air and he expected winged bird-like creatures to swoop out of the sky at any minute.

Marko yanked Max into one of the larger tents. He took a torch by the entrance and started the tent on fire as they ran through. They exited the back and did the same to the next. They continued running in and out of tents, setting them on fire. Soon an entire section of the camp was burning and the smoke clouded the already hazy sky.

After entering what seemed like the hundredth tent, Marko stopped and pushed Max behind one side of the entrance as he hid behind the other side.

Max peered at the hornets' nest raging outside. The place was going nuts. Everyone was scrambling in different directions. Some were searching for them, while others were putting out fires.

"What do we do now?" Max whispered.

"We need to get back to the cave."

Marko waved Max farther back into the tent as a large man approached. He stepped through the door and sniffed.

Max froze as the man turned towards him and their eyes met. Then the man's eyes rolled back in his head and he fell unconscious to the floor. Marko stood over him holding a short black stick. He dragged the man deeper into the shadows.

They waited a few more minutes. The fires were spreading and the smoke was growing thicker. Marko looked up at the sky.

"We need to head west." Marko pointed.

"Which way is the cave?"

Max's heart sank when Marko pointed in the opposite direction.

"Why do we need to head west?"

"Because the smoke is moving west and it will give us cover. We need to keep out of sight until things settle down." Marko glanced at Max's hand. "I forgot about your injury when I had you put that stuff on. It must have burned like crazy."

"It still does."

"I'm sorry, but it had to be done. Now let's get out of here." Marko moved to the back of the tent, lifted up the bottom and they slipped away.

They walked along a narrow pathway between the backs of two rows of tents. Max watched his footing so that he didn't trip on the guide ropes unlike Marko who navigated them without paying obvious attention. Angry shouts and calls rang out everywhere.

When they arrived at the last tent Marko paused to check the pathway. After a moment, he ran across the road into another alleyway with Max on his heels.

Halfway down the alley, Marko motioned Max to wait. He ducked into a tent and emerged with a torch in his hand, which was used to start the surrounding tents on fire. He waved Max to follow and they continued on their way. Marko torched every tent they passed. When they reached the end of the alley they stepped out into the main thorough-fare.

Judging by the size of the tents, Max decided that they must be near the center of camp. Marko eyed a grand tent and threw the torch onto the middle of its roof. The fire spread with several sparks jumping onto the surrounding tents as they marched away.

Max was having difficulty breathing. Not only did he have the smoke to contend with but the stuff on his face still reeked. Various creatures passed them but the low hanging smoke made it hard to see. Everything was hazy, gray and distorted. No one paid them any attention.

After walking for a while, the tents decreased in size again and the smoke-thickened air thinned out. Either the wind wasn't pushing the smoke this far or the fires were out. Max decided it was a combination of both. He was sure they were using magic to extinguish the fires.

They walked without interruption until a tall beast with a wolf-like head stepped into the street, blocking their path. He was a foot taller than Marko with muscular, hairy arms. "Who are you and where are you going?"

"None of your business," Marko responded, his hands sliding into his poncho.

"I've got my orders, so it is my business. You better answer before someone gets hurt." The beast crowded Marko in a threatening manner.

Marko's hand exploded out of his cloak like lightning. His movements a blur as his short black stick crashed down on the beast's forehead. Just as fast as the stick appeared, it disappeared. The wolf-like beast stared straight ahead as it fell.

The crowds huddled around campfires eyed them as the beast collapsed. They looked surprised that the beast fell, but with the poor light and the speed of Marko's hand, they didn't seem to know what had happened.

"Can't hold his liquor," Marko said to the onlookers.

Marko nodded for Max to follow. As they approached the edge of the camp, cries fractured the night air.

"Lower your hood." Marko removed his hood.

"What?"

"Do it, now! Show them we have nothing to hide," Marko ordered and Max obeyed.

Max was surprised that Marko had somehow disguised his face. He could have sworn Marko wasn't wearing anything a moment ago. Now, he wore something like a mask or had used a spell to make his face look distorted.

A piercing shriek rang out above their heads and grew louder. A gargoyle-like bird flew past and then disappeared.

A group of the enemy organized like fighting troops hustled up the street towards them. Marko continued to march straight ahead at a steady speed. Max held his breath as the soldiers marched by. They didn't slow down or look like they were interested in them. He exhaled when the group was out of sight. Before they reached the edge of the camp, Marko turned south.

Why did Marko turn? It was only a short distance and they would have been out of the camp. Max wanted to ask Marko so badly that he coughed to get his attention. Marko didn't respond but continued walking in a southerly direction.

"How are you holding up?" Marko asked after a time.

"I'm getting tired and my hand hurts. Hey, why didn't we leave the camp?"

"Because it would be too obvious if we were spotted circling the camp." He took a water skin from under his cloak and handed it to Max. "After you take a drink, use some to clean your wound."

As Max rinsed his hand, the pain lessened. He was ready for a break. They had been walking for hours, and his feet were sore. "What are we going to do now?"

"We will turn east soon. We shouldn't have any trouble until we try to leave the camp."

Max noticed how hideous Marko looked. His eyes were like a rat's with a nose that looked like something had cut off the tip. He had long fangs that were a decaying black and yellow color. "You'll have to teach me that spell some-day."

"Spell? What spell?"

"The one that changed your appearance."

"Oh, yes, I forgot," Marko said. "We'll have to ask Yelka." He took the water skin from Max and drank.

Marko led Max south before turning east. There was less excitement in the camp now. The only smoke in the air came from campfires. The enemy had extinguished the burning tents.

The pain in Max's hand was growing in intensity. He wondered if it was the smelly stuff or that he hadn't taken his medicine. He tried focusing on what they were going to do once they got back to Grandpa's. He hoped somebody had heard of the Zeenosees, so they could rescue Cindy. He prayed she was all right.

Max wondered what time it was. It was still dark but with the hazy sky it could be early morning. All he knew was that it seemed like they'd been walking for days and he was tired.

After what felt like an eternity, the edge of the camp appeared less than a mile away. They hadn't passed anyone for a while and Max hoped they would escape without incident. The sky was turning a dull gray, a hint morning was approaching.

When they were only yards away from the edge of camp, Marko led Max into a tent. Before Max could speak, Marko held a finger to his lips and pointed to the sleeping occupant. He waved Max to follow and they ducked under the back of the tent so that they were behind the tents again.

Marko put his mouth next to Max's ear. "They're watching the border."

Marko negotiated the narrow path between the back of the tents with cat-like ease. Max struggled with the ropes as he had before. After a short time of moving parallel with the border, Max heard voices.

As they drew near the end of the tents, Max and Marko had to freeze a couple of times as someone passed by on the border ahead. They hid behind the last tent separating them from the desert.

The voices, which before were only a murmur, were now strong and clear. They were discussing how a spy had penetrated the camp. By the sound of it, there were a lot of guards and they weren't happy.

Marko and Max started jumping across pathways and hiding behind tents in an effort to find an area without guards. It took them a few minutes to find a place the enemy patrolled only intermittently. The real benefit was a mound of dirt outside camp that would provide cover.

Marko watched the guards' every move. It appeared he was timing when they passed by and how long before they returned. Finally, Marko held up his hand as a signal to get ready. When Marko dropped his hand, they bolted for the mound of dirt across the border. Once there, they paused to see if anyone had noticed. After several moments of watching the guards continuing their normal patrol, they figured they were safe.

Marko whispered in Max's ear, "See that pile of rocks about thirty yards away?"

Max nodded.

"When I move, follow me."

Marko studied the guards again. "Go," he whispered and like a cheetah he ran towards the rocks with Max right behind him. They continued running from cover to cover until the camp was no longer in sight. They hustled to the cave to get their things. Marko changed his appearance back to his old self.

"So, you know where Cindy is?" Marko asked as they retrieved their packs.

"Well, I know the name of the people who have her. They are called the Zeenosees."

Marko's expression told Max that it wasn't good news.

"You know who they are?"

"Yes, I know."

"And?"

"They are a race who likes blood sports." Marko pulled his communicator out of his cloak.

Max watched with interest as Marko adjusted the dials. "Are you telling Grandpa we're coming?"

"Yes, and to open the gateway." Marko lifted the communicator.

"I wish I knew how to use my communicator."

"There hasn't been any time to teach you, with all the recent events."

Marko placed the communicator back under his cloak. He seemed to produce a lot of items from beneath that cloak. Max wondered how many things he had hidden under there.

They slung their packs over their shoulders and were heading for the cavern entrance when the ground rumbled and everything went dark as if someone turned off the lights. The darkness was so complete they couldn't see anything.

Marko's voice echoed, "*Prizgaj*," and a fireball flew from his hands towards the mouth of the cave. The entrance was blocked!

15

Grandpa's Adventure

Marko launched another fireball. It floated across the cavern so slowly Max thought it was never going to hit the wall. As the fireball glowed, Marko started searching the ground. Before Max could ask him what he was doing, Marko had found a long leg bone. He tore a piece of cloth from his shirt and wrapped it around the end of the bone before the slow moving fireball hit the wall and went out.

"*Prizgaj*," echoed again through the darkness and the cloth on the end of the bone ignited.

"What are we going to do?" Max was starting to panic.

"You're going to take your medication. I'm going to tell your grandfather we're running late and to keep the gateway open."

"How are we going to get out of here?"

"Don't worry. This might work to our advantage," Marko said. "It's good that your enemies think you're trapped." He stabbed the torch into the ground and pulled out his communicator. His fingers flew over the dials and then he put it away. He took the torch and examined the cave.

Max swallowed the pill by washing it down with water. "Can I wash this smelly tar stuff off my face?"

"Yes." Marko held the torch in front of him and moved towards the back of the cave.

Max poured water onto his hands and rubbed it on his face. The instant the water touched the gooey stuff, its stench strengthened. His injured hand burned when he touched it. The substance was like glue and wouldn't come off. Max figured he'd have to wait until he got home to get clean.

"What are you doing?" Max asked.

"The smoke is escaping in this direction. There is a hole somewhere. Grab the packs."

Max gathered up their things and joined Marko.

Marko handed the torch to Max and began moving rocks from a pile against the wall. The smoke, which had been slowly disappearing through the pile, began to flow faster as Marko rid the area of more rocks. He removed stones until a stream of light shone through a small opening.

It took Marko no time at all to create a hole big enough for them to crawl through. When Marko was outside, Max passed him the packs and then climbed from the cave. They emerged on the back side of the cave's entrance.

Marko checked the area for the enemy. "I think we're alone."

"Because they didn't expect us to get out?"

"Maybe." Marko waved Max to follow and they cautiously made for the gateway.

More than hearing or seeing any signs of pursuit, Max felt it. The hairs on the back of his neck stood on end as high-pitched shrieks filled the air.

"Run," Marko yelled and they started to sprint.

Max glanced over his shoulder, as several gargoyle-like animals descended out of the sky. They were half the distance to the gateway when their pursuers caught up to them. The sharp talons on their hands and feet were their weapons.

Marko drew his sword as did Max. He barely got it out of its sheath when Marko pushed him away from the claws of an attacker. When he hit the ground he rolled onto his back to protect himself. A few feet away, Marko fought with four gargoyle-like monsters. His blade was a blur as he slashed them. The creatures made the mistake of getting too close only once. Marko's sting was painful and resulted in severe wounds. He was like a cornered snake striking. Several of them tried to attack Marko's back but all who tried retreated howling in pain.

Max stayed on his back and used his sword for protection. Two of the winged nightmares attacked him but he fended them off.

The attackers retreated after several more had been wounded. Marko ran to Max and pulled him to his feet. "Stay in front of me." They dashed towards the gateway.

The creatures made one more attempt but flew away with mortal injuries.

As they ran, Max took the crystal out of his pocket and located the gateway. They charged up the hill and dove through it. Grandpa turned off the machine as they landed on the floor.

"I see you've been busy," Grandpa said. "And, holy cow, Max, you stink." He stepped back and plugged his nose. "You have information about Cindy?"

"Yes," Marko answered, "and it was Max who overheard it. You would have been proud. We went into the enemy's camp and joined a rally they were having. Max snuck right up on stage in the middle of their leaders."

Grandpa didn't say anything but Max could tell by the look on his face he was impressed.

"The Zeenosees have her," Max said.

"*The Zeenosees*," Grandpa repeated ominously. He exchanged a quick glance with Marko.

"I already told him," Marko said. "I didn't see the point in hiding it from him."

"A wise decision," Grandpa agreed. "Max, you need to get cleaned up, you stink. When you get back we'll talk."

It took Max a while to clean the black, smelly substance off his hands and face. He showered twice. He thought he got it all off the first time until he looked in the mirror. He grabbed an apple and headed back up to the third floor. As he climbed the steps, exhaustion caught up to him. Two nights without sleep was taking its toll.

When he entered the room, Yelka and Olik were there. They were in a heated discussion but quickly fell silent.

"What's going on?" Max asked with raised eyebrows.

"The enemy contacted us and they want to trade Cindy for Hudich." Grandpa handed Max a scroll of paper. "This was thrown into the front yard. We were making plans."

Max read the scroll. It stated what Grandpa had said, but the most disturbing thing he read was:

> *If our demands aren't met within 3 days*
> *Cindy will fight to the death in the Zeenosees'*
> *great arena.*

"What!" Max exclaimed.

"We will keep Cindy out of that arena. We were just agreeing to the stratagem," Olik said.

"What is the plan?"

"We're going to get her back," Grandpa assured him and shot Olik a sideways glance. "You don't need to concern yourself with all the details."

"I want to know the details. What are they?" Max demanded.

"We definitely won't give up Hudich. At least not totally," Yelka spoke up.

"Who is this Hudich?" Max asked.

"He is the one with enough power to help our enemy gain victory," Olik said. "We trapped him years ago in a world called Pekel."

"What will happen if he is freed?"

"With his magical powers and poisoned mind, the war would escalate dramatically," Yelka replied.

"We've agreed on a plan," Grandpa said. "You need to go get food and water. You and Marko will be leaving soon."

"Leaving for where?"

"You'll be going to the world where Cindy is. I figured out her miscalculation from Mir and I can open the gateway into the world of the Zeenosees where she went through."

"What are you going to do, Grandpa?"

"I'm going on a trip of my own. But don't worry about me. Yelka will operate the gateway."

"You're going after this Hudich, aren't you?"

"Yes. Now go get your stuff."

Max went downstairs to get the things they'd need. When he got back upstairs, Olik was gone.

Marko helped pack their supplies. Compared to how exhausted Max felt, Marko looked well rested. Max wondered if he ever slept.

"We're together again." Marko handed a pack to Max.

As soon as they were ready, Grandpa fired up the gateway. The mirror started revolving and picked up speed.

"What's the plan?" Max asked. He had many questions and everything was moving too fast. He wanted to know every detail. What was Grandpa going to do and what was his and Marko's role?

"Marko will explain everything. For now, you're going to try and locate Cindy," Grandpa said. "Remember. . ."

"Do exactly what Marko says," Max finished.

Grandpa turned to Marko. "If you locate and free Cindy, let us know immediately."

Marko nodded and stepped through the gateway.

"Be careful, Max," Grandpa said, and put his hand warmly on Max's shoulder.

"You too." Max realized his grandfather was embarking on his own perilous adventure. He hugged him, said good-bye to Yelka, and then followed Marko.

Max stepped down from the gateway and bumped into Marko, who stood motionless. Only yards away, a massive animal with shaggy hair watched them. It looked like a giant sheepdog brought back from the dead. The most frightening thing was its rows of razor-sharp teeth.

"What is it?" Max whispered.

"I'm not sure," Marko replied out the corner of his mouth.

The animal stared at them while sniffing the air with great huffs through its black nose. It crept towards them with its head lowered.

"I don't think it's going to attack," Marko whispered. "Its posture is submissive." He stepped towards the animal with an outstretched hand.

The creature approached Marko. Max's heart pounded and his mouth went dry. He didn't understand how

Marko could hold out his hand toward something that could remove his arm with one bite. Max slid his hand to the hilt of his sword. He didn't want to take any chances and if he had to help Marko, he wanted to be ready.

The animal was inches away from Marko's hand. It moved closer and took a whiff of Marko's scent. Then it touched its nose to Marko's fingers.

"Impossible." Marko jerked his hand away.

"What? What?" Max asked as Marko placed his hand on the creature's head. They remained still for what seemed like hours to Max. Why was Marko touching this hideous beast?

Finally, Marko lowered his hand. "His name is Ell and he knows Cindy."

Joe shut down the gateway after Marko and Max left.

"You're sure you want to do this?" Yelka asked.

"No, but we need to." Joe gave her a reassuring smile.

"You haven't been to Pekel in years. Are you sure you'll be able to find Hudich in two days?"

"If I know Hudich, he'll find me. I'm sure he is in charge. He wasn't when we put him there, but he had gained control the last time I visited."

"I thought magic was useless in Pekel."

"That's not entirely true. Magic lives in us, but the atmosphere of that world makes it difficult to utilize. After enough time in Pekel and with enough practice, one could learn to control it. I'm sure Hudich has realized that."

Joe took his communicator out of his pocket to see it flashed a message. "Olik is ready." He turned on the gateway. Once it was open, Olik came through.

"Did you get it?" Joe asked him.

From his backpack Olik produced a flexible tube a few feet long and an inch in diameter. It was transparent, with a strange gold clasp on one end. "If you secure this around his neck we will know his location at all times. It will also keep him from using magic. At least not without causing himself a considerable amount of pain."

"The trick will be to get it on him," Yelka said, her face lined with worry.

Olik held it out for Joe to see. "You fasten it with the clasp which has a one-of-a-kind key." Olik demonstrated the clasping mechanism. "Here is the key. I suggest you keep it safe. Once the collar is clasped and locked, it will automatically adjust to the size of the person's neck."

Joe took the items from Olik. He practiced fastening and unfastening the clasp. When he was satisfied on how to use it, he put it in his pack.

"I also brought you this." Olik handed Joe a gun.

"Thanks." Joe took it. "I'll need all the help I can get."

"Are you sure you don't want me to go with you?" Olik asked.

"No, it will be better if I'm alone. We don't need to give them the possibility of more hostages." He placed the pack on his shoulders and nodded to Yelka.

Yelka adjusted the dials on the control panel and the gateway flashed brighter as it changed worlds. She faced Joe with a stern look. "If you need help contact us immediately."

"I will," he said. When Yelka continued to glare at him, he added "I promise."

Olik gave Joe a firm handshake. "Good luck."

"Thanks." Joe picked up a walking stick, gave them a wave, and entered the gateway.

Joe stepped down into a wooded area. The sky was clear and a breeze blew gently through his hair. The night air was fresh with the smell of wild flowers and the gurgling of a stream could be heard as it flowed nearby. Joe surveyed the area, trying to decide which direction he needed to go. It had been five years since his last trip here, but it was a world he would never forget. He thought it foolish not to remember every detail of Hudich's prison. It was the world in which he trapped Hudich so he could protect others.

He took a notebook from his pack. On the inside cover was a map. He hoped Hudich hadn't chosen a new home since his last visit. During the twenty years since he'd trapped him, he'd made several visits to check up on him. As the years went by, it was more difficult to visit because Hudich gained more power. Not enough to escape Pekel but enough to control it. After a narrow escape on his last trip and the incident with his son, Joe gave up his inspections.

After studying the map, he started walking towards Hudich's last known place of residence. It was the best piece of land here. So, why would he move?

Joe searched for a road he had drawn on his map. It took him a few minutes to find it. Turning east he increased his pace. He didn't try to hide. He wanted Hudich to know he was here. Since they only had three days to save Cindy, there was no point in playing hide and seek. Besides, it would be impossible to sneak up on Hudich in his guarded castle and place the band around his neck.

No, I need him to put it on willingly.

A rustle in a nearby tree brought him to a halt. A massive raven-like bird sat on a branch. Suddenly, it stretched its wings and cried out, "Kerwah, Kerwah," then took off and flew east.

He'll soon know I'm here. He followed the flight of the bird.

He walked at a brisk pace, expecting trouble at any moment but to his surprise, nothing happened. He rounded a bend in the road and came to the end of the trees. A short distance farther on he reached the edge of a hill. The road wound its way down a steep slope into a valley with a wide river flowing through it.

Joe stopped to study the valley. In the center of the vale stood a giant castle with high towers and a protective rock wall. The river flowed straight towards it and then split to form an island on which the castle sat. The drawbridge was up. The castle appeared deserted. Not a single light glowed in any window and no guards patrolled the walls.

Maybe he has moved after all. Joe needed a closer look. If Hudich wasn't there, he would have to find a way to get his attention quickly. If he had to search for him, he wouldn't know where to begin.

It took a while for him to descend the road leading into the valley. The road was so steep that if he hadn't brought his walking stick, he wouldn't have any skin left on his backside.

Even though he hadn't seen anything suspicious, his heart raced and his mouth was dry. He tried to convince himself the symptoms were the result of the difficult decent but he knew it was more than that. All of his senses were operating on high. Every time the breeze rustled the weeds, he jerked towards the sound.

The river was silent as it meandered along. It was at least a hundred feet across before it divided around the castle.

As he reached the castle, it sprang to life. Torches ignited in every window and all along the walls. The drawbridge crashed down, chains rattling. A squad of Trogs on horseback poured out and surrounded him.

Their thick green skin with its sparse coarse hair was visible in the torchlight. Yellow eyes mounted on fat round noses stared at Joe while long pointed ears flapped in the breeze.

A massive Trog with nasty yellow teeth coaxed his horse forward and lowered his spear to Joe's chest. "What do you want, old man?"

Joe swallowed and his heart jumped into his throat. "I'm here to see Hudich."

The Trog kicked Joe and almost knocked him off his feet. "That's Lord Hudich, old man."

They stared at each other for a few moments. "Bring him," the Trog ordered.

Several Trogs dismounted and overpowered Joe. They knocked him to the ground and kicked him repeatedly. Then they removed his pack and tied his hands behind his back. When he was secure, they set him on his feet. "Move," one commanded as they marched him into the castle.

Once inside, they covered his head with a hood so he couldn't see. Twice he caught his foot on something protruding from the floor and went down. After several minutes of walking, his escorts shoved him into a room so violently he stumbled and fell again. This time no one yanked him up. A door slammed and then there was silence.

Joe used the floor to wiggle the hood off his head. He was in a fair-sized room, which contained a long wooden table and several chairs. Moonlight filtered in through a row of stained-glass windows, bathing half the room in a soft glow. Two wooden doors on opposite ends of the room appeared to be the only entrances or exits.

He rolled to the nearest wall, placed his back against it and struggled to his feet. His ribs screamed with pain where the Trogs had kicked him.

"It isn't fun is it?" a deep voice spoke from the shadows.

"What isn't?"

"Getting old. You aren't the man you used to be," the voice continued. "I, however, will be around long after you're gone, as you know, my kind have longer life span."

"Yet, my kind live in the better world." Joe returned his own jab in response to the *old* remark.

"I have a feeling that is about to change."

"Not if I can help it, *Hudich*." Joe emphasized his name.

Suddenly, an incredible force struck Joe in the stomach, doubling him over and dropping him to his knees. It took him a moment to regain his breath and climb back to his feet.

"That's *Lord* Hudich, old man. I have developed my skills in this forsaken place. Something I'm sure you have not."

"Perhaps, but I'm not forced to live in this place." Joe aimed at Hudich's ego.

Wham! Another blow hit Joe in the abdomen and he dropped to the floor again gasping for breath.

"Your place of residence has officially changed, *permanently*!" Hudich laughed.

"Not if you want yours to change." Joe winced as he gained his feet.

"What are you talking about?"

"A chance for you to leave this place."

"What makes you think I want to leave?"

Joe decided not to answer. He wanted Hudich to mull over the possibility of leaving Pekel. The desire to rule and control dominated Hudich's thoughts and that was not possible here. He might rule Pekel but here his power was limited.

"I'm listening," Hudich said after a few moments. "But if I don't like what I hear you'll be staying, forever. And, let me assure you, they'll be the worst days of your life."

"Like you said, I'm an old man." Joe let a long pause go by before speaking again. He could feel Hudich's impatience growing and his breathing quickening in anticipation. "Your followers are holding someone of great importance to me."

"And?"

"They want to trade you for this person. They've given me three days to make the trade or they will kill my friend."

"Are you willing to die for this person?"

"Yes."

"I know you and you are not telling me everything. If you are willing to die for your friend, you have more conditions."

"Yes, where is my pack?" Joe gasped at a stab of pain from his bruised ribs.

Out of the shadows a leg and then another became visible. Tiger-like feet with sharp claws moved into the faint light, as Hudich stepped towards the table. Then a long muscular arm flashed out of the shadows and dumped the contents of Joe's pack onto the table. The items scattered in all directions.

With his face still hidden in the shadows, Hudich rummaged through the objects as if he didn't recognize any. He examined the gun for a moment,
"I've seen this object before." Joe swallowed the lump in his throat, fearing Hudich might know what it was, but he placed it back on the table. Hudich held up the collar and examined it. After checking the other objects, he threw the pack down on the pile. "What do you want with this stuff?"

"To take you to the world of the Zeenosees, where I will trade you for my friend."

Hudich moved back into the shadows. Joe could hear his breathing and figured he was pondering what he had heard.

"How do you intend to do this?"

"Among my things is a collar you will have to wear." Joe stepped towards the table. "Once the trade is made I will remove it."

"What does this collar do?"

"It will make it so you can't use magic." Joe jumped to the point. He didn't have anything to gain by trying to fool Hudich.

"Why would I submit to wearing your collar, old man?"

Joe heard the threat in Hudich's voice. He was not someone to toy with and he was dangerous even without the full use of magic. "These are my terms. You will wear the collar and I will transport you to the land of the Zeenosees. The collar will ensure you will behave yourself during our journey. Once we make the trade I will free you." Joe paused to get a feel for Hudich's reaction. "To show you how serious I am, I let you capture me. I'm willing to be your prisoner until I die, if you don't want your freedom."

"You have three days to make the trade?"

"Yes, after that you will be trapped here, forever! And, as you so eagerly pointed out, you will live a lot longer than I will."

Hudich stepped toward the table. One hand held Joe's pack open below the edge of the table as the other swept the objects off and into the pack. "I'll keep this for a while." Hudich turned away from the table and left through the door at the far end of the room.

After the door closed, Joe let out a sigh of relief. He moved to one of the chairs and sat down. He twisted and turned his hands to test his bands. The sharp pain in his wrists told him the ropes were tight.

He wasn't comfortable in this position. Gritting his teeth he slid his hands under his butt and to the back of his knees. Sweat formed on his forehead as he battled the pain in his wrists and ribs. Exhaling all the air from his lungs, he pulled one of his knees to his chest and slid his hands over his foot. A gasp echoed off the walls as he moaned with pain. He paused for a moment and repeated the step bringing his hands in front of his body.

He wondered how long he would have to wait. Exhausted, he laid his head on the table. Before he could fall asleep, the door at the far end of the room opened with a bang. Joe sat up, staring into the gloom.

Hudich stepped close enough that his body was visible in the light, but his head remained in the shadows.

"Have you made a decision?" Joe asked.

"Yes. I intend to find out how willing you are to die for your friend."

16

The Retrieval

"I don't think you need that." The Sheriff uttered strange words as the clamp over Cindy's mouth fell to the floor with a clank.

"Sheriff," Cindy said in disbelief. "How did you? What are you doing here?"

"Looking for you, of course." The Sheriff's grin spread from ear to ear. "It's lucky I found you. Who knows what the Zeenosees had in store for you. They love to make sport of creatures they catch."

Cindy was relieved to see a familiar face, even if it was an unfriendly one. She hoped it meant Grandpa and Max knew where she was. "What do you want with me?"

"To keep you safe. If that old fool Joe does what he's told, that is how you'll stay."

This didn't sound like it was all bad news. The way he referred to Grandpa indicated he probably knew where she was.

"I'll see they bring you food and water."

"What do you mean he knows Cindy?" Max asked.

"He can talk?"

"I wouldn't call it talking, more like communicating." Marko touched Ell's head. After another few minutes he removed it. "He says she saved his life, twice, and he was bringing her to this spot when she was captured. He came here hoping someone would come looking for her."

"Can he help us?" Max asked.

"Yes, he knows where she is."

Max stepped closer to Marko, adrenalin rushing through him. How did Cindy get involved with this hideous creature? "Can I talk to him?"

"Yes. You need only touch his head."

Max crept towards Ell. His hand was shaking as he placed it on Ell's head.

Hello. Ell spoke to him.

Hello. He wanted to ask more about Cindy but his mind was blank.

I'm Ell. What's your name?

Max. Max pulled his hand away. It was weird talking with thoughts. How many other creatures could communicate this way?

Marko placed his hand back on Ell's head. When he removed it, Ell took off into the jungle and they followed.

Joe didn't receive any further visitors during the night. When morning arrived, a Trog entered with a tray of stale bread and water. Joe would have preferred the food in his pack, but to keep up his strength, he ate what they gave him. He tried to sleep but couldn't, the floor and the table were too hard for comfort.

The sun shone through the windows, illuminating the entire room, allowing Joe to inspect his prison. He didn't want to escape yet, but if his plan failed he might have to.

He had just checked the windows for loose panes, when the door opened. Two fully armed Trogs entered and eyed him suspiciously.

"Come," one ordered in a guttural voice.

They waited for Joe to cross the room then parted for him to walk between them. The Trogs walked behind Joe, barking out directions as they went. The castle was a massive network of tunnels, hallways, and staircases. They directed him under an archway into an open courtyard with balconies set all around.

"Wait here." They cut the ropes from Joe's hands with a knife and then disappeared through the open archway. The instant they left, a gate crashed down blocking the way they had entered, sealing Joe inside.

The courtyard had gated archways at both ends and a pair of wooden doors on either side. There were torture areas with chains and racks along one of the walls. Wind-torn and sun-faded cloth awnings covered the balconies overlooking the small arena.

Joe's wait was short. The balconies began to fill up with Trogs and other horrifying creatures. Once seated, they started mocking and throwing things at Joe. He didn't want to give them the satisfaction of seeing him grow angry, so he remained calm and motionless. A few objects made contact but bounced off without any real effect.

A hushed silence fell over the crowd as Hudich arrived and sat in the center balcony. The shadow cast by the awning kept his face hidden. At one time, Joe thought light caused Hudich physical pain. Later, he learned that Hudich only liked his victims to see his face right before he killed them.

A slew of Trogs waited on Hudich's every whim. One filled his glass while another, a runt, wrote down his orders and still others rushed around doing who knows what.

A door on the side of the courtyard opened and a Trog entered carrying Joe's pack. He walked to the center and dumped the contents on the ground. Everything was there: the gun, the collar, the water skin, the food, a knife and other items. The Trog left and the door closed behind him.

Joe looked at the items and then at Hudich. He couldn't fight the feeling that this was a test. *He wants to know something.*

The runt standing next to Hudich moved to the edge of the balcony. "Lord Hudich has decided that you will fight the Hark." This brought cheers from the audience. "Once the Hark is released, you may use anything in your pack. If you can get to it." He laughed and the crowd roared again. He then returned to Hudich's side.

Through the far gate, Joe watched several Trogs lead in the Hark with chains attached to long poles. A fearsome, muscular beast that could walk on two legs or four, it had tough, leathery, tan skin with red stripes running across its back. Each finger and toe had a long razor-sharp claw. Its claws were not as big as the fangs protruding below the upper lip. A crocodile-like snout separated its green eyes and wide, pointy ears.

They guided the Hark under the gate and it let out a roar that turned Joe's blood cold. A cheer from the crowd followed.

Another group of Trogs hustled in carrying pikes and surrounded the Hark. The ones escorting the beast pulled a lever on their poles, which released the beast. The Hark tried to attack its escorts, but those with the pikes kept it away from them.

A couple of times, the Hark threw itself onto the tip of a pike. The pain enraged it more as it tried biting and ripping the guards.

Joe watched the scene and wondered if he should start moving towards his backpack, knowing he couldn't beat the Hark to it. Then a voice inside his head warned him. *This is a test. It isn't about dying for Cindy.*

Joe noticed the runt and Hudich were discussing something. Then, the runt walked to the front of the balcony again. "Release the Hark." The crowd cheered as the guards stepped away.

The Hark raced towards Joe at a blinding rate. Joe stood motionless. He could see the Hark's fierce eyes. As it drew near, it uttered a roar that drowned out the noise of the crowd.

Joe waited until the Hark was about to leap. "*Izginem se.*" He disappeared and dove to the side. The Hark slammed into the gate, thrashing and tearing at the air with vicious force where Joe had been.

Joe jogged along the wall. He knew he wouldn't be able to stay invisible for long. On his previous visits to Pekel, he discovered he could use the invisibility spell for short periods. He figured it was because magic was in him and the spell worked on himself. The drawback was, in Pekel, he couldn't make the spell last.

His backpack lay where the Trog dropped it but he decided to avoid it. Suddenly, his hands became visible. Behind him, the Hark howled as it spotted him.

The Hark scattered dirt and rocks as it sprinted after Joe. Before it reached him, Joe disappeared again. He didn't know how long he could keep this up. The more energy he used the harder it would be to stay invisible. He raced towards the guards with the pikes. About three-fourths of the way there, he became visible again. As before, the Hark let out a blood-curdling roar and rushed him.

Joe's heart pounded and his breath came in labored gulps. His muscles screamed for him to stop and sweat streamed down his forehead. This time the Hark didn't leap but charged straight ahead. Between the Hark's new strategy and his own hard breathing, Joe struggled to cast the spell.

He didn't clear the Hark's outstretched claws as one tore the back of his arm, spinning him in a circle. Joe tried to keep his footing but went down.

The Hark ripped and bit at the empty air. It was only seconds before the Hark located its prey. Joe lay only feet away. The Hark crept to its victim and let out a wicked roar as if saying its prey couldn't escape this time.

"*Nehaj*," Hudich called and the Hark froze in its tracks. Time stopped and the crowd fell silent.

The guards rushed into the courtyard and surrounded the Hark with their pikes at the ready. Joe looked up to see Hudich standing with his hands extended. A guard grabbed Joe by the back of the shirt and dragged him away as the Hark regained its motor functions and tried to attack its captors.

"Take him to his room," Hudich ordered as Joe was yanked to his feet.

Another Trog joined the first and they escorted Joe out of the courtyard. As they went under the archway, the crowd booed and threw rocks and rotten fruit. Joe slid his hand over the back of his arm. His sleeve was soaked with blood. He touched his fingers to the wound and discovered a deep gash, perhaps three inches in length.

"Can I get something for my wound?" Joe asked but a harsh grunt was the only response.

Joe couldn't tell if they were following the same route back to his room. The size of the castle made it impossible to remember the directions they were taking. When they arrived, the Trogs opened the door and let him enter. Joe was thankful they didn't shove him in.

Joe went to a window and cautiously rolled up his sleeve. He used the window as a mirror to inspect his wound. He was tearing off a piece of his shirt to use as a bandage when the second door opened.

Hudich entered and walked to the table dropping Joe's pack onto it, and quickly stepped back into the shadows. Joe got a brief glimpse of Hudich's face. He had solid red eyes like an albino rat and his skin, black as night, clung to his skull like stretched plastic. It resembled a black skull with fangs hanging below his lip line.

"Why are you here?" Hudich sounded curious.

"I told you. I'm here to take you to the land of the Zeenosees and trade you for my friend."

"And who is this friend?"

"No one you know."

"Why the land of the Zeenosees, old man?" Hudich's voice rose. "That doesn't sound like something you planned."

"It wasn't. My friend was captured by your followers."

Hudich remained in the shadows without speaking. Joe could hear him breathing but otherwise he made no movement. "You may have your things," Hudich broke the silence and then left the room.

Joe took his pack and found the first aid items he always carried. He cleaned and dressed his wound before eating some fruit, a granola bar and drinking water.

After his meal, he tried to sleep. In the past few days, he had slept little and felt groggy. He found a somewhat comfortable spot on the floor in the corner. It wasn't long until his exhaustion gave way to sleep.

A violent shake woke him. In the faint light, Hudich stood over him. His surprise caused him to flinch as a hand clamped over his mouth.

"Shh." Hudich held a finger to his lips. "You can trade me for your friend, old man, but you have to do what I say until we are out of here."

Joe nodded. The situation in Pekel must be a lot different for Hudich to be sneaking around. He wondered how long he had been asleep. Only torchlight filtered through the windows, which told him he had slept the entire afternoon.

Hudich released Joe's mouth and handed him a black cloak. "Put this on. It should help hide you in the dark."

Joe climbed to his feet. He stretched to ease the stiffness in his legs. As he put the cloak on, he noticed Hudich appeared nervous as he watched the doors. Joe slung his pack over his shoulder and winced as his wound protested. "Ready."

Hudich led him to the door where he paused to listen. "Wait here," he whispered and then left, closing the door behind him.

Joe didn't wait long until the door reopened and Hudich's head appeared. "Come."

Joe followed Hudich down a torch-lit hallway. They made several turns and stopped many times to listen. Joe had never before seen Hudich anxious. He sensed Hudich was afraid. The Hudich he had known always carried himself with disdainful arrogance. Now he was creeping around like a mouse avoiding a cat.

After slinking down more corridors, Hudich took a torch from a wall bracket and opened a door to his left. They entered a wide, dark hallway and Hudich closed the door behind them. The path ran straight ahead for a short distance and then turned into steep descending stairs.

The sharp angle of the staircase was awkward so Joe used the handrails to keep his balance. Hudich descended the stairs with ease. He never turned to verify whether Joe was still there.

"Where are we going?" Joe's whisper echoed off the walls.

Hudich glanced over his shoulder and shot Joe an angry look and put a finger to his lips warning him to remain silent.

They continued their descent. When the stairs ended, the ground was no longer stone but hard soil with pools of water on its potholed surface. Water dripped from the stone walls and ceiling and moss grew on every surface like a green fuzzy rug.

They tramped along, stepping in puddles. Hudich stopped once to listen but Joe couldn't hear anything above all the splashes.

"Are we under the river?" Joe ventured.

"Yes, this tunnel leads to a cave in the hillside north of the castle."

Joe didn't know why Hudich answered now when he wouldn't on the stairs but he was dying to ask more questions. "Why all this sneaking around?"

"I need tell you nothing, old man."

Joe didn't push Hudich further. Right now, he was willing to go with him. He might change his mind or try to kill Joe, if he continued to irritate him. He remembered that Hudich needed to put on the collar, before going through the gateway. This was an important piece of the plan. "What about the collar?" He didn't want to annoy Hudich but he didn't want him to forget about it either.

"That can wait." The irritation in Hudich's voice rose. "We may need to fight before we get out of here, and I will need what little magic I have."

Joe couldn't stop himself. "Who will we have to fight?"

"The Trogs. They will not let me leave willingly."

Joe wondered how *Lord Hudich* had turned into the prey of his own army. Maybe the Hudich he had once known wasn't as powerful as his enemies thought.

Before he could ask another question, they reached the stairs on the other side of the river and started climbing. These were worse than the first. There weren't any railings and the steps were steeper and broken in several places. Hudich climbed without any problems but he had to stop and wait for Joe several times. Joe crawled on his hands and knees so he wouldn't fall backwards.

When they reached the top there was a round stone door. Hudich extinguished the torch and they waited in the dark while Hudich listened.

"The Trogs have crossed the river. They don't know about this tunnel."

"Why is your army after you?"

"Do not test my patience." Hudich threatened and Joe let it go.

The sound of a latch clicking echoed off the walls and then Hudich pushed open the stone door. A flood of moonlight and starlight created a gray landscape. Hudich led Joe out of the tunnel. They were on a hillside above the valley floor, which appeared to be full of fireflies flickering everywhere as the Trogs searched by torchlight. Several Trogs were at the base of the hill and moving in their direction.

"Where to, old man?" Hudich whispered.

"Up and to the South." Joe pointed.

They began climbing. To keep hidden from searching eyes, they both remained hunched over as they moved. Joe glanced over his shoulder and saw Trogs ascending the hill.

He was having trouble keeping up with Hudich, breathing hard and perspiring heavily. He hadn't exercised much over the last couple of years, and age was catching up with him. Joe took out his communicator and adjusted the dials.

"What are you doing?" Hudich growled as Joe slowed to use the device.

"I'm telling my friends to turn on the gateway. I think it wise to have it open when we get there."

Just as they reached the top of the hill, they were spotted by the Trogs. Shouts of excitement rolled like a tidal wave through the searchers, as they began moving in their direction. Joe and Hudich started running at full speed. Joe tripped and went down several times and in each instance Hudich picked him up.

By the calls of their pursuers, Joe could tell they were losing ground and the gateway was still some distance away. He didn't know how long he could keep sprinting. In mid-stride, he removed his pack and fished around for the gun. He was going to need it to get them out. He shoved the gun in his pocket, and swung the pack onto his shoulder.

"How much farther?" Hudich asked.

"About a quarter mile." Joe gasped for air.

After several more minutes, they reached the trees and then the road. The trees didn't conceal them for long, as the gap between them and the Trogs was shrinking. The whole area behind them was full of flashing lights and harsh yells as the army continued the chase.

Suddenly, a line of torches appeared in front of them as Joe waved the crystal around. He didn't know if the gateway wasn't open or if all the approaching torches were making it difficult to locate. He took the communicator from his pocket, it was flashing; Yelka had received his message. "We need to stop. I can't locate the gateway like this."

"If we stop, we're dead," Hudich growled over his shoulder. "They know my magic is limited and they will tear us apart."

Joe was losing energy fast and stopped. Hudich noticed Joe was no longer following and whirled around. "What are you doing, you old fool?"

Joe ignored him and continued using the crystal. He located the gateway and knew they weren't going to reach it before the Trogs overtook them.

"It's that way about fifty yards." Joe pointed in the direction of the gateway. He pulled the gun out of his pocket as he jogged forward. Hudich let him pass.

"Hudich," called a Trog from the army which had now surrounded them.

Joe and Hudich halted as a gigantic Trog pushed his way into the circle.

"Where you go, Hudich?" the monster asked in his guttural voice.

Hudich looked like a cornered animal ready to strike. Joe gave him a chance to respond but when Hudich didn't speak he stepped forward. "He's coming with me."

The head Trog eyed Joe and then roared with laughter, which caused the entire army to burst out as well. "You have no say here, old man."

Joe stepped closer, pointing the gun at the Trog's head. "This weapon will kill you before you know it."

Again the army laughed. "You be one who dies and Hudich will return to castle."

Joe took aim at the shield the Trog carried and pulled the trigger. There was a flash of light and the blast tore the shield away with such force it knocked over several soldiers behind him. The rest of the army took several steps back.

"Now, if you don't mind, we'll be going." Joe pointed the gun at the gigantic Trog's chest. "So back up." He fired a shot at a nearby tree, shattering it into a hail of sparks and splinters. Then he returned his aim to the Trog.

The Trogs backed up even more as Joe turned to Hudich. "On your knees." He moved towards him.

Hudich knelt with a surprised look on his face. Joe kept pointing the gun in all directions, which caused the Trogs to spread out farther.

"Take off your hood and hold out your hands," Joe commanded.

Hudich, who still looked shocked, obeyed his orders. Joe placed his pack in Hudich's outstretched arms and, while pointing the gun with one hand, he retrieved the collar from the pack with the other. He got behind Hudich and fastened the collar around his neck. He dug the key out of his pocket and locked the collar in place.

"Get up." Joe placed the key back in his coat and then used the crystal to relocate the gateway. The flash showed it fifteen yards to his right, within the midst of the Trogs. He continued waving the gun around to keep them back.

"You think—" the main Trog started to speak when Joe pointed the gun at his feet and fired again. The ground erupted, throwing dirt, grass and rocks through the air. The force of the blast slammed the main Trog to the ground and those behind him raised their shields to protect themselves from flying debris.

"I think what?" Joe had to show he was in charge.

He could tell Hudich was surprised at the situation. "I'll bet you thought you were going back to the castle," Joe said in a hushed voice so only Hudich could hear.

Joe noticed the Trogs had backed up several more feet. He still needed them to retreat another twenty yards. He didn't have much time. In a rush, he and Hudich wouldn't stand a chance. The gun would only take out three maybe four before they would overpower him.

"The gateway is to our right about fifteen yards," Joe continued whispering. "We need them to back up. Then we will have the element of surprise because they don't know it's there."

"What are you going to do?"

"I have an idea. No matter what I do, keep moving to the right. When you get close enough, we'll leave." He glanced at Hudich, who gave a slight nod, and then wheeled around, aiming the gun at the group of soldiers to his right.

"You," he shouted, singling out one at the front. "What are you looking at?" He stormed in his direction.

The crowd of Trogs in his path tripped over each other trying to scramble out of his way. The one Joe approached stuttered, "Nuthin."

When Joe was only feet from the pile of Trogs, he turned to his left. This time he fired a shot at the feet of several he had singled out, blasting dirt over the whole crowd. "I told you I'm taking him and I won't have any interference." He headed towards them. The group stumbled as they fled from the crazy old man.

Joe worked the whole army, ranting and raving about apparent looks they were giving him. When he moved towards one side of the circle, the entire army retreated. Hudich continued creeping towards the gateway.

After Joe's last outburst and having fired the gun, he was heading back towards Hudich. With the crystal out, he waved his hand through the air and located the gateway. Hudich was only feet from it and could reach it before the army grabbed him.

"Enough," shouted the head Trog, causing Joe to turn towards him. "I no think you can kill us all."

Joe aimed the gun straight at him but kept walking towards Hudich. "No, but I can kill you."

"We see," the Trog said as Joe reached Hudich.

"He is going to attack," Hudich whispered.

"Yes," Joe agreed. "It is two feet to your right. When I fire the next shot follow me."

Joe pointed the gun at the gigantic Trog and then he lowered it and pulled the trigger. As the Trogs flinched, Joe bolted past Hudich and dove into the gateway. Hudich followed.

17

The Surprise

Mouth hanging open, Yelka stared at Hudich who stood only feet from her. She backed up until she bumped into the gateway console.

"Shut off the gateway." Joe ordered.

Yelka snapped to. She had trouble closing the gateway while fumbling with the controls and eyeing Hudich at the same time.

Hudich, aware of her inspection of him, covered his head with his hood. "That was very cunning. I can always count on you to be clever, old man."

"Got you out of there didn't it?"

"You must be Yelka," Hudich smiled disarmingly.

Yelka gazed without responding.

"Have you notified Marko?" Joe asked.

"Yes, he told me to have you go northwest at this bearing." She gave him a piece of paper. "He said he would wait for you."

"Good." Joe handed her the gun. "Keep an eye on him while I take care of some things." Joe left the third floor and went to the kitchen to get more food and to fill his water skin. He was about to return upstairs when a scream filled the house followed by a heavy thud. Pack in hand, he bolted upstairs. Hudich was on the floor struggling for breath.

"I told you that collar would keep you from using magic." Joe shook his head. "I can't blame you for trying."

"Like I said," Hudich climbed to his feet, "you are clever. Like the game you played in the courtyard. How could you know I wouldn't let anything happen to you?"

"I knew you wanted to leave but you also wanted to see if I had anything up my sleeve. I hoped your desire to leave was strong enough that I wouldn't have to show all my cards. I didn't realize you were not only a prisoner to Pekel but also to the Trogs."

"Yes," Hudich spat.

"They wanted you alive. They needed you?"

"Yes, to remain in power."

"And what does that mean?" Joe raised his eyebrows.

"For the same reason you put me there, I had become a prisoner. The Trogs gained power with me leading them. The magic I could do frightened their enemies into submission. They soon realized there were limits to my powers and their fear of me diminished over time. Individually they were terrified but collectively they knew they could kill me. They needed me to give the illusion to our enemies that I was strong and in control. When their enemies realize I'm gone, the war for power in Pekel will begin."

"Now I understand." Joe moved to Yelka.

"Everything is ready." Yelka returned the gun to Joe.

Joe slipped Yelka the key to the collar. "Keep this safe," he whispered in her ear. "I will send new coordinates for the gateway, so we can make a quick exit."

Yelka slid the key into her pocket and went back to the control panel. She turned on the force field and then the gateway. "Be careful."

As the mirror transformed into its usual ball of light, Joe pointed the gun at Hudich, "After you."

Hudich stepped through the gateway and Joe followed.

Cindy had sat unattended in her cage for a while, when two Zeenosees showed up driving a machine with an extendable arm. The extension arm lifted her cage off the ground and carried it while the rest of the vehicle hovered just like all other Zeenosee crafts.

The complex inside the mountain was vast. They passed hundreds of glass rooms full of Zeenosees performing various activities. Some appeared to be doing data processing, others sat in what looked like business planning or training meetings, and still more busied themselves in military supply rooms. Smaller hovercrafts sped everywhere. Soon Cindy's hovercraft arrived in a stadium-sized cavern with a ceiling several hundred feet above her.

The hovercraft glided towards the far side of the cavern, where all sorts of creatures sat on isolated platforms that protruded from the face of the cavern wall. A bottomless pit separated the platforms from each other and from the main cavern. The craft slowed down as it approached the edge and stopped in front of a narrow unoccupied platform.

Standing on the main cavern floor in front of each platform was a small control panel. They resembled parking meters along the edge of the main cliff. Some platforms were larger than others and the width of the pit that separated them varied as well.

The Zeenosees set Cindy's cage down with one of its ends hanging over the drop-off. One Zeenosee climbed on top of her cage and opened a door to the end over the drop-off. Cindy hated heights and felt a twinge of panic. She hoped they weren't going to make her leap to her death.

The other Zeenosee moved to the nearest control panel. He pushed a button and a ramp shot out of the cavern floor under Cindy's cage and extended to a platform, making a bridge between the platform and the main cavern. The Zeenosee who had been on top of the cage jumped down. He disappeared behind the hovercraft and returned with one of the spears Cindy had seen them use on Ell.

The Zeenosee standing beside the panel spoke to her but his words were nonsense. He then said something to the Zeenosee at the back of the cage, who stretched out the spear and touched Cindy's shoulder. There was a flash of blue light and a pop. Cindy felt a rush of pain and she let out a scream. She jumped to her feet, rubbing her shoulder. The Zeenosee was speaking again and motioned with his hand towards the bridge. Cindy hesitated when she felt another shooting pain, this time on her backside, causing her eyes to tear up. She didn't want to get shocked again and hustled to the ramp.

Cindy was about to run across the ramp, when she noticed the depth of the drop-off. No bottom! The cliff walls were not only steep, but they were smooth as glass. She didn't want to cross but out of the corner of her eye she spotted the Zeenosee about to shock her again, so she ran the distance at a sprint. When she reached the platform she continued all the way to the wall as crossing the bottomless pit had left her shaken.

The Zeenosees withdrew the bridge and then sped away in the hovercraft.

After calming her nerves, she explored her narrow platform. She counted a distance of about twenty feet running along the side of the mountain, which was so smooth Cindy decided it must be man-made, or Zeenosee-made. She then counted another twenty feet from the mountainside to the edge of the cliff. Lying on her stomach, she tried to find the bottom of the drop-off without success.

She noticed the creatures to her left staring at her. "I know," she told them. "You haven't seen anything like me before."

Ell led Marko and Max to the edge of a large Zeenosees' city. The only thing that broke up the never-ending metropolis was a mountain exactly in the center. Marko and Max built a blind, just as they had done in Mir, except this one was large enough to hide Ell along with them.

After the hiding place was finished, Marko went into the city to gather information. The sun was setting when he returned. He carried a small animal carcass about the size of a cat, which he gave to Ell, and then sat down with his back against a tree.

Max wondered what had possessed Cindy to help this hideous creature, but looking at its razor sharp teeth made Max glad that Ell was on their side.

"She is definitely here," Marko said. "There is much talk of the new creature being held in the city."

"You're sure it's Cindy?"

"Yes, I spoke to a Zeenosee who had seen her. He said she is in the heart of that mountain."

Ell stared at them with his head cocked to the side as if he had something to say, so Max walked to him and placed his hand on Ell's back.

"He says they use the prisoners for blood sport," Max informed Marko.

"That is not their plan for Cindy. They want to trade her for Hudich."

The three companions sat in silence as they ate a cold meal. It was an hour later when Marko's communicator began to flash and he read Yelka's message. "Your grandfather is on his way," Marko said. "Why don't you get some sleep while I wait for him."

Max was exhausted and didn't have any trouble taking Marko's advice.

Max awoke the next morning to find that Grandpa had arrived with his prisoner. Hudich sat against a tree with his hood concealing his face. Grandpa and Marko were discussing something in hushed voices. Ell watched them as he lay against the blind. Max could tell by his posture he was frightened.

As Max climbed to his feet, he noticed Hudich watching him. He couldn't see his face but he could feel eyes boring into him. He went near Grandpa and Marko, both for safety and to find out what was happening. They didn't notice him right away, but continued their discussion, which involved Marko taking a message into the city.

"We want the exchange to take place here." Grandpa noticed Max standing by them. "Morning Max."

"Morning," Max replied. "What's going on?"

"Marko is going to deliver a message that says we'll make the exchange here, outside the city. And only Alan and one driver should come with Cindy to make the exchange."

"Do you think they'll agree?" Max asked.

"Yes, they want Hudich."

"We were also deciding on the time of day when the exchange should take place," Marko said. "I believe it should be at dusk when visibility is low."

Grandpa appeared to ponder Marko's statement. "That means it is low for us too."

"We will have time to study the layout," Marko added.

Grandpa nodded. "Excuse me, Marko. I want to talk to Max alone."

Marko wandered back to where Hudich was sitting.

"Interesting friend Cindy made." Grandpa motioned towards Ell.

"Yes." Max told Grandpa about Ell and how he had helped Cindy. He also explained how Ell wanted to move to another world. "Can we help him?"

"I think so. Now, I know you want to help Cindy, but I don't want you around during the exchange."

Max started to protest but Grandpa held up a finger to silence him. "We can't afford to give them any more hostages." Grandpa took out his communicator and entered some information.

Marko moved to where he could keep watch. Ell remained as close to the blind as possible, sniffing the air every once in a while.

"There. I told Yelka to move the gateway between those two trees." Grandpa pointed to an area a short distance away. "I want you and Ell to hide by the gateway. If there is any trouble, you are to leave. Yelka will turn it on before the exchange."

Max started to object but Grandpa held up a hand to silence him. "I don't want any arguments, or you will go now."

Max sighed and kept quiet. He followed Grandpa to Marko and listened to the final details of their plan. They agreed to make the exchange in front of the blind. Marko took a few items out of his pack and then took off towards the city.

Grandpa and Max returned to the blind to eat. Grandpa told him how he had brought Hudich from Pekel. Hudich grunted every now and then, indicating his displeasure with parts of the story. Max tried to get a glimpse of Hudich but he kept his face hidden.

They took turns keeping watch. Hudich and Ell remained where they were all day. Max and Grandpa staked out the area where the trade was to take place and Grandpa gave Max extra instructions.

It was early afternoon when Marko returned. Max was on watch and Marko appeared as if out of nowhere only feet from him. "Wow," Max exclaimed at the site of him. "Could you have made it past me without being seen?"

Marko smiled and continued walking. Max wanted to hear Marko's news and followed. They ducked behind the blind and Marko took a drink from a water skin.

"It's done," he said. "They'll be here at sunset."

"Only Alan, Cindy and a driver?" Grandpa asked.

"Yes," Marko replied. "I would have been here earlier but I had to lose a tail."

They spent time reviewing their plans. Grandpa and Marko would wait with Hudich. Marko would exchange Hudich for Cindy while Grandpa would have his gun ready in case anything happens. Once they met Cindy and made the trade, Marko would return with Cindy.

"We won't have much time after the exchange before more troops arrive," Marko said.

"I know," Grandpa responded. "Yelka will open the gateway before the exchange. We will leave immediately after."

"Good," Marko added.

"Max," Grandpa said. "It's time for you and Ell to go."

"Go?" Marko looked surprised.

"They're going to hide by the gateway. If there is any trouble they will leave."

Grandpa turned to Max. "I think you need to see something before you go. You need to see the face of our enemy. This is the only reason I haven't sent you home already." Grandpa took the gun out of his pocket, walked to Hudich and yanked off his hood.

Max looked at Hudich's black skull-like face and felt a surge of uneasiness flow through him as if an ominous shadow hung over him. Hudich locked eyes with Max and he could feel an evil force there. He didn't know why but something else bothered him. A voice was yelling inside his head but he couldn't make out the words. There was something familiar about Hudich. He had seen him before. "I know—," he muttered.

"Are you all right?" Grandpa asked.

"Uh, yes." Max continued to stare at Hudich. *Where have I seen him? Why is he so familiar? The stranger, the stranger on the bus, he resembled the stranger. But that isn't the only place. Where else do I know him from?*

"Max!" Grandpa yanked Max out of his thoughts. "I want you and Ell to hide. Now!"

Max walked to Ell, placed his hand on Ell's head and explained what Grandpa wanted them to do. Max led Ell down to the trees next to the gateway.

"I'm going to have one last look around." Marko went to check the area again.

Max could see Grandpa standing next to Hudich. Hudich replaced his hood but Max could still picture his face. The more he thought about it the more nervous he felt. He was glad to have Ell with him even though the creature was fidgeting.

Time crawled as they watched and waited for Cindy's arrival. Then the engine of an approaching hovercraft broke the silence.

Marko returned and stood next to Grandpa. Grandpa aimed the gun at Hudich who climbed to his feet. They moved to the other side of the blind, out of Max's sight.

Suddenly, Ell's head began jumping back and forth. He sniffed the air and looked in all directions. Max put a hand on his side.

There are Zeenosees approaching from behind us.

Behind us? Max's heart stopped.

Yes, and others from the sides.

That would mean. . . Max didn't finish his thought. The voice that had been screaming in his mind became clear. He knew where he had seen Hudich before, only it wasn't Hudich. It was another member of Hudich's race.

We've got to help Grandpa!

Get on. Ell lowered himself to the ground and Max scrambled aboard. Ell exploded towards Grandpa.

"Grandpa," Max screamed. "It's a trap." But the thundering engine of the hovercraft stifled Max's warning.

Grandpa, Marko and Hudich watched the hovercraft as it drew near, carrying Alan, Cindy and a pilot. The craft set down a stone's cast from where they waited. Alan stepped out and helped a blindfolded Cindy down the ramp.

Grandpa jabbed the gun in Hudich's back. "Don't do anything stupid and you'll be free."

The hovercraft engines shut down. In the silence, Max's cry echoed through the jungle. "Grandpa, it's a trap!"

Everyone turned as Max and Ell charged towards them.

Marko's hand slammed down on top of Grandpa's forearm with his short black stick. Grandpa cried out as his bone snapped and he dropped the gun. As Max got closer, he could see Marko, only he had changed. He looked like Hudich.

Marko raised his hand to deliver another blow to Grandpa when Ell slammed into them, sending Marko as well as Hudich flying like bowling pins.

Grandpa retrieved the gun with his good arm and fired a shot at the ground in front of Alan. A spray of large debris flew into Alan and knocked him to the ground. "Run, Cindy!"

Cindy ripped off the blindfold and sprinted the wrong way. Max could tell she didn't know which way to go. "Cindy!" Max yelled to draw her attention. Ell immediately ran towards Cindy.

Suddenly, the jungle sprang to life around them, both on the floor and in the air. Hovercrafts and ground troops closed in from all sides.

When Ell reached Cindy, Max lowered his arm. Catching each other by the hand, Max swung her onto Ell's back. She wrapped her arms around Max so tight he had trouble breathing.

Find Grandpa.

Hudich bolted towards Alan's hovercraft and freedom. Grandpa and Alan fought a magical battle. Sparks and lightning bolts exploded everywhere as each cast a volley of spells and the other blocked them. Max noticed Marko moving in behind Grandpa. The face he had now was the same one he had worn in Tabor in order to evade the people in the enemy's camp; the same face as Hudich.

Anger burned inside Max like an inferno. He extended his arms, "*Premakni*." The spell caught Marko unprepared, lifted him off the ground and hurled him backwards. He landed with a crash and gasped for air. Their eyes met and Max could feel his hatred. Marko was consumed by evil, something Max had not believed possible.

Get Grandpa. Max thought and Ell leapt forward.

Grandpa and Alan continued their battle of magic spells; neither overcoming the other.

Marko was back on his feet and running towards Grandpa. Marko was fast but not as fast as Ell. They were going to reach Grandpa first.

Zeenosee troops were pouring out of the jungle while the sky was a sea of hovercrafts racing in all directions. They appeared to be confused by the situation unfolding before them.

"We've got to help Grandpa," Cindy yelled into Max's ear as they sped along.

"I surprised Marko once," Max said. "Maybe we can catch Alan off guard, too."

"On the count of three." Cindy began counting. When she reached three they both cast the *premakni* spell.

Alan was quick enough to block their spell but it drew his attention away from Grandpa. Grandpa landed a blow that shot Alan through the air like a cannonball, rolling end over end.

"Grandpa," Max yelled as they approached.

Grandpa turned toward them and made ready to climb onto Ell's back. Ell skidded to a halt and Cindy and Max reached out to help him aboard.

Before Grandpa could get onto Ell, an object struck him in the back of the head and knocked him unconscious. Max recognized Marko's black stick as Grandpa fell.

Marko charged towards them when *premakni* rang in Max's ear. Again the spell lifted Marko off the ground and launched him several yards away. Max knew Cindy had cast the spell.

Down. Max ordered Ell who knelt.

Max jumped off Ell's back and tried to lift Grandpa. With Cindy pulling from the top and Max pushing from the bottom, they managed to get him on Ell. Max was climbing back up, when he spotted the gun lying on the ground only feet away and bolted for it. Max knew they would need the gun so he dove for it.

"Max!" Cindy yelled but it was too late.

Alan got back to his feet and rejoined the fight. His spell caught Max with full force right before he reached the gun. It threw him several yards. Max crashed into a tree and managed to hold onto it so he didn't fall to the ground. Although the impact jarred every bone in his body, he knew that latching onto the tree saved him from hurtling into the dirt below.

Cindy spurred Ell in Max's direction. The jungle was full of Zeenosees and other creatures. They encircled them, closing off all chances of escape.

In their efforts to reach Max, Cindy and Ell forgot about Marko. He recovered from Cindy's spell and closed in on them in a rush. Marko held a long tree branch in his hands, which he jabbed vertically into the ground in front of them.

Ell couldn't dodge the obstacle. It took out his front legs and catapulted him and his passengers. They hit the ground, tumbling as they bounced out of control.

Marko advanced. His blade flashed in the lights shining down from the hovercrafts.

"Cindy, look out." Max hollered as he descended the tree. He drew his sword and sprinted after Marko.

"Premakni," Cindy screamed with outstretched hands. This time Marko was ready. He dove out of the way of the spell and sprang right back to his feet.

Marko was about to overtake Cindy when Ell banged into him knocking him sideways. Ell stood between Marko and Cindy like a mother grizzly guarding her cub. The fur on the back of his neck stood on end and his razor-sharp teeth were exposed.

Ell's fierce display didn't faze Marko. He whipped his sword around in front of him as if daring Ell to make the first move.

As Max approached them, a group of Zeenosees emerged behind Cindy and picked up Grandpa's limp body. Cindy, whose attention was on Ell and Marko, cried out as hands clutched and bound her.

Cindy's shout caused Ell to turn his head. Marko took advantage of the opportunity to strike and swung down on Ell's head. Marko's face reflected great surprise when his sword struck Max's blade with a clank. Max had prevented his blow.

"You've proven yourself a worthy student," Marko sneered and then unleashed a series of strikes that Max scrambled to block. As he retreated, he lost his footing and tripped. He raised his sword to obstruct Marko's last swing.

Ell, seeing Marko's back to him, lunged forward with his mouth wide open. Before he could reach him, two deafening booms shook the ground and cords wrapped up Ell's legs. He fell over with a thud.

All of a sudden, the sword flew out of Max's hand. Alan had cast a spell that threw Max's sword into a tree.

Marko ended his attack on Max and walked to the now helpless Ell. "You have caused enough trouble. And you are no longer necessary." Marko raised his sword high in the air.

"No!" Max screamed as pain exploded in his head and everything went dark.

18

A Leap of Faith

"Max, Max, are you all right?" Cindy asked.

Cindy's face came into focus as he stared up at her. She was cradling his head in her lap as they sat on a platform connected to the side of a cliff. "Wha. . . What happened?" Max moaned.

"You were hit in the head."

Max could see tears in her eyes. "Ell," he gasped with horror. He tried to sit up but it made his head throb even more.

"Ell's fine." Cindy said. "He's on the next platform."

"And Grandpa?"

"They took him about fifteen minutes ago."

Ignoring his dizziness, Max climbed to his feet and noticed the platform was separated from the main cavern by a drop-off. Then he saw the other platforms with a variety of creatures. Off to their right Ell sat alone on a platform.

Max picked up his pack from where it lay next to him. He found the medicine for his hand and took it for his head. "How did they get us over here?" He continued to search through his pack.

"With a ramp that's controlled by that thing sticking out of the ground. What are. . ?" Cindy started to ask with raised eyebrows.

"Found it." Max pulled out his communicator. "Didn't they search my stuff?"

"They did, but Marko said the communicator was useless to you."

"It was, until yesterday when Grandpa showed me how to use it." Max winked. "Now we need to figure out how to get across the drop-off and find Grandpa."

"Good luck."

Max ignored her sarcasm and started searching for a solution. "Did they say why they took Grandpa?" He studied the drop-off.

"It had something to do with a collar. I didn't know what they were talking about. Grandpa mentioned something about trading our freedom for a key."

Cindy watched Max surveying an area between the mountain and the edge of the cliff. He moved his hands like he was about to cast a spell and then counted the number of steps from the wall to the drop-off.

"What are you doing?" Cindy asked.

"I might have figured out a way across."

Joe stood in another chamber under the mountain with Hudich, Alan, Marko, and others who were all staring at him.

"Where is the key?" Hudich paced around the room.

Joe could feel Hudich's anger. "I told you. I will trade the key for our freedom." He stared straight ahead at no one in particular.

Hudich stopped in front of Joe and backhanded him across the face. "I'm growing tired of you, old man. Is that what you gave Yelka before we left?"

"Maybe. Maybe not." Joe ignored Hudich's slap.

Marko stepped forward. "I could take care of Yelka." He changed into his human form. "She trusts me. Besides, she should have guessed something has gone wrong by now."

"I agree," Alan said. "I think we should deal with Yelka. I'm sure he left the key with her. Once we have the key and Marko disposes of Yelka, we will have everything we've always wanted."

Hudich appeared to be considering this as he continued pacing. "Even if she doesn't have the key we can gain control of the gateway." Hudich came to a halt. "Do it."

"I'll need to go back to the jungle." Marko took out his communicator. His fingers moved rapidly over the dials and then he waited for a reply. After several minutes without a response, he re-entered the message.

"What's wrong?" Hudich asked his voice full of impatience.

"I don't know. He must have set up some kind of signal with her. She's not answering." Marko transformed back into his hideous self.

"You've thought of everything haven't you, old man?" Hudich roared raising his hand to strike Joe again.

Right before his blow landed, Joe uttered, "*Premakni*," and threw Hudich backwards into the wall. "Do not touch me again."

Alan stepped forward, threatening. "And you will not attack my master."

The tension in the room was so thick; Joe could feel its weight crushing him. Everyone glared at him as if they could squeeze what they wanted out of him. Joe remained calm as he stared down his captors.

"I have a better idea," Hudich said. "He may not be concerned at the threat of losing his own life, but how about a loved one's life."

"That's an excellent idea." Alan grinned and his eyes gleamed with wicked delight. "We have the leverage, I suggest we use it."

Joe realized their intentions and tried to hide his emotions, but he knew he wasn't doing a very good job.

"Marko," Alan said. "Go get Max. You have such a good relationship with the boy. Meanwhile we'll discuss the location of the key with Joe."

Marko looked from Alan to Hudich, who nodded his approval and Marko headed for the door.

"Marko, don't be too gentle with the boy." Hudich said with a devilish smile.

An evil smile spread across Marko's face as he turned into his human form.

"How do we get across?" Cindy asked with a sigh. "I have been racking my brains about this for two days. I find it hard to believe you know a way."

"Well," Max hesitated. He was sure Cindy wasn't going to like his idea. "I will run and jump."

"You think you can jump across this thing?" Cindy motioned towards the pit.

"Let me finish. I'll run from the mountainside and when I reach the edge I'll jump. When I do, you'll cast the *premakni* spell. You should be able to throw me way across the gap. I saw you launch Marko twice this distance."

"I don't know." Cindy shook her head. "If I mess up, we won't get a second chance because you'll be dead."

"Grandpa needs our help and if we don't get out of here soon, we'll never leave."

Cindy didn't respond. Max could tell she was thinking it over, her pale face showed her concern.

"Well?" he asked.

"Okay, but you can't start until I say so."

"Agreed. I'll tell Yelka what's going on."

Cindy nodded and took a deep breath. Her hands were shaking. "I can't picture you clearing the gap, and if I don't see it, it won't happen."

Max didn't answer. He moved back to the mountainside and took out his communicator. Moments after he sent Yelka a message, she responded.

"Marko tried to contact her," Max said.

Cindy shot him a look that said *let me concentrate.*

Max looked at Ell, who had been watching them the whole time. He could tell Ell wondered what they were doing but he couldn't communicate with him. Max waved at him hoping he would understand such a gesture.

Max was waiting for Cindy to get ready when someone appeared at the other end of the cavern. As he approached, Max could see it was Marko.

"Cindy," Max hissed. "Marko's coming. It's now or never."

Cindy looked up to see Marko heading towards them.

"I'm going." Max sprinted towards the drop off.

Max heard Cindy gasp as he ran towards the edge. A wave of fear flooded through him as the edge drew near. He launched himself off the edge.

"*Premakni,*" Cindy yelled.

The spell threw Max across the gap and he landed on the main cavern floor with plenty of room to spare. As Max rolled to his feet, he saw Marko sprinting towards him but he still had to cross the vast cavern.

Max ran to the console and noticed there were only two buttons. One was to extend the ramp and the other to retract it. He pressed the top button and nothing happened so he pressed the bottom one. The ramp started to extend towards Cindy.

"Look out!" Cindy screamed as Marko closed on Max.

Max wanted to draw Marko away from Cindy, so he darted away from him in the opposite direction across the cavern. Marko gave chase with his black stick in hand.

Ell raced back and forth at the front of his platform. His roars echoed off the cavern walls.

"Where are you going?" Marko hissed.

Suddenly, Max felt a sharp pain in the middle of his back where Marko struck him with the stick. Max fell, face first. He stifled a scream and closed his eyes to hold back the tears. He flipped onto his back with his hands extended, "*Prizgaj*." A ball of fire exploded from his hands and enveloped Marko as he tried to dive away. Marko hit the floor and rolled several times to extinguish the flames that had ignited his clothes.

Max was on his feet racing towards Cindy, who had crossed the bridge.

"Behind you!" Cindy hollered.

Marko was in pursuit, smoke rising from his charred clothing. He transformed into his dark self and drew his sword.

"I was told to bring you back bruised and battered." Marko increased his pace. "They didn't say what I could or couldn't do to Cindy."

"Cindy, run!" Max called. Another sharp pain erupted in the center of his back as Marko hammered him with the hilt of his sword, knocking him flat.

"*Premakni*," Cindy called with her hands extended.

Marko tried to dodge the spell but didn't get completely out of the way. It hit him in the side, spinning him around, but he stayed on his feet.

When Max reached Cindy, he took hold of her out-stretched hands and pulled her after him. As they fled, Max noticed movement at the entrance of the cavern.

Ell let out another roar which Max interpreted as a warning. Max shoved Cindy as hard as he could to the side. She went down in time to avoid Marko's sword. Max felt another sharp pain in his kidney as Marko kicked him, sending him to the ground. Marko turned on Cindy, who was lying on the cavern floor.

"*Pridi*," Max yelled and Marko's sword flew from his hand into Max's. Marko shot Max a look of complete hatred.

"Move away from her," Max warned through gritted teeth and moved in front of Cindy. "How could you betray us? I thought you were our friend."

"Do you know how long it took me to get Joe, his heir and Hudich in the same world together," Marko responded. "It was years of doing good and taking orders from that lesser life form you call Grandfather."

They eyed each other for a moment and then Max pointed the sword at Marko threatening him.

"You know you can't stop me," Marko said.

Max held the sword at the ready and waited for Cindy to get to her feet. Behind Marko, Max could see Ell circling his platform across the pit.

"You see, Max," Marko smiled. "I have the sword I gave you." Max's sword appeared in Marko's hand and he lunged forward with a powerful stroke Max barely blocked.

"*Pochasi*," Max called as Marko attacked again. Suddenly, Marko was thrown into slow motion. He moved so sluggishly Max blocked his advance with ease and then he advanced on Marko. Marko looked shocked. For the first time, Max felt Marko was afraid. He continued his onslaught, driving Marko towards the drop off.

As Marko reached the edge he threw off Max's spell on him. His expression changed from panic to rage as he howled with furry, preparing to attack. He sprang towards Max with incredible speed.

Max dropped his sword and brought both hands up, "*Premakni.*" The spell threw Marko across the drop off into Ell's open jaws.

Ell bit down and thrashed his head from side to side, snapping Marko's body like a whip. Ell then released the lifeless body into the gorge below.

Max and Cindy stared into the pit when a roar from Ell caught their attention. A couple of prison workers were making routine checks and appeared unaware of what had transpired.

Cindy pulled Max down close to the ground. "I don't think they knew Marko was here," she whispered. "Set Ell free when you hear me coming. I have an idea." She took off along the ledge away from the tunnel that opened into the main cavern before Max could say anything.

"How will I hear her coming?" he muttered as he tried to hide behind the slender console. In a couple of seconds, Cindy was no longer in sight. The Zeenosees were halfway across the cavern talking casually to each other, when an earthshaking commotion echoed off the walls.

The Zeenosees exchanged confused looks and then moved in the direction of the noise. The sound continued to grow with each passing moment. It sounded like a stampede was heading their way. Suddenly, Ell roared to draw Max's attention. Max pushed the button to extend the ramp to Ell's platform.

Max watched for Cindy as Ell bounded across the ramp. Ell took the back of Max's shirt in his teeth and threw him up onto his back. Max was startled at the move but quickly gripped Ell's fur when he landed. Ell bolted after Cindy. She appeared, sprinting towards them. She extended the ramps to each of the platforms, releasing the prisoners as she went. The panicky Zeenosees scrambled towards the tunnel entrance with the escaping prisoners hot on their heels.

Max lowered his arm as they reached Cindy and helped her climb aboard.

To the entrance, fast! Max told Ell.

Ell raced ahead of the escaping prisoners. The two workers disappeared into the sea of fleeing beasts.

More Zeenosees appeared in the tunnel ahead, drawn by the commotion. Ell charged through the guards sending them flying in all directions. One guard managed to pull an alarm bell before Ell smashed into him. The earsplitting siren pierced the compound as the three raced through the tunnel and unprepared Zeenosees dove out of the way. In Ell's wake, a wave of creatures swallowed up the Zeenosees.

"Where are Marko and that brat?" Hudich growled as he stomped back and forth.

"We told him to rough up the boy," Alan reminded him.

Suddenly, they heard the alarm bell ring and everyone snapped to attention, looking for the cause of the warning signal.

"What's happening?" Hudich roared.

A Zeenosee burst into the room, "The prisoners are escaping."

"Which prisoners?" they asked together.

"All of them."

"*Izginem se.*" Joe disappeared and moved behind Hudich. He shadowed his every move.

"Find the old man!" Hudich ordered. "And find Marko!"

Alan cast spells around the room in an attempt to make Joe visible but none found their mark.

Max, Cindy, and Ell entered the main hangar, which opened to the outside world. Zeenosees scrambled everywhere and an armed group gave chase.

"*Premakni*," Max yelled, knocking most of them backwards.

"*Premakni*," Cindy copied, throwing the rest aside.

"We've got to find Grandpa!" Max said.

I can find him. Ell began sniffing the air.

More creatures entered the hangar with Zeenosees in close pursuit. It was a full-fledged battle. The speed of the prisoners' escape didn't give the Zeenosees time to organize.

Max took out his communicator. "I'm telling Yelka we need an exit."

As Zeenosees left the room where Joe was, he attempted to leave with them. He was in the doorway when Alan's spell exposed him.

"Behind you," Alan yelled, but fortunately, the alarms and the fighting drowned out his voice.

With Alan, Hudich, the Sheriff and a few others on his heels, Joe zigzagged down the hallway doing his best to avoid the spells being thrown at him. One connected and he went down. Joe landed on the ground, unable to break his fall with his broken arm. He rolled over with a gasp, his wounded arm beneath him. With gritted teeth, he tried to get up.

Before he could stand, Alan reached him. He had the gun pointed at him. "Don't tempt me, old fool."

Joe raised his one good arm.

"Now, you are going to give us the key," Alan commanded. "Or you are going to watch Max and Cindy die. I'm sure when the Zeenosees get this mess cleaned up they can arrange a match where Max and Cindy are the main event."

Ell led them through a several tunnels while being chased by a group of armed Zeenosees. All around them, Zeenosees were overpowering and capturing the escaped prisoners.

"We don't have much time!" Max shouted. "We can't fight the entire Zeenosee nation."

Suddenly, in the corridor ahead, there stood Grandpa, holding his hand in the air. Max clamped his hand over Cindy's mouth to keep her from calling out, and with his other hand he pointed at Alan.

Max then told Ell what he wanted him to do and Ell bounded towards Grandpa.

"What are we going to do?" Cindy whispered.

Keep going. Max thought to Ell.

Grandpa, Alan, Hudich and the others looked up to see Ell barreling towards them. They had no time to react before Ell was on top of them. He didn't slow down but snatched Grandpa up in his teeth by the back of his shirt like a mother lion transporting her cub.

Alan and Hudich were stunned as Ell carried Grandpa away. They joined the Zeenosees in their pursuit.

To the hangar. Max urged Ell.

Joe swung like a rag doll as Ell dashed through the complex. Around every corner they acquired more pursuers. They passed several groups of soldiers guiding captured prisoners back to their cells.

"Grandpa, are you all right?" Max called down to him. He could tell by the look on his grandfather's face that he was in pain.

"Tell me when it's over," Grandpa Joe answered, as he clutched his broken arm against his side and closed his eyes.

Zeenosees blocked their path ahead, but Max scattered them like leaves. "*Premakni!*"

Ell turned and bounded down so many hallways that Max no longer knew where they were and hoped that Ell could find the hangar. Just as he was thinking that Ell must be lost, they ran out of the tunnel and into the main hangar.

Ell ran across the open space of the hanger floor, dodging the enemy as he went. It was like watching rush hour in a major metropolis. Hovercrafts landed everywhere bringing reinforcements. Ell was working his way along the edge of the cliff when a mighty boom shook the walls.

Ell howled in pain and went down, skidding. His passengers were thrown in all directions. Max saw that Ell had been shot in the front leg.

Joe slid across the floor and his feet went over the edge of the cliff. "Max!"

Max and Cindy ran, caught him before he fell and helped him up.

"Joseph," Hudich roared. "You shall give us the key or you shall watch your grandson and his friends die. Starting with this hideous beast."

Max, Cindy and Grandpa Joe stood in front of Ell as he lay on the hanger floor. Max put his hand on Ell's shoulder to comfort him. He looked down into Ell's eyes and gave a wink.

Joe stepped forward guiding Max and Cindy behind him. Zeenosees closed in on all sides except where the cave opened behind them. Several hovercrafts watched their every move from the air only yards outside the opening.

"There is nowhere left to run." Alan moved closer. "The game is over and you've lost. Give us what we want and I will see to it that your deaths are painless."

"I've never trusted you," Joe spat.

Alan pointed the gun at Ell, "Give us the key or your monstrous friend will be the first to go."

"No." Max jumped between Alan and his grandfather. "I can get you the key. Just don't hurt Ell."

"This thing has a name?" Alan crinkled his nose as if a horrible stench filled the air.

"Yes," Max said. "I will give you the key if you let us go."

"There will be no going for any of you." Hudich said. "There will only be less pain when you die. Alan, shoot the beast again to show him what we mean."

"No," Max cried. "I will get it for you."

"You can't give it to them." Grandpa protested.

Max took out his communicator. "Yelka has the key and she will only respond to me."

"Max!"

"I know what I'm doing. Trust me." It took all Max's strength to keep from smiling. He stepped closer to Alan. "I will have Yelka open the gateway over there." He pointed to a spot behind Alan. "I will go and get the key."

"That's all you will do," Hudich snarled. "If you don't return quickly, know they will suffer horrible deaths."

Max nodded and began entering information into the communicator. When he was finished, he waited. Then a light began flashing in response. "It will open any second."

Everyone watched the area Max had indicated.

Suddenly, Max spun towards Grandpa, Cindy and Ell. His hands shot outward and he yelled, "Premaknite." The spell lifted the three off the hanger floor and threw them over the edge of the cliff. Before Max sprang after them he registered the looks of shock and disbelief on all their enemies' faces. He had thrown his friends and grandfather off a cliff!

When he reached the edge, Max took one last look at Alan and Hudich. He gave them a knowing smile and then jumped.

19

Summer Ends

Max fell through the gateway and landed on top of Ell, Cindy and Grandpa. Yelka stood wide-eyed her mouth open. It appeared she wasn't expecting to see Ell or the way they dropped through the gateway instead of walking through it.

Grandpa chuckled joyfully as Cindy helped him off the floor. "Well done Max. Where did you get the idea to open the gateway on the side of a cliff?"

"On the side of the. . ." Yelka stammered.

"I thought, where can I open the gateway so we can go through without them stopping us," Max replied.

"Yelka, did you realize where you placed the gateway?" Grandpa beamed.

"No, but I thought those coordinates were strange," Yelka responded with a confused look. "Can I ask who that creature is?"

"This is Ell." Cindy placed a hand on Ell's giant head. "He helped me survive in the jungle and then led Grandpa and Max to me."

"He communicates by touch," Max added.

"Come Yelka," Cindy smiled. "Touch his head."

Yelka looked at Grandpa, who gave her a nod. She then walked to Ell and placed her hand on his head. "Oh my," she uttered after a few minutes.

They spent the next hour mending Grandpa's broken arm and Ell's wounded leg. Grandpa suggested moving Ell to Yelka's world where she could look after him until they could find a more suitable world. Yelka was in whole-hearted agreement.

They all traveled to Yelka's world to introduce Ell to his new home. They showed him where Yelka lived and where to find water. After Cindy informed them that Ell was an omnivore, Yelka led Ell to a spot where wild fruits grew in abundance.

When the time to say good-bye arrived, Cindy placed her hand on Ell's head with moist eyes. *You will always be my friend.*

Come visit me whenever you can.

I will. I promise.

Then Max and Grandpa took their turns saying good-bye. They also agreed to visit Ell often.

Ell followed them back to the gateway and watched them leave. Yelka accompanied them back to Grandpa's house so she could help them deal with Cindy's mom and dad.

They discussed what to do about Cindy's parents as they ate dinner. She couldn't just show up after being gone for days and not have a story. They didn't need to worry about the police because they had been involved in her disappearance and so were currently not waiting near Cindy's house. Finally, they decided honesty was the best choice.

"This war affects everyone. We need all the help we can get," Grandpa stated.

Later that evening, they went to Cindy's parents and explained everything in great detail. It was a rollercoaster of emotions. Cindy's parents were elated she was back, angry with the sheriff and Alan, and shocked by the explanations. It wasn't until Cindy showed them some magic and Grandpa showed them the gateway that they were convinced.

Her parents' last reaction shocked Max the most. He was expecting them to forbid Cindy from seeing him again. Instead, they wanted to help because they, too, had been feeling something dark and mysterious connected with the town. They wanted to know how they could protect themselves and wanted to be involved. They even set up times when Yelka could teach all of them magic.

The next few weeks went by faster than Max wanted. Although he missed his mother, he was going to miss Grandpa and Cindy just as much.

Yelka showed up every day to help Max and Cindy practice their spells and Cindy's parents to learn spells. They all traveled to Yelka's house a time or two and visited Ell, who was doing much better, and his leg was almost healed. Yelka did not teach them any new magic but kept encouraging them to practice every day, even during the school year.

Now that they no longer had a weapons teacher, Grandpa asked Olik to instruct Max and Cindy in math and science. They thought his lessons were boring in comparison to magic and weaponry, but Grandpa kept insisting that Olik's instructions were just as important. "Everything in the universe is governed by mathematical principles," he would say.

Grandpa insisted they also practice everything Marko had taught them. Max showed Cindy the sword techniques Marko had given him while Cindy's parents had forbidden her to come over.

Max did miss Marko, at least the good Marko that he had known and trusted. He had thought that they were friends and Marko's betrayal hurt Max.

Max and Grandpa repaired all the broken windows and painted over all the graffiti on the outside of the house. The place finally looked better than the day Max arrived.

Max was dreading the day he would have to leave. He wondered what Cindy would do without him. She would have to go to school with no friends and everyone, including the teacher, against her. The thought that she might flunk because of a biased teacher crossed his mind several times.

One night, a couple of days before Max was to leave, Grandpa and Max sat silently at the dinner table. Grandpa had prepared spaghetti and meatballs, but neither one of them had much of an appetite.

"Grandpa," Max broke the silence.

"Yes?" Grandpa looked up from his barely eaten meal.

"Did you suspect Marko of being a traitor? I mean, Yelka only responded to my communicator."

"I don't know if I suspected him, but I did find a reason not to trust him. It was the stuff he gave you to put on your mark. I found it curious that he had something that temporarily negated the enemy curse; a powder which even Yelka didn't know about. I told Yelka to respond only to your communicator because I was afraid my communicator, and Marko's might be confiscated. I hoped that Alan and the others wouldn't think you had anything important in your pack since you are young. I was right." Grandpa studied Max's reaction. "Any other questions?"

"Are people in danger because I didn't let you bring Hudich back with us?"

"No, Max," Grandpa said with surprise. "What makes you think that?"

"I thought the goal was to rescue Cindy without having to trade Hudich. Now, Hudich is no longer trapped in Pekel."

"Well." Grandpa rubbed his chin. "Hudich merely traded one prison for another."

"What do you mean?"

"That collar Olik made. Hudich and his followers do not possess the technology to take it off. They have relied too much on magic and ignored the other stuff. Technology is one of our greatest advantages. He is now trapped in the land of the Zeenosees because that collar keeps him from using magic. In a way, his new prison is worse than his old one. He could do a little magic in Pekel, but now he can't do any."

"What if they get the collar off?"

"I don't think that will happen anytime soon. Maybe that will be our next adventure," Grandpa smiled. "You can help me devise a plan to move Hudich back to Pekel. At least with that collar on, we can track his movements."

"So, trapping him there wasn't a total loss?"

"No, there is a chance that they will get the collar off before we can move Hudich, but we still have time."

Max started feeling better and took a couple of bites of spaghetti. "Then, we have to try and get him back to Pekel?" Max asked between mouthfuls.

"Yes, we have to try. You don't need to worry about that right now. You'll have plenty to worry about when you get home."

Max didn't like the sound of that. He didn't hate school but he didn't want summer to end. He could learn more from Olik than he could from any school teacher.

The next day during their morning chores, Larry and his friends showed up. It was their first encounter with the enemy since returning from the land of Zeenosees. Larry and his friends rode their bikes to Grandpa's house. They skidded their bikes to a halt next to the fence whooping and hollering. It was exactly like the first time Max had seen them. They were as rude and obnoxious as ever.

"Is little Maxie going home to his mommy?" Larry called. "Now, Mindy won't have anyone to play dolls with."

This brought howls of laughter from the rest of the gang as they sat on their bikes glaring through the fence.

Cindy went up the steps and disappeared into the house. It appeared to Max that she had had enough of Larry and his friends. Max couldn't blame her. She had been through a lot this summer.

"What, Windy going to cry?" Larry laughed with the rest of his gang.

Grandpa and Max continued to work ignoring Larry and his friends.

"I'm proud of you," Grandpa whispered.

"Thanks." Max piled up the weeds they had pulled. "Why?"

"For not letting that hot-aired buffoon get to you."

"I figure he isn't worth it."

Larry and his friends persisted in yelling rude comments. Not getting the response they had hoped for, they gave up. As they turned to leave, Cindy was suddenly standing next to Larry.

"What do you want?" Larry puffed out his chest in a threatening manner.

Grandpa and Max stopped to watch what was happening. Neither of them saw how Cindy got behind Larry, but there she was right next to him. Max's adrenaline started pumping and he was ready to act if Larry did anything.

"To make sure Grandpa didn't lie," Cindy said with a smirk.

"What's that supposed to mean?" Larry glanced at his friends with a confused look.

"This." Cindy punched Larry as hard as she could in the nose, breaking it.

Larry went down crying and bleeding profusely while Cindy faced down the others. When they saw the expression on Cindy's face they all took off down the street. Larry cowered away, holding his nose with one hand and dragging his bike with the other. Once he was out of Cindy's reach, he got on his bike and rode away.

Cindy noticed Max and Grandpa staring at her. She meandered through the gate and rejoined them picking up weeds.

"Where did that come from?" Max stared at her.

"Oh, I didn't want Grandpa to be a liar." Cindy shrugged her shoulders. "He told Larry's dad and the sheriff I broke Larry's nose. I didn't want to disappoint them."

Grandpa chuckled and a smile crossed Max's face.

"Besides, I figured I owed them for all the trouble they caused me."

"I only have one question," Grandpa said. "Did you use the invisibility spell to get behind them?"

"No, I went through the house and out the back gate." "Don't worry." Grandpa said. "You'll both conquer that spell sooner or later."

The next two days grandpa didn't make them do any lessons. He told Max and Cindy to go out and play. He knew they wouldn't see each other for many months and said they should have some fun.

They spent time everyday playing catch and hiking around the hills behind Grandpa's house. They talked about all the things they had learned and done during the summer. They avoided talking about Max leaving because it made them sad. Cindy admitted that it was going to be difficult once he was gone. She made Max promise to write at least once a week.

They noticed the Night Shade down the street had disappeared. Grandpa was the first to point it out. They decided that the enemy must be busy trying to get the collar off Hudich. Grandpa conceded that the drawback to Hudich not being in Pekel was that he had contact with his followers again. No one could reach him in Pekel, but now that he was in the land of the Zeenosees, Hudich could be once again involved with the enemy's plans.

On the night before Max's departure, Grandpa entered his room and sat on the edge of his bed. Max didn't feel like sleeping and was happy to see his grandfather. Max was a raging sea of emotions. One minute he was excited to be going home to his mother and the next he was depressed because he would miss Grandpa, Cindy and the others.

"Max," Grandpa said.

"Yes?"

"I want you to promise me you will only use magic for self defense or when you are practicing. There are enemies out there who will be drawn to any magical activity."

"I promise."

"I also want you to study hard in school. All the magical talent in the world and all the defensive training won't make up for a poor education. I don't know if you fully understand why I brought you here this summer but I needed to train my replacement."

"Replacement?"

"Well, I'm not going to live forever and I need someone to maintain the gateway when I'm gone. You saw a glimpse of the battle we're in. It is a much larger war than you know. This gateway is our best weapon. If the enemy gained access to it, all creatures everywhere would fall under their control. Everyone would be a slave to their will."

"I think I got the picture when they kidnapped Cindy."

"Yes, they want power and they will do anything to get it. It's my job to make sure they don't get it, and will be yours one day."

"I understand."

"I want to make sure you do. I need you, and so do good people everywhere. I know I kind of thrust a lot on you, but you are my last hope. I wish I had other options."

"Don't worry Grandpa; I'll try not to let you down."

"I know. And last but not least, I want you to know how proud I am of you." Grandpa got a little misty. "You showed great character this summer. You were brave, courageous and ingenious. If it wasn't for your quick thinking, a lot of things could have gone wrong. If Hudich had escaped without that collar, we would all pay a heavy price."

Max didn't know what to say. He blushed and felt embarrassed because he didn't think of himself as being courageous. He thought he had done what anyone in the same situation might do.

"Anyway." Grandpa patted Max's knee. "Try and get some sleep." He turned off the lights and left the room.

Max's last day dawned leaving him feeling exhausted. He hadn't slept well because of all the emotions that were running through him.

Cindy came over before breakfast. Max could tell she was depressed. He tried to act as if it was any other day and didn't bring up the fact he was leaving.

Yelka showed up soon after breakfast but she didn't stay long. She gave Max a lecture about practicing his spells and how she expected him to be better next summer than he was now.

When it was time for him to leave, they began the long walk down to the bus station. His departure was a lot different than his arrival. No one dressed in black followed them and there wasn't any chanting. None of them spoke.

They arrived at the bus stop fifteen minutes before it was time to board.

"Do you have everything?" Grandpa was more trying to make conversation rather than find out if Max had actually packed properly.

"Yes." Max couldn't find anything to say. He was going to miss them and he felt bad for Cindy. He had friends back home. Cindy didn't have any friends here.

They sat without speaking, letting the minutes slip away and finally the time arrived for Max to go. Max gave Grandpa a hug and told him good-bye. He wanted to give Cindy a hug and hadn't decided if he should when she initiated it. She squeezed him so tight he couldn't breathe.

"Remember, you promised to write me every week," she said.

"I will."

"You need to get going," Grandpa urged. "Don't worry about Cindy. I will look after her."

"And I'll look after him," Cindy pointed to Grandpa.

Max sat where he could watch them as the bus pulled away. They were waving frantically as he left. Then it hit him, he probably wouldn't see them for the duration of the school year. He didn't know if he would visit during the holidays or not.

Suddenly he had a depressing thought. He just had the most exciting summer of his life and he couldn't tell anyone about it. He finally had something interesting to write about for the required school essay, "What I Did on My Summer Vacation" and he couldn't write a word of it.

I guess I will have to make it up, as usual.

Spell Pronunciations and Definitions

Stress marks: [bold type] indicates the primary stressed syllable, as in news·pa·per [**nooz**-pey-per] and in·for·ma·tion [in-fer-**mey**-shuhn]

pridi (pri·di) [**prē**-dē] – Moves objects towards you.
zaspi (za·spi) [zä-**spē**] – Causes sleep.
prizgaj (pri·zgaj) [prē- **3g ī**] – Use to create fire.
ugasni (u·ga·sni) [$\overline{oo}$-**gä**-snē] – Use to extinguish fire.
premakni (pre·ma·kni) [prā-**mä**-knē] – Moves objects away from you.
vstani (vs☐ta☐ni) [$\overline{oo}$s-**tä**-nē] – Stops moving objects.
pochasi (po☐cha☐si) [pō-**chä**-sē] – Slows moving objects down.
izginem se (iz☐gi☐nem☐ se) [ēz-gē-n ām-sē] – Makes one invisible.
prikazi se (pri☐ka☐zi ☐se) [prē-**kä**-zē] – Makes one visible.
izbrisi znamenje (iz☐bir☐si☐zna☐men☐je) [ēz-**brē**-shē **znä**-menyē] – Removes curses.

Symbols and their examples:

ē	**bee**
ä	**fa**ther
3	vi**si**on
ī	**pie**, **by**
$\overline{oo}$	**boot**
ā	**pay**
ō	**toe**

Printed in the United States
116573LV00002B/10-15/A

9 780979 720215